The residue of evil lingered in the air

Like a suffocating blanket, a wave of heat wrapped around her, making her feel as if the air were too heavy to drag into her lungs. Sabrina didn't want to breathe this atmosphere at all. Not when an ancient, wicked aura seemed to reach out toward her like poison gas drifting through a battlefield.

"Do you feel it?" she asked, wrapping her arms around her shoulders.

Dan shrugged. "The graveyard's got you spooked."

Sabrina stepped back and her heel came down on something hard nestled in the grass. A bolt of electricity shot through her. All the way to the tips of her red hair, causing it to stand on end around her face.

She looked down at the rounded white stone, smooth but for a faint image of a star scratched on its surface.

Could it be? With the realization, her breath turned shallow. "It's been cursed."

REBECCA YORK

A *USA TODAY* bestselling author, Ruth Glick published her one hundredth book, *Crimson Moon*, a Berkley Sensation, in January 2005. Since 1997 she has been writing on her own as Rebecca York. Her novel, *Killing Moon* was a launch book for Berkley's Sensation romance imprint in June 2003. Her latest 43 Light Street book was *The Secret Night*, in April, 2006. In October she launches the Harlequin Intrigue continuity series SECURITY BREACH with *Chain Reaction*.

Ruth's many awards include two RITA® Award finalist books. She has earned two Career Achievement awards from *Romantic Times BOOKclub* for Series Romantic Suspense and Series Romantic Mystery. *Nowhere Man* was the *Romantic Times BOOKclub* Best Intrigue of 1998 and is one of their reviewers' "all-time favorite 400 romances." Ruth's *Killing Moon* and *Witching Moon* both won the New Jersey Romance Writes Golden Leaf Award for Paranormal.

Michael Dirda of the *Washington Post Book World* says, "Her books...deliver what they promise: excitement, mystery, romance."

Between 1990 and 1997 Ruth wrote the Light Street series with Eileen Buckholtz. You can contact Ruth at rglick@capacces.org or visit her Web site at www.rebeccayork.com.

REBECCA YORK
Trial by Fire

HARLEQUIN®

TORONTO • NEW YORK • LONDON
AMSTERDAM • PARIS • SYDNEY • HAMBURG
STOCKHOLM • ATHENS • TOKYO • MILAN • MADRID
PRAGUE • WARSAW • BUDAPEST • AUCKLAND

ISBN-13: 978-0-373-36058-1
ISBN-10:   0-373-36058-4

TRIAL BY FIRE

Copyright: © 1992 by Ruth Glick and Eileen Buckholtz

www.eHarlequin.com

Printed in U.S.A.

CAST OF CHARACTERS

Sabrina Barkley—She was drawn into a world of danger and evil where only one man could save her...or condemn her to an eternal hell.

Dan Cassidy—This assistant state's attorney was out to get more from Sabrina than her knowledge of the arcane.

Sara Campbell—As word of her healing powers grew, she found herself in grave danger.

Duncan MacReynolds—He was bewitched by a red-haired lass.

Lillias Weir—She'd come a long way for revenge.

Hilda Ahern and Gwynn Frontenac—Two wealthy widows whose seemingly harmless enthusiasm could be steering them into the path of trouble.

Erin Morgan—Sabrina's assistant would do anything to help her boss, wouldn't she?

June Garrison—How deeply was she involved with Dr. Davenport?

Dr. Luther Davenport—Was this charismatic director of the Andromeda Institute running an upscale con game or was he masterminding a diabolical murder plot?

Prologue

Preparation was everything. Preparation and a heightened awareness of the dark currents that ebbed and flowed through the affairs of men. Currents you could use to your advantage, if you knew the ancient formulas. Currents that could sweep you into oblivion if you made the wrong move.

"Grant the success of this venture." Murmuring an incantation, the Servant of Darkness stepped through the door of the hidden chamber.

Black curtains were the backdrop of power here. They hung from floor to ceiling around the elongated room, shrouding walls and windows and even the door—shutting out what others called reality. Making a cocoon of solitude, and a nexus of power. For there was only one person who entered this secret place and came out alive.

There were no electric lights. Only dozens of long white tapers made in the ancient way from the fat of slaughtered animals and fitted into antique brass candelabra.

A table opposite the door held an open brass bowl. It was full of oil. But the oil was only an inert medium. The important part was the viscous liquid tinged a delicate pink, streaking the contents like the faintest trace of blood.

"For I will see the face of mine enemy." The Servant of Darkness went down on bended knees before the open bowl and offered a few words in the ancient formula. There were many ceremonies that could be performed in this private refuge. The one tonight was of special, urgent importance.

"And I will smite any who come to challenge my power. From the past and from the present."

There was a moment of silence while the feeling of strength and energy mounted. Then a practiced hand struck a long thin match and touched the flame to the oil. The fuel flared up, and as the mixture ignited, the essence of rotten cherries billowed forth, along with a strong mind-altering drug.

It wasn't a pleasant smell. Yet the occupant of the room leaned over the bowl and breathed deeply, welcoming the momentary sense of dislocation in time and space that the hallucinogen brought. For the unprepared, it could be a terrifying experience. For the initiated, the disorientation would clear away almost at once. Soon it would be replaced by the sure, sharp vision that had served for so many years.

Still on bended knees, the sorcerer approached the inlaid table in the exact center of the chamber. A large square of white silk—the only bit of cloth in the chamber that wasn't black—was mounded in the center.

Knowing fingers caressed the fabric, slick and smooth as a serpent's belly. Then the silk was whisked away to reveal the centerpiece of the room. A perfect sphere of pure crystal. Ten inches across, it rested in a dark metal stand.

"I will see the face of mine enemy," the Servant of Darkness repeated. This time it was a command—a gathering of forces.

The candle flames flickered in the mysterious depth of

the crystal ball, reflected in an endless pattern. Then, among the flames a face appeared.

It was a woman's countenance, hauntingly delicate and framed by a wreath of long red curls. Even the spray of freckles across the nose and cheeks had a winsome appeal.

Sara Campbell. Oh so pure. Oh so innocent.

The sorcerer hunched forward, staring down fixedly at the image shimmering in the crystal, watching the features blur and change subtly. As the face reformed, the skin became clear and translucent. The hazel eyes altered to sea green. The straggly brows were almost tamed.

Different.

Yet the same, for the superficialities were insignificant. More important was the vital spirit of Sara Campbell. The will. The soul within. Sara Campbell might be dead. But her essence had been reborn in a woman living now. In Sabrina Barkley.

"The cycle comes around again. But the master grants a second chance," the cruel voice intoned.

Yes! In this life, things would be different. But first, the two images must be brought together. Merged. Fused. The woman from the past. And the woman of the present. When Sabrina Barkley finally understood the full extent of the horror, she would be destroyed for all time. And the Servant of Darkness would glory in the victory.

Chapter One

In the dim light of the parking garage across from 43 Light Street, Sabrina Barkley folded her hands on the steering wheel and rested her head on her arms for a moment. Although she usually arrived at work full of energy, for the past few days she'd awakened feeling as if she'd spent the night running from an unseen pursuer. The dragging fatigue was accompanied by a sharp sense of anxiety that pressed her shoulder blades taut against the car seat.

Sabrina drew in a deep breath and let it out slowly. She wasn't going to indulge in a case of the jitters now. She had too much to do. Straightening her shoulders, she strode across the street to Sabrina's Fancy, the lobby shop she'd opened on a shoestring a few years ago.

As she walked in the door, her assistant, Erin Morgan, gave her an appraising look. "Hmm. Which is it? Good news or bad?"

Sabrina forced a laugh. "Both. Remember those proposals I've been writing to hotels and restaurants?"

"Of course."

"Well, the hospitality manager at the Harbor Court Hotel called yesterday afternoon. They're featuring local crafts people in some of their promotions, and they've ordered two hundred and fifty of my bath-herb-and-soap baskets to put in their suites for the Mid-Atlantic tourism conference.''

''Way to go!''

''Now all I have to do is find the time to make them up.''

''You could hire some helpers.''

''You're right. I keep forgetting I'm doing well enough for that. But I'd better sit and figure out what extra supplies I'll need.''

''I'll take care of things out front.''

''Thanks.''

As Sabrina crossed to her office, she gave silent thanks once more for Erin Morgan's quiet strength, although she knew her assistant felt just as lucky to be working here as she was to have found her. Erin's husband had been one of the casualties of the Gulf War, and she'd told Sabrina more than once how relieved she was to find a job that allowed her to support her young son and still work on the college degree that was so important to her future plans.

Sabrina closed the office door. A year ago she'd started to decorate the small room but had never really finished. It was dominated by the former school library table she used as a work surface and the antique pigeonhole desk she'd picked up in Fells Point at a going-out-of-business sale. Also squeezed into her private domain were a sofa where she sometimes snatched an afternoon nap and a narrow bookshelf crammed with reference volumes. Well, so much for Victorian elegance. At least the packets of herbs in the storage boxes always smelled good.

Usually Sabrina functioned well in the comfortable clutter, but now that she was alone again, another wave of uneasiness washed over her. Scraping back the desk chair with a jerky motion, she sat and felt her body sag again. After a few moments she made an effort to pull herself together and get to work. She hadn't spent years building up her business so she could fall apart when she got her first big chance to show her stuff.

The seminar on small-business strategies she'd taken last month had suggested that when you were planning a new venture, you should write down all the ideas that came to you, without worrying about details. Kind of like brainstorming with yourself. That was worth a try.

After squaring off at the desk, she picked up a pen and began to scribble on a white pad of paper. Color schemes. Scents. Textures. Herbs. Dried flowers. Unusual? Rosemary. Angelica. Lace. Satin ribbons. Too feminine? Lemon balm. Pastel tissue paper. Excelsior. White lacquer baskets.

At first the thoughts followed each other in rapid succession. Then the inspiration dried up. Sabrina fidgeted restlessly on her chair. All at once it was stuffy in the little office. No—suffocating. Although she dragged several deep breaths into her lungs, it seemed the oxygen didn't help much.

Sabrina tried to focus on what she'd written, but as she bent over the paper, the lines of script blurred. Alarm settled like a lead weight on her chest, pressing the air out of her chest.

The sensation became more acute as the whole room wavered. For an awful moment, currents of heat seemed to ripple through her head, playing over the surface of her brain like static electricity. Frantically her fingers gripped the shaft of the ballpoint pen she was still holding. Then her hand began to move across the page again. But this time the writing instrument took control—as if it were a magic wand and she were under some strange spell. Words and sentences flowed from the tip of the pen. Against her will, they dragged her away with them. Away to another time and another place.

...at the very moment Sara stepped out the door, a screeching raven dived toward the roof of the little cottage.

"No! Get ye gone." Dropping her basket, she rushed at the creature, flapping her apron. But to no avail. The bird circled the chimney before flying off toward the pines at the edge of the clearing.

Heart blocking her windpipe, Sara stood trembling in the little farmyard.

A raven so close to the house. A bad omen.

It was even more terrible if one of the huge black birds went round the chimney. A warning of death.

Gran had been sick this past fortnight. But she wasn't going to die! She couldn't!

"What is it, child?" a weak voice called from within.

Sara poked her head back inside, seeing the old woman covered with rough wool blankets and lying on her bed in the far corner of the cottage. "Just a bee buzzing my face," she fibbed, curling her bare toes in the muddy ground by the door. "Are ye sure naught will trouble ye while I'm gone?"

"Aye. Just get that wintergreen to soothe my old bones, and I'll be bonny. And gather some mountain thyme and coltsfoot. We'll be needing those, as well."

Torn, Sara hesitated.

"Go on, lass."

"Aye." Knuckles white against the dark basket handle, she started toward the craggy mountains. Yet once she was out in the heather with the wind picking up her red hair and the sun warming her lightly freckled face, she acknowl-

edged how sick she was of the dank stone cottage after a week of rain.

First she gathered wintergreen. Then she picked some of the other plants she'd learned to make into healing potions or use to flavor their simple food. She knew all the best places to look, and her basket was quickly full. Then above her on the side of the cliff, she spied a patch of rock speedwell. Gran was partial to the deep blue flowers, each petal with a crimson line at the base.

Setting her basket on a flat slab, Sara began to climb. When she reached the first ledge, she went on to the next. Few of the other village girls would have taken such chances, but timidity had never been one of her virtues. Minutes later, she smiled in satisfaction at her prize, a bouquet that would brighten their humble table. Needing both hands to scramble down, she tucked the flowers in the bodice laces of her wool dress.

She was still twenty yards from the valley floor when she heard hooves pounding across the rocky ground. The animal was dark and magnificent—a destrier, one of the highly trained battle horses. The rider must be a laird from the castle, judging from his rich cloak and fine leather boots. He was having trouble with the mount, yet he might have kept control of the beast if one of Sara's bare feet hadn't slipped on a patch of loose stone.

"Beware," she cried out.

He looked up just as the rocks rained down the side of the mountain toward him.

Too late.

As the missiles struck the horse, the animal screamed and bucked. Horrified, Sara saw the rider tossed into the air, his fall broken by a clump of gorse.

The horse galloped on. The man lay motionless.

Dead.

The omen had been meant for him.

Sara looked around. No one had seen the accident. If she ran right home, the lairds would never know what she had done. Yet even as the cowardly thought surfaced, she moved toward the still figure.

He lay sprawled on his stomach. Kneeling, she grasped him by the shoulders and rolled him over. His eyes were closed, and gold-tipped lashes lay softly against his tanned cheeks. When she touched his face to brush away the dirt, she sensed the first hint of the man's beard that hadn't fully grown in. His age couldn't be much more than her own fifteen years.

As her fingers touched his skin, he groaned.

He was alive!

With the skills Gran had taught her, she began to assess the damage. His white lawn shirt was covered with dirt. Of more concern was the torn leg of his britches. It was soaked with blood above the knee. Her hands were tearing at the fabric when strong fingers locked around her wrist.

"A wood sprite." His eyes were open now—and as blue as the stained glass in the window of the cathedral. With a shaky hand, he reached out and touched her fiery tresses. His fingers dropped to her shoulder and trailed slowly down to the bright flowers she'd tucked into her bodice. When he rustled through the foliage, she felt the pressure against her breasts. No one had ever touched her so familiarly. For a moment the breath froze in her throat as she gazed down at the hand. It was broad and well-formed—a foreteller of toughness and power to come. She couldn't move. Then, summoning her own strength, she brushed the fingers away.

"Be still," she ordered. "You've been hurt."

He moved his head and groaned, then tried to pull away from her. "You threw rocks down on me."

"Nay. It was but an accident. I meant you no harm. Please. I'm a skilled healer," she said, overstating her abilities a bit. "Let me help you."

He closed his eyes and lay back with a sigh while Sara retrieved her basket. Luckily she'd gathered some verbena. A poultice would start the healing of his wounds.

At a nearby stream, she tore several strips of cloth from her petticoat and dipped them in the cold water. Then, back at the lad's side, she began to clean his thigh.

Although she saw him clench his teeth as she picked embedded gravel from his flesh, he didn't cry out.

"You're from the castle?" she asked to distract him from the pain.

"I—"

"SABRINA! SABRINA!" His hand was on her arm. Shaking her. But he was hurt. Where did he get the strength? She stared at the hand in utter confusion. Too small. Too feminine.

"Sabrina. What's wrong?" An anxious voice floated toward her from somewhere close by. Her gaze fluttered from the hand that gripped her arm to a face that was vaguely familiar, but not a man's. It belonged to a red-haired lass.

Sabrina fought a rising sense of panic. Her eyes bounced from the intruder to the room and back again as she tried desperately to get a fix on reality. The young woman kneeling beside her. The place. The time. Herself.

It took every ounce of self-control to hold back a scream. She was trapped here. But who was she? Where was she? What was she supposed to be doing?

"Hey, are you going to pass out on me or something?"

The familiar voice and the urgent question were like a lifeline, and she clutched at them with all her strength. Inch by inch, she pulled herself to firmer ground.

"Jo?" she finally managed, her voice high and reedy as she stared at private detective Jo O'Malley. Her friend. "What are you doing out in the mountain pass?"

"Mountain pass?"

From the expression on Jo's face, Sabrina knew she must have said something outrageous. She looked away, praying for a safe place to rest her gaze. This time the room made more sense.

It belonged to her, Sabrina Barkley. And she was in the little office at the rear of her shop. Profound relief swept over her. Somehow she felt as if she'd just escaped an unspeakable fate, and she didn't even know what it was.

"You looked like you were in a trance."

"No. Really." Sabrina sat up straighter and cleared her throat, even as she wondered exactly what she was going to say. "I was, uh, using a brainstorming technique I picked up at a small-business seminar." To her surprise, she sounded almost coherent. Encouraged, she continued, "I guess I just got carried away."

She was still congratulating herself on her quick recovery when her eyes flicked back to the pen still clutched in her hand and the lines of script slanting across the page in front of her. A woman climbing rocks. A man falling from a horse.

The handwriting was familiar but the words seemed to have sprung from nowhere. Or her subconscious. Her heart started to pound. My God, what had she written? Reflexively she slapped a herb-seed catalog down on top of the pages.

"You don't have to make up a cock-and-bull story about

what you're doing. I didn't know you were into writing fiction. But that's pretty good stuff. Lots of nice description.''

"Hmm?"

"That historical novel. I guess you were pretty into it, huh?"

With a profound sigh of gratitude, Sabrina let the misconception stand. "I feel kind of silly, getting all wound up in, uh, something I'm writing."

"I know what you mean. Sometimes that happens with the crime fiction I'm working on."

Sabrina had forgotten Jo wrote detective stories. Now she gave her friend a conspiratorial smile. "So don't tell anybody you caught me, okay?"

"Sure. I understand. It's hard to show your work when you're just getting started." Jo pursed her lips, stood, and leaned on the edge of the worktable. "I was going to ask you a favor. I wish I hadn't barged in like this."

"Jo. It's okay. Honestly."

"Well, a friend needs a special favor."

"Dried bouquets?"

"No, he needs to borrow some of your expertise."

"With growing herbs?"

Jo sighed. "I guess there's just no good way to introduce the subject. It's got to do with the Graveyard Murders."

Sabrina couldn't repress an involuntary shudder. The strange murder cases had been headline news in the *Morning Sun* off and on for weeks. When the first article had appeared, she'd read the whole thing with a sort of morbid curiosity. But the story had given her a very spooky feeling that had made her studiously avoid any of the later accounts. "Is one of your clients involved?"

"No, but the assistant district attorney assigned to the

case is trying to get a lead on some of the evidence, and I thought you might be able to help him.''

Sabrina's fingers curled around the edge of the chair seat. The trapped feeling she'd thought she had under control had come screaming back.

Murder. The occult. The first newspaper article had given her the sense of something evil growing and thriving in a dark, obscure corner of the city. She'd been thankful it didn't involve her. Now she felt as if it had crept a step closer. But she didn't want to tell that to Jo, not when she'd successfully convinced her friend she was okay. And she didn't want to give in to the sense of dread she felt. Really, it was probably left over from whatever had happened to her with that story she'd been writing.

So she hid her reaction behind a flippant tone. ''If this is another one of your attempts to fix me up with an eligible bachelor, forget it. That computer-designer friend of Cam's couldn't talk about anything but chips and parallel processors.''

''This is on the up-and-up. You've heard of Dan Cassidy, haven't you?''

Sabrina thought for a moment. ''The guy who was leading the fight to take back the streets from the big-time drug dealers last year?''

''Yes.''

''I've read about him. He's supposed to be tough. So what exactly does he need from me?''

''Dan's looking for an expert opinion.''

''On what? I don't know anything about drugs. Except for some of the herbal compounds. And they aren't going to command big bucks on the street.''

''It's better if *he* tells you what he wants,'' Jo hurried on. ''He's springing for lunch at Sabatino's.''

"Did you tell him it was my favorite restaurant?"

"Of course."

Jo must have sensed her wavering. "Twelve-thirty," she said.

"Oh, all right. We can walk over together."

"Um, I can't. I'm testifying in one of Laura's child-abduction cases." Laura Roswell was a lawyer who also worked in the building. Married last month, she was finally getting back to a full schedule after a honeymoon on the West Coast.

"It's just you and Dan," Jo continued. "You'll like him."

"I don't have to like him. This is supposed to be business."

"Okay. Forget that part. But you need to know what he looks like so you can find him. He's got blond hair and blue eyes. He told me to tell you he's wearing a gray suit and a blue-and-gray rep tie."

Sabrina looked down at her own jade green caftan woven with gold threads. "We should make a striking couple."

"Sweetie, you can ditch him right after lunch if you want."

Sabrina watched her friend disappear through the open doorway. Then, almost against her will, her eyes were drawn back to the seed catalog she'd slapped on top of the pad of paper on her desk. Getting up, she closed the door very softly. Her heart started to pound again as she moved the catalog and began to scan what she'd written.

"Color schemes…herbs…satin ribbons…"

As she continued to read, a knot of tension grew in her stomach.

"…at the very moment Sara stepped out the door, a

screeching raven dived toward the roof of the little cottage.''

The knot expanded, pressing against her diaphragm. The story was so vivid. So real. Where had it sprung from? Then a memory came racing back into her mind like a rescue vehicle with sirens blaring. She'd done this same sort of thing a long time ago. As a kid, when she was feeling sad or unhappy or needed to escape, she'd go out behind the woodpile and tell herself little stories about a girl who lived in a cottage in the mountains with her grandmother. That explained what had happened a few minutes ago. She'd been insecure about the big hotel commission, so she'd regressed or something. Instead of buckling down to planning herb baskets, she'd started writing a romantic tale about another woman from a different time and place.

Sabrina pursed her lips, silently admitting that this had been different. As a little girl, she'd sought the solace of the stories when she was unhappy. This time, it was more like some outside force had compelled her to write. In fact, to be perfectly honest, she couldn't actually remember having composed this vignette.

Sabrina grimaced, feeling suddenly as if bony fingers were pressing into her shoulder. She knew no one was there. Still, it was all she could do to keep from looking over her shoulder. Pushing back her chair, she crossed to the bookshelves and stood with her arms folded, facing the room.

She wished she hadn't said yes to Jo. Instead of blowing her valuable time meeting some guy for lunch, she should be focusing on the work she had to do and also finding out if Erin needed any help. As she stepped into the front of the shop, she found her assistant restocking their inventory

of culinary herbs. Her rich brown hair hid her face as she
bent over the box of plastic packets.

"I hear you're meeting one of Baltimore's VIPs for
lunch," she said.

Oh great, Sabrina thought. Now if I cancel, I'll have to
explain myself to three people. But what exactly would she
say? She didn't really want to talk about the strange feeling
that had been hovering over her all morning.

THE LOCKUP DOORS slammed shut behind Dan Cassidy.
This time he was on the outside of the grim gray walls that
surrounded the Baltimore City Jail. Pausing, he rolled his
broad shoulders and sucked in a deep draft of the unfettered
air, letting the breath out slowly. It didn't matter why you
were inside the jail. You always emerged totaling up your
sins and feeling grateful for your freedom.

This morning, he should also be feeling overjoyed that
he had Raul Simmons behind bars with a signed confession
to the Graveyard Murders. Everybody else was satisfied
with the way things had turned out. After finding one of
the victim's wallets at Simmons's house, the police had
been happy enough to turn the case over to the district
attorney's office. And the mayor was pressing for a quick
conviction before the fall election.

Dan strode across the parking lot to his car. As far as he
was concerned, there were too many things that didn't add
up. Like the witchcraft angle, for example. Every time he
tried to get Simmons to talk about casting spells and performing rituals, the man just smiled his secret smile. It
might be the ploy of a coy sorcerer. Or the refuge of a man
who didn't know a broomstick from a toad's tongue.

Pausing with his fist on the door handle, Dan considered
another loose end. The Sabrina Barkley connection. A

crumpled gold-foil token with her logo had been found in a victim's pocket. It had taken a week of digging to tie the exuberantly stylized double ess to the lobby shop at 43 Light Street. After that, he'd had her checked out. On the surface, she was an upstanding if slightly eccentric member of the business community. But he'd always gone with his hunches, and the more he sifted through the information he'd accumulated about her, the more he felt as if something didn't add up.

The direct approach—the one he'd always taken in the past—would be to bring her in for questioning. He couldn't explain to himself why he was hesitating. Why he'd asked Jo to set up an appointment with Ms. Barkley. All she was supposed to think was that he wanted to use her for background on the case. Maybe he'd learn something about witchcraft by talking to her. It just wasn't his main agenda.

Realizing he was sitting in the car with the engine idling, Dan shifted into reverse and pulled out of his parking space. Ten minutes later he was back in front of the stately marble elegance of the Clarence Mitchell Courthouse. From the outside, it looked a heck of a lot better than the jail. Inside, it was a crowded rabbit warren. Luckily, as an assistant district attorney, he rated his own office, even if it was barely big enough for a desk, computer, filing cabinets and visitor's chair.

His secretary, Edna Strause, gave him a summary of the crises he'd missed while he'd been interviewing Simmons. However, there was one piece of halfway-good news.

"Ms. Barkley will meet you for lunch," Edna reported.

"Fine." He ignored the speculative look in his secretary's eyes and closed the door to his office.

It was a relief to loosen his tie and shrug out of his suit coat. Still, it wasn't easy to get down to work. On most days, he thrived on his job. He liked the hectic pace, the hard-fought trials, the negotiations, and especially the satisfaction of bringing criminals to justice. But not when the police dumped a half-baked case in his lap and expected him to produce something a judge could swallow.

AFTER ALMOST A WEEK of clouds and showers, sunlight was finally flooding through the fan transom over the entrance to 43 Light Street. A good omen, Sabrina told herself firmly as she pulled open one of the heavy brass-and-glass doors.

She started briskly down the hill toward the inner harbor. However, during the three-quarters of a mile walk to Baltimore's Little Italy—a neighborhood of row houses where almost every corner sported a restaurant, deli or bakery—her pace slowed considerably. In her enthusiasm for the sunshine, she must have misjudged the effects of the heat and the humidity, because by the time she reached the restaurant's black and white tile entry, she was feeling a bit like a wilted amaryllis in a 110-degree greenhouse.

Usually the aroma of onions sautéing in olive oil and chicken simmering in tomato-wine sauce made her mouth water. Today as she followed the maître d' past street scenes of old Baltimore to Dan Cassidy's table, she fought against a slight feeling of queasiness.

As they approached a darkened corner, the maître d' stepped out of the way and gestured toward a man seated at a table. The man's face and shoulders were in shadow. In fact, from where she stood, her best view was of a pair of long legs crossed at the ankles and protruding from under the table. It should have been an easy pose, yet as her eye traveled upward, she noticed that his fingers were tightly gripped around his water glass. When she took a step closer, he leaned forward and looked up.

God, she thought, he looked like Robert Redford in *Legal Eagles.*

Redford had spotted her. He stood, towering over her. Their eyes met, hers uncertain, his appraising.

"Ms. Barkley?"

"Mr. Cassidy."

His hand was extended, and she automatically reached to grasp his palm. As their flesh touched, a jolt of unexpected sensation went through her. Not something physical, exactly. More like an electrical charge right to her brain. It brought disorientation, a wave of heat across her skin, and something she couldn't name. Something from deep, deep in her subconscious.

Sabrina blinked as she recognized the sensations. They were similar to what had happened this morning, when the stupid list had turned into a scene from a historical novel.

Cassidy must have caught the odd expression on her face. "Are you feeling all right?"

For the second time today, she smiled and lied. "Just reacting to the weather, I guess." She drew herself up straighter. "I understand you need some help on a case."

"Yeah. I need some insights, all right. But maybe we should have some lunch before we discuss murder."

Chapter Two

Well, at least he had a sense of humor. Or maybe it wasn't meant to be a joke.

While Cassidy studied his menu, Sabrina studied him, scanning his face, trying for the quick insights she often gleaned.

Cassidy was too tall to play Redford. And too tough. The left side of his square jaw was marred by a small scar. And there was a ready-for-action way he carried his body that didn't quite go with the conservative suit and tie.

The blue eyes hidden from view as he gazed down at the menu wouldn't soften the effect. Sabrina couldn't say the same for his lashes. They were like gold fringe dipped with dark ink.

The waiter came and took their order. As soon as he'd left, her attention turned back to her companion. With a wry inner laugh, she realized she wasn't tuning into anything more than the very masculine physical package across the table from her. Dan Cassidy might make her feel off balance, but that didn't mean she wasn't attracted to him. Focusing her concentration, she tried to reach for something deeper, and came up against an almost-impenetrable wall. His guard was up. Against her? Or was he always like this with strangers? At the very least, she had the feeling he didn't like asking for advice.

He glanced up suddenly, discovered her watching and gave her a piercing look she felt all the way to the pit of her stomach.

"Jo says you're in the herb business," Dan said.

"Yes. I started growing them and researching old uses."

"So how did you get from herbs to the arcane?"

"I'm not exactly into the arcane. I hope that's not what Jo told you."

"She said you have a lot of talents. And now you have your own business?"

"Yes."

"What do you sell?"

"Herb products. Some jewelry. Dried flowers." She gestured with her hands. "Anything that catches my fancy. That's how the shop got its name. So what makes you think I can help you?"

Dan didn't answer. He was staring at the double gold ess charm dangling from her bracelet. "You sell those?"

"It's my logo. I put a foil one in with each purchase as a personalized touch."

"Why a double ess?"

"I got to playing with my name and liked this design."

"The charms must be expensive."

"Not really. I get thousands at a time."

"So your business must be doing pretty well."

"I can pay the bills."

"How did you get started?"

His rapid-fire questions went beyond casual interest. In fact, they made her feel as if she were on the witness stand, and she had the odd sensation that he already knew most of the answers. Still, it was difficult not to respond.

"When I was a kid, my family lived in a little community on Stony Creek. I had a crazy old aunt who loved the shore. She used to park herself at our house every summer for a couple of weeks. The rest of the family hated her visits because the place was already pretty crowded. But I'd sit there fascinated when she'd read my palm and tell my fortune from my tea leaves. When she died, it turned out that she had a pretty nice nest egg socked away in the bank. She left it to me."

"Lucky you. So what do you see in my palm?" Cassidy asked unexpectedly.

Sabrina glanced up at him, aware of a challenge in his blue eyes. At the same time, she remembered the jolt when they'd shaken hands. She wanted to brush off the request. Really, this was silly. She only had a passing acquaintance with palmistry, but Cassidy was offering her an opportunity to prove to herself that the previous reaction had been nothing more than the culmination of her own nervous anticipation. She reached for the large hand he'd extended, cupping it between her smaller ones.

At first neither one of them moved—or breathed. The touch of his warm, dry skin had a strangely mind-emptying effect. When she finally remembered what she was supposed to be doing, Sabrina cast her eyes downward toward his palm.

"Will I get a conviction in the murder-one case I'm putting together?" he asked.

The edge of mockery in his voice brought her back. All at once she thought she understood where he was coming from—why he'd asked so many questions. He wanted to find out whether she was out in left field before he told her about the case. Maybe she'd give him something to think about. "Your life line is very curved and your head line is almost ramrod straight. That's a classic setup for conflict."

"Like what?"

She traced her finger along the crease that made a semi-circle around his thumb. The Mount of Venus at the base was pronounced—a sign of sensuality. She wasn't going to tell him that. Or that he had a strong primitive streak. Not in so many words.

At her touch, his muscles contracted. She wanted to search his face again. Instead she kept her head tipped downward and moved his hand into better light. Now she could see a definite break near where the life line began.

"Did you have a life-altering event in your childhood?"

Sabrina felt his whole body tense and knew that she'd touched a raw nerve. But when her eyes flicked to his face, it was carefully blank. Like a closed door that was marked private.

She swallowed. "Really, we don't have to keep on with this."

The tense look softened into a knowing smile. With his other hand, he took her thumb and pressed it against the pad of skin below his index finger. "Aren't you going to tell me about my Mount of Jupiter?"

Any speculations about his early life were swept away by prickles of sensation that started where he held her thumb against his flesh. She'd felt nervous since she'd met the man, and she fought to deny the response. "Yours denotes assertiveness. Competitiveness. A respect for hard facts. A tendency to scoff at what you don't understand. Am I getting warm?"

She looked up, ignoring the way his blue eyes bored into her. "Why didn't you tell me you'd done this before?"

To her surprise, he laughed, but he didn't let go of her hand. In fact, neither one of them moved.

"We had a palm reader up on a grand-larceny charge six months ago. She kept trying to convince me that my destiny would work out for the better if I reduced the charge to petty theft."

"And?"

"I guess if she could really predict the future, she'd have stayed a step ahead of the police."

Sabrina raised her chin. "We both know making predictions about specific happenings in the future from looking at a person's palm is about as scientific as running the presidency based on astrological predictions, but each person's hand is still unique. And lines etched there reflect not only physical attributes, but character and personality." She pointed to the fourth finger of his left hand. "There's a very faint mark at the base here. Either you got tired of your class ring, or you took off a wedding band a couple of years ago."

He didn't move a muscle. "Divorced."

They became aware that they were still holding hands and that the waiter had arrived with their food.

Dan took his hand back. She folded hers in her lap.

Halfway through the meal, Cassidy cleared his throat. "Sorry. You're right. I wasn't being fair. This case is putting a lot of pressure on me, but I shouldn't have taken my frustration out on you."

"Want to tell me something about it?"

"Yes. Do the names Ian Alastair or Bette Kronstat mean anything to you?"

Sabrina thought hard. Ian? Did she know an Ian?

She looked up to find Cassidy watching her closely. "No. I don't think so."

"They're the two victims of the Graveyard Murders. We didn't know their names initially, because neither one was found with any identification." He looked around the room. Most of the lunch crowd had cleared out, and the nearby tables were now unoccupied. "I'm sure you've read something about it. Kronstat was found first. Then Alastair. In different graveyards."

Sabrina's fingers wadded the napkin in her lap. "Wasn't there supposed to be a ritual aspect to the murders?"

"Yes. And we've got a confession from a guy who says he did it. The problem is, I'm not sure I believe him." Reaching down beside his chair, he brought out a glossy photograph. "Would you mind taking a look at this?"

In the dim light, Sabrina couldn't see any details. "It's not a body or anything, is it?"

"No. Just a strange symbol."

The assurance didn't make her feel any less apprehensive as he handed the picture across the table. Looking down at the photograph, Sabrina found herself staring at a crude drawing carved into a charred wooden board. It was a wide open, unblinking eye. The sight of it wiped out everything else she'd been feeling. It seemed to be focused on her with a malice that she could feel all the way to the marrow of her bones.

"The evil eye," she breathed.

"What?"

"The evil eye," Sabrina repeated. "It's an almost universal symbol. Every culture has it. The idea is that certain men and women have the power to kill or make you sick or give you bad luck just by looking at you."

"That's ridiculous!"

"Of course. We know that today. But centuries ago when

somebody who was perfectly well suddenly fell deathly ill, it was an explanation that people could understand.''

''And when they decided whose evil eye had caused the malady, what happened?''

Sabrina grimaced. ''The person—usually a woman—was likely to be accused of witchcraft. In some countries she was hanged. In others, she was burned.'' As Sabrina said the last words, she could hear the horror in her own voice.

Dan gave her a sharp look. ''What does that have to do with a murder in Baltimore at the end of the twentieth century?''

''There are plenty of superstitious people who believe in hexes and curses. In the Middle East, you can still buy amulets to ward off the evil eye. For that matter, there have always been a few people who thought they could get ahead in life by tapping the power of…of…the dark forces. Even in this country, there are modern witches and devil worshipers.''

''So you think, rightly or wrongly, the murder victims were tried and convicted of witchcraft and executed by some vigilante group?''

''I don't know.''

''I'd like to take you over and show you where the most recent body was found and where this eye was in relationship to it.''

''You mean if I don't have anything more pressing this afternoon, you'd like to take me to visit a cemetery where someone didn't bother to bury the latest corpse?'' she inquired.

''You could put it that way.''

A simple yes or no would do, she thought. Yet under the table, Sabrina clutched the wadded napkin as she tried to grapple with conflicting emotions.

Cassidy had raised her curiosity. It wasn't as strong as the fear that if she helped him, she'd be getting herself into something that, for want of a better word, she might label evil.

The assistant district attorney was waiting for an answer.

"I'm sorry," she heard herself say. "I just don't think I want to get any more involved."

Disappointment flashed on his face, then a polite mask dropped into place. "You're perfectly free to decline, of course." Reaching in his pocket, he fished out a small leather case. "Here's my card. If you change your mind, give me a call."

"I will." But she knew she wouldn't.

His expression was unreadable as he watched her hurry away from the table.

Dan Cassidy's face was still impassive as he headed for the side street where he'd parked his car. A public prosecutor who didn't have a poker face was like an investment planner without a tax shelter. It was only when he'd climbed into his car that the mask slipped.

Back to square one. Or almost. He wasn't sure what to think about Sabrina Barkley. So maybe Ian Alastair had made an innocent purchase at Sabrina's Fancy. Or maybe someone had given him a bar of her bath soap. But there'd been a slight hesitation before Ms. Barkley denied knowing him. And that wasn't all. She'd been nervous all during lunch. Why, if she didn't have anything to hide?

Still, she'd given him something to think about.

The execution of a witch. Had Simmons gone after someone who'd frightened him? Or was he taking the fall for a group? Or was Ms. Barkley deliberately trying to throw him off the scent? Trusting her insights might raise more questions than it answered.

Dan sighed. As he glanced down at his hands on the steering wheel, his eyes went to the place where the gold band had circled his flesh. The line was practically invisible. Ms. Barkley had sharp eyes.

But her personal insights had been the more disturbing part of the palm reading. Perhaps his own reactions were coloring his judgment. Sabrina wasn't the only one who'd been off balance during lunch. He hadn't just been thinking about the murder investigation. He'd been reacting to the fiery autumn hair, the clear green eyes, the sexual awareness that he could feel zinging back and forth between them when she'd been holding his hand.

As he recalled the pressure of her warm flesh against his, he acknowledged the sensations hadn't all been sexual. There'd been something more. Something that had made him edgy. Her picture hadn't been included in the packet of information he'd collected on her, but he kept feeling as if he should recognize her, anyway. Had she been called to jury duty? Had her name come up in connection with one of his previous investigations? Had he seen her in the crowd at the Crab's Claw Pub down in Fells Point?

None of those sounded right. Because he wouldn't have forgotten her if he'd met her before.

His mind went back to the palm reading, and he grimaced. There weren't half a dozen people who knew about the tragic event that had changed his life. Yet one glance at his hand and she'd seen something he'd thought was invisible. Would she have mentioned it if she'd been worried that he was suspicious of her?

It didn't make sense. But he could certainly understand

her turning him down. Well, if she thought this was the last she was going to hear from him, she better take another look at her tea leaves.

SABRINA WAS MAKING some real headway on the Harbor Court Hotel plans when there was a knock on the door. Erin leaned into her office and asked in a low voice, "Is it all right to tell Hilda and Gwynn you're here?"

"Of course. I'll be right out."

Hilda Ahern had been a customer of Sabrina's since she'd sold homemade vinegars and jellies at her Howard County house, and she'd introduced her friend Gwynn Frontenac to the joys of herb teas and exotic spices.

The two ladies were both wealthy widows in their sixties who filled their days with volunteer work, long lunches at the Women's Industrial Exchange, and a never-ending stream of harmless enthusiasms.

Sabrina greeted the two customers with a smile. Hilda was short and thin and wore sporty junior clothing. From twenty feet away, the outfits looked appropriate. But when you saw her up close, you realized that even a couple of face-lifts and nightly application of expensive estrogen cream couldn't rejuvenate skin that had been overexposed to the sun.

Gwynn was tall and gave the impression of a steamship plowing through choppy waters. While some women her size dressed in dark colors, she was partial to large splashy prints, primary hues and broad-brimmed picture hats.

"I stopped in for some of your tarragon vinegar and that divine lavender soap," Hilda began.

"Of course."

"By the way, what herbs would you recommend for the heart? I've been having some palpitations at night," Gwynn inquired.

Sabrina paused with her hand on the vinegar bottle. "You really should ask your doctor about that," she murmured.

"Oh, *doctors,* what do they know? My internist's just going to attach a bunch of electrodes to my chest, give me another one of those beastly stress tests and charge me five hundred dollars for the torture. And he's not going to find anything."

"Perhaps you should try Dr. Davenport. He's much more sympathetic to sensibilities of refined women like us," Hilda put in. "I've got some free tickets for his lecture tomorrow." The smaller woman shuffled through her fanny pack and brought out two bright pink cards, one of which she handed to Sabrina. "You should come too, hon. He's so knowledgeable about the mind-body connection. I know you'd pick up some pointers."

"How thoughtful of you, Hilda," Sabrina said. "I've heard interesting things about him. I will try to make it."

Before they left, Gwynn leaned toward Sabrina. "It's a long ride back to Ruxton. Can I borrow your little girls' room while you ring up the sale?" she asked, laying her credit card on the antique oak counter.

"Of course. And be sure to try the new hand cream I've put out." She didn't have to tell Gwynn the facilities were through her office, since it was a standard request.

Sabrina and Hilda were chatting when the other woman returned, rubbing rosemary-scented cream into her hands. "This is quite nice. Can I get a bottle?"

Sabrina added it to the sixty dollars' worth of purchases already on the slip. After the door had closed, she glanced at Erin and found her assistant looking uncomfortable.

"What's wrong?"

"I don't like to repeat gossip."

"I'm not going to spread it," Sabrina assured her.

"You're not really going to get mixed up with Luther Davenport, are you?"

"Why not? What have you heard about him?"

"My mother told me one of her friends went to a free lecture and ended up giving a donation she couldn't afford to his Andromeda Institute."

"A lot of my customers are excited about him, and I'm curious."

"Well, leave your checkbook home."

"I can take care of myself." Yet even as she spoke the reassurance, she silently admitted that she hadn't been doing a very good job of it today.

Bustling back to her office, she got out several boxes of herbs to see how much she'd need to purchase for the Harbor Court project. But now that she was alone, with the pungent smell of thyme, lavender and lemon balm filling the room, her thoughts drifted back to the encounter with Dan Cassidy at lunch. Once again she felt the disturbing prickles of sensation dancing on her skin.

Sabrina dropped the sprigs of thyme on the desk, unaware that she was scattering the tiny leaves. Images flickered in her head. The horseman. The mountain. Dan Cassidy's face. Good grief. Somehow meeting him was getting mixed up with the story she'd been writing.

Struggling to wrench her mind back to the task at hand, Sabrina looked down at the herb sprigs forgotten on the surface of her desk.

She gasped. A malevolent eye stared back at her.

Reason told her it was just an arrangement of twigs and stems, but the illusion was too strong to shake. With a jerky brush of her hand, Sabrina swept everything onto the floor and then sat looking down at the mess she'd made. The eye was gone, scattered at her feet. But the feeling of disquiet persisted.

With a sigh, she went to get the broom. But as she passed the bookshelves, her steps halted in front of the collection of reference books she'd purchased over the years.

Something. Something tugged at her memory. Did it have to do with the story she'd been writing? Or with what she and Dan had talked about at lunch? Or the pattern she'd just seen?

Running her finger along the spines of the books, she paused at one called *The Secret Tradition.* It was a history of the black arts, written in the eighteenth century. The author, one Silas Purves, had evidently been a believer, and Sabrina had been surprised at some of the nonsense presented as doctrine. She felt a little shiver on the back of her neck as her finger rested on the volume.

Not her preferred sort of reading. But it had been part of a box of books she'd bought at an estate sale.

Sabrina wanted to turn away, but some outside force kept her rooted to the spot in front of the bookcase. The same force seemed to guide her arm as she reached up and pulled down the musty tome. It fell open in her hand, and she found herself staring at a wood carving that was remarkably similar to the photograph Cassidy had shown her. And the eye that had just materialized out of dried herbs on her worktable.

Sabrina's chest tightened in a painful spasm. Somehow she stopped herself from dropping the book on top of the pile of dried greenery. Instead her fingers curled around the worn binding.

After several erratic heartbeats, she was able to bring her gaze back to the crude picture. This time a block of wood with the eye was propped up against a tree. In front of it was a dead man laid out on the ground with his arms folded across his chest. But his face was contorted, his tongue sticking out as if he'd died of some terrible agony.

Sabrina turned her head away to shut out the horrible sight. Was she going to see this disturbing image everywhere she turned?

Perhaps the text would give her some clue about what was going on. Covering the picture with one flattened hand, she began to skim the accompanying passage.

> Witches often project their powers by the use of symbols. A representation of the evil eye can be just as deadly as the look itself—for it extends a witch's evil sphere of influence beyond her person.
>
> A body found in the vicinity of such a symbol should be presumed to be the victim of a witch's malice.

Sabrina stared at the passage with distaste. Silas Purves wrote with the strength of conviction. Probably he was sorry he'd been born too late to be a member of the witch-trial court. Sabrina sniffed derisively. Why would the witch be stupid enough to leave such an obvious calling card? You'd only do that if you were darn sure of your power. The sniff turned into a little shudder.

She started to shove the book back and stopped. In good conscience she couldn't pretend she'd never seen the pages. Based on their brief conversation, Cassidy had wondered if the individuals he'd found dead in the cemetery had been tried and convicted of witchcraft. This passage seemed to be saying just the opposite. Which meant that he might be wasting time pursuing false leads.

Maybe she should tell his secretary so he could have

someone come over and pick the book up. That would discharge her obligation, and she wouldn't have to actually talk to the man.

Sorting through the clutter that always seemed to multiply in her purse, she dug out the card and dialed the number.

ERIN HAD ALREADY LEFT for the day when the bell over the shop door jingled. Sabrina looked up from behind the counter to find herself swallowed up by Dan Cassidy's disturbing blue gaze.

Neither one of them moved. Then he seemed to realize he'd been staring and began to look around the shop, his eyes cataloging natural cosmetics, potpourri and handmade jewelry.

"So this is Sabrina's Fancy."

"Yes."

He picked up a stylized foil ess from beside the cash register and held it against the charm that dangled from her bracelet. Instead of putting the foil letter back, he slipped it into his pocket and cleared his throat. "I was surprised you called."

"I didn't expect you to show up in person."

"I was all out of herb tea."

"You don't drink herb tea."

"Maybe I'll take it up," he countered.

"I'll make sure you leave with a starter kit."

"Can I see the book?"

Sabrina bent, pulled the dusty volume from the shelf under the counter and opened it to the place she'd marked.

Instead of going right to the passage, Dan picked up the tome, looked at the gold lettering on the spine and flipped to the title page. "*The Secret Tradition.* Do you do a lot of witchcraft research?"

"No. I don't like the subject. This is really the only book I have. There's actually some useful information on herbs buried in the text."

Dan turned to the marked section, studied the picture carefully and then began to read. When he finished, he closed the book and laid it back on Sabrina's desk. "Perhaps I've been making the wrong assumptions in the murder investigation."

Sabrina shrugged. "At least this is something else to consider."

"Like maybe a modern witch in Baltimore is trying to extend her evil sphere of influence. Do you know any practicing witches in the area?"

"If I do, they haven't confided in me about their midnight activities. But I told you, there are people all over the country who call themselves witches. Men and women. Most of them say they're connected with an ancient tradition of natural practices. White magic. Or good magic, if you want to call it that. There might be somebody around here who dabbles in the black arts."

"But we both know magic is a big con." He was baiting her again.

"Is it? Then why does a person who knows he's under a *hungan*'s hex curl up and die?"

"What's a *hungan?*"

"A voodoo priest."

"It's fear of the curse that kills."

"So in a sense, the magic did work. It's just like a doctor who gives a hypochondriac a placebo and tells him it will make him feel better. If the patient wants it to work, it just might do the trick."

The assistant district attorney looked perplexed. "You keep coming up with logical arguments for the illogical."

Sabrina laughed. Cassidy might be skeptical, but he was sharp. "I guess I like to play devil's advocate."

"An interesting choice of words, under the circumstances." He cleared his throat. "I don't want to keep pushing you on this. But it's obvious you know a heck of a lot more about witchcraft than I do."

"The subject makes you uncomfortable," she shot back.

"Yeah."

"You think it's all a bunch of mumbo jumbo."

"Yeah." His eyes continued to meet hers.

"You don't like working with someone you consider a nut."

He flushed slightly. "Opinions can change."

Sabrina lifted her chin. "All right, I'll go to the cemetery with you."

FROM THE PASSENGER SEAT of Dan's car, Sabrina watched him loosen the knot of his tie, slide it from around his neck and toss it into the back seat. "You don't mind if I get out of uniform, do you?"

"Of course not."

His suit jacket followed the tie, folded rather than tossed. Suddenly he looked less civilized, as if the nine-to-five trappings had actually been some kind of disguise. When he leaned over to adjust the temperature control, a gold chain with a primitive-looking medallion swung free. In the center was a blazing sun.

He straightened, and it settled back against the golden hairs curling at his neck.

Sabrina's fingers were drawn to the charm. They closed

around the gold disk and held it so that she could see it better.

"That's very old, isn't it? Where did you get it?"

"Family heirloom. Do you know what it's supposed to be?"

Sabrina smoothed her thumb over the design. "In ancient times it was widely believed that man prayed from his heart, the center of his emotional life. That's probably a good-luck charm symbolizing the link between the heart and the sun."

"Interesting."

When she realized the heel of her hand was resting against the front of Dan's shirt and that the gesture was much too familiar for such a short acquaintance, she dropped the ornament.

"It was my grandfather's. He brought it along when the family emigrated from Scotland."

"Scotland?"

"You've been there?"

"I—no."

"Me neither." There was a wistful look in Dan's eyes. "When I was a kid, I used to have a great time at grandpa's place in the country. He left the charm to me, and I started wearing it." He seemed a little embarrassed by the explanation. Or maybe it was the liberty she'd taken.

They both turned away from the intimacy. Sabrina busied herself with the lap belt. Dan started the engine.

Before they reached the city line, he turned off Frederick Road into an area of small red-brick town houses that looked as if they'd been there since the early fifties. It was all very uniform and very middle class until they came to a forbidding stone wall topped by a wrought-iron fence. The road crested a small hill, and Sabrina peered over the

wall, staring at old trees and rows of gravestones. Many
were elaborate monuments obviously erected in the last
century. But the obelisks, angels and crosses were black-
ened by years of exposure to the elements, and there was
a certain run-down look about the place.

Sabrina studied the houses on the other side of the wall.
She definitely wouldn't want to live there. It might be all
right during the day. At night she'd imagine all sorts of
flickering shapes in the shadows under the trees and behind
the tall monuments. She'd always half believed in ghosts.
Her friend Laura Roswell's adventure at Ravenwood last
year had reinforced her conviction that a restless spirit
might reach out from the grave and try to affect the affairs
of the living.

She was about to wrench her gaze away from the ram-
shackle city of the dead when a flicker of movement that
was both furtive and swift caught her eye. She didn't know
she'd gasped until Dan Cassidy slammed on the brakes.

Chapter Three

"What's wrong?" Dan asked sharply.

"I thought I saw someone sneaking around down there."

"Where?"

Sabrina pointed toward an area thick with gravestones. They both stared silently and intently, but nothing else stirred.

"Maybe it was a shadow," Sabrina murmured, wishing she hadn't gasped and given her nervousness away.

Dan nodded and started the car again. But Sabrina kept her eyes trained on the graveyard until the road dipped too low for her to peer over the wall. Perhaps she really had only seen the shadow of a tree branch animated by a sudden puff of wind. But try as she might, she couldn't shake the notion that something more sinister was waiting on the other side of the wall.

"Ever been here before?" Dan asked as he pulled up at the gate. He was scrutinizing her again in that intense way she'd come to dislike.

"No! Why are you staring at me?"

"I'm wondering why you're so nervous."

"I don't like this place. Okay?"

"It's kind of run-down, isn't it?" He nosed the car into

the stone arch that guarded the entrance. Further progress was blocked by a locked gate.

Sabrina wished she was somewhere else. But it was much too late to back out now.

"I'll only be a minute." Dan got out of the car and headed toward the nearby caretaker's cottage. The stone building looked like something out of Grimms' Fairy Tales. Irrationally Sabrina's palms grew moist as Dan disappeared inside. She kept her eyes on the door until he reappeared, followed by a bent old gentleman carrying an iron key that must have weighed a couple of pounds.

"Honk loud when you get ready to leave," he instructed. "If you don't want to get locked in, remember I'm not gonna be around tonight after eight. Got a meetin' down at the church."

Locked in! Sabrina's eyes darted to her watch. When she saw it was just a little after six, she sighed with relief. They should have plenty of time to finish their business and get out again.

"You haven't had any more trouble, I assume," Dan asked as he stood beside the car.

"I haven't heard a peep out of the residents, but then my ears ain't too good no more. Didn't hear a thing when that guy got dragged in here and laid out like the main event in a satanic ritual."

The casual remark set Sabrina's teeth on edge. It also gave a focus to her disquiet. She and Dan had come here because of a murder, and she'd wondered whether dark forces were involved. Well, the residue of evil lingered in the air like something palpable. She glanced at Dan. Didn't he feel it?

"The police will continue to patrol the area," he told the caretaker as he climbed back into the car. "But be sure to call the precinct if there's even a hint of anything suspicious.''

When the gate clanked behind them, Sabrina felt as if she'd just been shut into a coffin. The narrow road winding between the rows of graves contributed to the claustrophobic effect. It had probably been built in horse-and-buggy days, which meant getting a hearse in here must be like shoehorning sardines back into the can, she mused as they rounded a tight curve flanked by a small mausoleum and a praying angel.

"Let's circle around the back of the site," Dan suggested. "That way we won't have to back up to get out."

Poised for a quick getaway, she thought. "Fine," was all she said.

"If we leave the windows open, it won't get so hot in here."

"Okay."

When Dan opened his door, Sabrina remained seated. She didn't usually wait for someone else to escort her out. Now she was in no hurry. As Dan helped her from the car and she stepped onto the dried grass, she felt a wave of heat and humidity wrap around her like a suffocating blanket, making her feel as if the air were too heavy to drag into her lungs. Yet she really didn't want to breathe this atmosphere at all. Not when an ancient, wicked aura seemed to reach out toward her like poison gas drifting through a battlefield. It touched every molecule of flesh on her skin and somehow seeped below the surface, too.

As if she could block out the disturbing sensation, Sabrina clamped her teeth together and wrapped her arms around her shoulders. "Do you feel it?" she asked, hearing her voice rise at the end of the question.

Dan glanced down at his shirtfront, which was already starting to stick to his chest. ''The heat? Yeah.''

Not just the heat, she almost screamed, her gaze bouncing off the grave markers and crosses and coming back to Dan. He was openly studying her.

''You look so pale. What's wrong?''

''Something. I don't know.'' She looked around again, this time more slowly, her eyes probing the long shadows blurring the edges of every gravestone and every tree, afraid she was going to spot whatever had been sneaking around before. Only this time it would be much closer.

''I think the graveyard's just got you spooked.''

''If that's what you want to call it.''

''Are you afraid of ghosts?''

Unwilling to answer, she shrugged, breathing shallowly.

''The site's over there.'' He pointed down the hill.

If Dan hadn't held her firmly by the arm, she would have hung back as they started down the slope toward the murder scene. She felt as if she were being towed along under water, every movement slow and heavy.

He drew to a stop in front of a large granite slab that was badly weathered. The base had shifted so that the stone listed to one side at a seventy-degree angle. Weeds ringed the area. In the center, instead of a mound was a rectangular depression.

''I guess they didn't pay for perpetual care,'' Sabrina muttered. Now that they were at the actual site, every one of her nerve endings was at screaming alertness. This spot was dangerous. Very dangerous.

''It's one of the oldest grave sites in the cemetery.''

Trying to come up with a rational explanation for the way she was feeling, Sabrina peered at the time-worn surface of the marker. Carved across the front, the name Ridley was barely visible. And the date. 1820? 1828?

"The victim was lying in the depression, with his head facing in the direction of the stone. His arms were folded across his chest," Dan told her. "The carving was propped against the headstone."

Sabrina felt the skin of her belly crawl as she pictured the body lying in the depression. "He was oriented like the man in the illustration," she murmured. "With the headstone taking the place of the tree."

"I wondered if you'd pick up on that." Dan reached toward her. Despite the heat and humidity, she moved closer to him. Her breath was even more shallow and irregular now, and the part of her mind that was still functioning knew it was in danger of shutting down.

"Bad vibrations?"

Sabrina was far beyond putting up any kind of front. "Yes." Unconsciously she took several steps back. As she did, the heel of her shoe came down on something hard nestled in the grass. A bolt of electricity seemed to shoot through her. She felt it all the way to her fingertips. All the way to the tips of her red hair, which stood on end around her face.

"What the hell—" Dan grabbed Sabrina's arm before she toppled over and eased her down to the ground.

She sat there in the weeds, looking around in a daze. The breath that hissed in and out of her lungs burned.

"Are you all right?"

"...hurts..."

"What?"

"My chest...hurts to breathe."

Dan was on his knees beside her, watching her face. The worry in his eyes made her struggle to relax her contorted features. After a moment, she could speak more easily. "It's getting better."

"Thank God." He stroked her arms and shoulders, smoothing down the strands of hair that floated around her face. Her eyes drifted closed, and her head flopped forward against his chest.

"What happened? Did you step on a live wire or something?"

"I don't know," she murmured into his shirtfront.

For several heartbeats he cradled her against himself, stroking her gently. When his thumb skimmed across her lips, her lids fluttered open, and she stared up into his blue eyes. They were as full of surprise and doubt as she imagined her own to be.

"It's my fault that happened to you," he muttered.

"No."

"I practically forced you to come here." His voice was gritty.

"I wouldn't have come if I hadn't wanted to help you."

An unreadable look crossed his face. "Are you sure you're okay?" he asked.

"I think so," Sabrina whispered.

"I want to find out what you stepped on."

Fear leaped inside her chest, and she grabbed his arm. "Be careful!"

"Don't worry."

Her pounding heart added to the pain in her chest as she watched him searching in the grass around the area where she'd been standing. He poked cautiously at the ground.

"Don't."

"It's okay." When he turned back to her he was holding a perfectly rounded white stone. It was smooth, except for the faint image of a star scratched into the top surface.

He peered at it doubtfully. "Maybe it had some kind of electrical charge. It's gone now."

Sabrina looked at the oval nestled innocently in Dan's hand.

Teeth clenched, she reached out and lightly touched a finger to the star. All that was left was a faint buzzing sensation like insect wings vibrating against a windowpane.

"You don't feel anything?" she whispered.

"What?"

"Tingling."

He shook his head, then looked from her to the stone.

"I'm not making the whole thing up."

"Of course not. I saw your hair standing on end like you'd stuck your finger into an electric socket, and I saw the way it hurt you to breathe." Dan turned the orb in his hand, looking at it from all angles.

Sabrina shuddered. "Put it down."

"What is it?"

"Something bad. Something that's been cursed."

"Cursed? How do you know? Are you saying a spell gave you that shock?"

Put that way, it sounded silly. She shrugged and struggled to her feet. When she swayed slightly, he reached out a hand to steady her. All she wanted was to get out of this place before anything else happened.

"Maybe there's another one." After making sure she wasn't going to topple over, Dan moved off through the weeds, his eyes focused on the ground. Seeing him hunker down, Sabrina hurried to his side. Another white shape nested in the grass.

"Don't touch it."

"Okay. I'll call the lab and tell them to use protective measures when they pick it up." She saw him hesitate. "I'll take you back to the car. Then I want to see if there are any more.''

Sabrina had felt as if she were balancing on a razor's edge ever since they'd arrived at the graveyard. The idea of going to the car and waiting there by herself made her throat clog. ''No, I'll help,'' she murmured.

''You feel well enough?''

''Yes.'' At first the assurance was a lie. Then as she began to walk around the site in the opposite direction from Dan, she did start to feel better.

It took half an hour to find seven more stones laid out in a pattern around and across the grave. The whole configuration was about twelve feet wide and twenty feet long.

''Nobody spotted any of these before?'' Sabrina asked doubtfully.

''Most of them are pretty far from the grave, and they just look like stones in the weeds, unless you step on one and it zaps you. Do you think they're like land mines or something? I mean, are they supposed to interfere with a search of the site?''

Sabrina drew in a deep breath and let it out slowly. Dan had been giving her odd looks and making pointed remarks since they'd met. Perhaps the best way to deal with him was to get his doubts out into the open. ''Maybe the stones don't affect most people the way they affected me.''

He turned to face her squarely. ''What do you mean?''

''It probably sounds like a new-age cliché to you, but sometimes I pick up vibrations from people—or things. Like for example, the minute we drove through the gates of this place I started feeling as if something evil was waiting to—I don't know—grab me.''

''I guess on some level, I did, too,'' Dan muttered. ''But I was damned if I was going to admit it.''

"I appreciate your telling me that."

"I don't like to give in to that sort of feeling."

"Neither do I," Sabrina agreed. "But something bad—or evil if you want to call it that—happened here. A ritual murder, to be specific. And the murderer is almost certainly the one who put those stones around the grave in a certain pattern."

Dan nodded.

"I was already sensitized by the aura of this place. Then I stepped on the stone and it was like a direct connection to what had happened." As she spoke, the hairs on her scalp stirred. "Does that make any sense to you?"

"Sort of. I think I can understand."

She'd been braced to have him laugh at her. Now she let out a long sigh.

"A pattern, yeah. So what do you think it means?" Dan asked.

"I'm not sure. Let's see what it looks like," Sabrina answered, glad the conversation was no longer directed at her. Searching through her purse, she found the notebook she always carried and began to sketch the configuration.

Dan watched her work. "Well, I still don't know what it is," he muttered when she'd finished the rough drawing. It appeared vaguely like an irregular rectangle, compressed in the middle. "Some kind of ancient coffin symbol?" he asked.

"I don't think so. Each stone has a star scratched into the top. And the one in the upper right-hand corner is slightly bigger than the rest," Sabrina pointed out.

"So?"

"I think it's the constellation Orion."

Dan looked again. "Damn. I didn't see it at all, but I guess you're right. It's one of the few I learned when I was a kid, but I never could figure out why it was supposed to be a hunter. It looks more like an hourglass to me. As far as I'm concerned, the only constellation that's shaped like what it's supposed to be is the Big Dipper.'' He shrugged. ''But you can look up in the sky and get any image you want just by connecting the dots in different ways.''

''That's a logical way of approaching it. But the ancient Greeks didn't see the stars the way we do. They felt various influences from different parts of the sky and made up stories and images to go with them.''

''How does that explain why someone laid out these stones around the body?''

Sabrina was a lot more comfortable talking about Greek mythology than what had happened to her when she'd stepped on the first star stone. ''Let me tell you a little bit about Orion. He was a giant hunter who kept bragging he could kill any living animal. Finally the gods got tired of his boasts, so they sent a huge scorpion to sting him to death. But Diana the huntress asked that he be placed in the sky. Naturally he was put directly opposite Scorpius, the scorpion, so he would never forget his fateful boast.''

''So he was killed by the gods,'' Dan mused. ''The murderer is looking less and less like the guy cooling his heels in the city jail.''

''Why?''

''He's just an unemployed steelworker named Raul Simmons, as far as I can tell. I think he found Bette Kronstat's wallet after she was killed. I'm willing to bet he claimed responsibility for the murders because he's mentally unbalanced.''

Sabrina nodded, but she was still focusing more on the present clues than the man who'd confessed to the crimes. ''How did the murder victim die?''

"Poisonous injection."

Sabrina felt a crawly sensation on her skin. "That fits, too. Like being stung to death."

"Well, we know the witch is into symbolism. What else about the mythology do you think is relevant?"

"When the ancients gazed at Orion, they felt his aggression and his human pride."

"How do you know so darn much?"

Sabrina flushed. "Do I?"

"Yes."

"I guess I read a lot."

"Lucky for me."

Before Sabrina could demur, Dan stroked his jaw thoughtfully. "Okay, so the victim could be someone who thought he could go up against the witch. Only she got him first."

"And laid him out in the middle of the Orion configuration to make a point."

Dan pocketed the original stone Sabrina had stepped on.

"You keep saying 'she,'" Sabrina observed. "A witch doesn't have to be a woman."

His eyes flicked away from hers. "I keep thinking of her that way."

"Do you picture her with a pointed hat and a broomstick?"

He laughed. "Sometimes."

"If it's not Raul Simmons, it could be anybody. Somebody sitting in front of a computer terminal right now. Or selling plates in the china department of Hecht's. Which reminds me. Did you check out the name Ridley?"

"Yes. The family died out."

By mutual agreement, they had started back in the direction of the car. As they climbed the hill and left the immediate area of the grave, Sabrina felt a profound sense of relief. She glanced at Dan, and he smiled.

She smiled back.

When they came abreast of the car, she stopped and wrinkled her nose. "Do you smell something funny?"

"Rotting flowers?"

"No, cherries, I think." The odor was quite unpleasant.

Dan nodded. "Maybe there's a tree around here, and nobody picked the fruit."

"That could be it," Sabrina answered doubtfully.

Dan turned on the ignition and closed the windows. The air-conditioning whooshed as it sprang to life. It should have cleared out the smell, but after several moments, Sabrina realized that the aroma was even stronger and somehow very compelling. And something strange was happening to her head.

"It's in here, not out there." For some reason, the observation ended with a bouncing little laugh.

"The cherries? So?"

"It's making me dizzy."

"Lighten up. You worry about stuff too much," Dan tossed off.

Sabrina gave him a slow smile. The fruity aroma didn't smell so bad after all. In fact, it seeped into her head like liquor soaking into a sponge cake. Now there was a seductive richness to the scent. A richness that made her breathe deeply.

"Nice," she murmured.

"Yeah."

Dan sounded close, but when Sabrina glanced at him, she found she was viewing him from far away, as if the driver's seat had suddenly migrated to the end of a long tunnel.

Somehow that was terribly funny, and she started to giggle uncontrollably.

"What?"

"Come back here." She reached for him. But her arms weren't long enough.

It was hard to think in a straight line. Hard to put one tiny little thought in front of the other.

Dan gunned the engine. With a jerk, the car shot forward. Some dim part of Sabrina's brain knew she should be alarmed, but she was having too much fun!

The road was narrow and twisting. As the vehicle picked up speed, Dan spun the wheel wildly, somehow keeping the car on the blacktop.

Then a tree seemed to jump in front of them.

"Watch out!" Sabrina shouted.

This time Dan couldn't move fast enough. The car slammed into the obstacle and came to rest with a jarring thunk. They both pitched forward. Sabrina's head hit the mirror. She cried out in pain. Then she was being snapped back by the seat belt.

A loud blaring noise filled the car. The horn. It wouldn't stop.

Dan swore.

Sabrina looked up. The scene around them blurred and then bounced into focus. She sucked in a terrified breath. The car was surrounded by a wall of flames.

Chapter Four

"Fire!" she screamed above the blaring noise. "Fire!"

"What?"

"Fire, don't you see the fire?" Sabrina shouted, pointing wildly toward the inferno closing in on the car.

Dan looked alarmed and craned his neck in all directions. "Where?"

Her hand swung in an arc.

When he didn't respond, Sabrina shrank down, pulling at the seat belt, trying to fold her body under the dashboard. Ever since she could remember, she'd been terrified of being burned. Now she and Dan were surrounded by a flickering red-and-orange barrier, and there was no way through. She didn't even consider that she might have conjured it up from her imagination. It was too real, too daunting.

A scream tore from her throat as the tongues of flame lapped at the windows, enveloping the car. Soon the heat would turn her skin to ash. She was in hell. In hell where she would burn forever. And there was only the terror, the consuming flames and the cloying, sweet smell of the cherries.

Then the focus changed like a telephoto lens finding its

range, and the scene was overlaid with a different hallucination. The grave markers around them were a crowd of people in old-fashioned costumes. Their faces were contorted in anger. The blaring horn was the yelling and jeering of the throng as strong arms reached to drag her toward the red-and-yellow blaze.

No. Get away. Before they tied her to the stake.

Unhooking the seat belt, Sabrina reached for the door handle and bolted from the car.

The evil-smelling flames licked at her hair, seared her skin, whooshed after her. They gained on her as she ran in a zigzag line; she wove unsteadily across the grass, the sound of the crowd speeding her legs.

Footsteps echoed behind her.

"Sabrina. Damn you. Wait!"

"No! Duncan. Save me. Save me."

Then, magically, as if her deep need had conjured up a savior, he was there, swinging her up into his arms.

He turned around, and all at once she knew that he didn't mean to rescue her at all. "No! No! Not the fire. Don't take me back to the fire." With a scream of terror that ended in a spasm of choking, she began to fight him as if all the demons of hell were dragging her into the inferno.

He was trying to hold her arms, trying to restrain her without hurting her. Still she fought against him, her mind spinning, caught between one illusion and the next, unable to find any reality besides the man who held her. She could hear him gasping in lungfuls of air, feel his fingers digging into her ribs, her shoulders, her hips.

"Stop. I won't hurt you, Sara. Never."

Yet even as they struggled, as their bodies brushed and collided in opposition, another stronger, more elemental force came into play.

Male and female—searching, seeking. And all the usual inhibitions had been stripped away by the drugging vapor that still enveloped them—still held them in its grasp.

The contact of man to woman generated sparks like flint striking steel. All at once the fire was no longer around Sabrina. It was in her.

Dan must have felt the change. "That's it. Don't fight me." His voice was thick. His grasp shifted from force to persuasion. Fingers pressed, kneaded, and began to roam in wide circles across her back and shoulders. Moments— or was it centuries—ago, he'd been trying to carry her to safety. Or into the flames.

Sabrina felt light-headed. Then she looked up at him, focused on the blue of his eyes, and gave a little sob of joy. She was in his arms again, after so many lonely years.

Still, the confusion lingered. For wild heartbeats she thought she might drown in the mysterious depths of his eyes. No, it was more like falling helplessly through layers of cloud cover toward the earth far below.

She heard the ragged edge of his breathing. It matched the painful movement of air in and out of her own lungs. Dan stared down at her, transfixed as if he were seeing her, really seeing her, for the first time. "So beautiful. So very beautiful." One hand winnowed through her wild red hair, slanting her mouth at an angle under his. The other arm pulled her tightly against him into a lover's embrace.

She felt the heat radiating from his big body, the taut muscles of his stomach, the pressure of his broad hands, holding her, trapping her.

Her fear was as great as before. Some part of her sensed terrible danger as though her very soul might flee her being if her lips met his. "No, please."

"You want this as much as I do."

"Yes," she sobbed.

She had to stop. Some small, frightened part of her tried desperately to pull away while there was still time. It was an impossible attempt. There was no way to resist her own desires. No way to resist the overwhelming rightness of being with him like this again. With a little moan, she twined her arms around his neck and pulled his lips down to hers. She'd ached for him. Pined for him. And it had been so long. So long. An eternity.

Familiar yet strange.

Shattering yet healing.

Overwhelming yet completely natural.

She felt him groan low in his chest. With that deep animal sound of half pain, half pleasure she knew it was the same for him as it was for her.

Her lips opened under his, inviting him to meld with her, to merge, to share his essence.

Joy leaped in her heart as he accepted the invitation. Then they were devouring each other hungrily. Kissing. Touching. Pressing aroused body against aroused body. He shifted her in his arms, pulling her to him as if he couldn't bring her close enough.

His hips moved urgently against hers, and she answered the shifting pressure, thrust for thrust. Her hands slid down his back even as she raised up on tiptoes, seeking to equalize their heights. Then she was trying to tug him down, toward the waiting bed of grass that spread out all around them.

Sabrina had forgotten the blaring of the horn. Until she and Dan were suddenly surrounded by bone-jarring silence.

"Where the hell is everybody?" a voice called into the sudden void.

She felt as if a large, rough hand had grabbed her by the

back of the neck and yanked. She tried to shake herself away from its clutches, tried to cling to the rich, sensual dream.

But illusion had vanished.

With a little cry of loss, Sabrina's eyes snapped open. She swayed, grabbed for something solid, and found herself clinging to muscular forearms.

It took several seconds for her to realize she was holding on to Dan.

His face was flushed. His chest rose and fell as if he'd been running hard.

"What?" The question tumbled from her lips. She wasn't even sure what to ask.

"Sa-Sabrina? I—"

She leaned forward, desperate to hear what he was going to say. Instead the same gruff voice intruded again, tearing and ripping at her mind like a saw ripping through silk. "There you are."

Dan looked up, his face mirroring the pain in her head.

A moment later an old man came dodging and puffing through the forest of grave markers.

The caretaker. From the graveyard. What was he doing here?

His eyes were wide. "Lord 'a mercy. In all my born days. Heard the horn. Thought you wanted me. Bad like. Then I saw the car plowed into a tree."

Dan shook his head. With fingers that weren't quite steady, he reached up and touched Sabrina's forehead. She winced.

"You hit your head," he mumbled.

He helped her sit, and she leaned back against a stone marker. Her thoughts were still spinning. When she closed her eyes, she saw flames dancing behind her closed lids.

Heart pounding, she opened her eyes again, and the fire disappeared.

"What happened?" she moaned.

Dan didn't answer. Instead he looked uncertainly back at the car.

So did Sabrina. "The rotten cherry smell…"

"When I started the engine."

"Then everything went fuzzy," she said uncertainly.

"Some kind of gas, do you think?"

It was hard to make sense of what he was saying.

"*Something* knocked us silly," Dan continued.

Sabrina nodded slowly, remembering the unpleasant odor and how spacy she'd started feeling right after she'd first smelled it.

"I'd like to know who the hell cherry-bombed an official government vehicle." He started to laugh and sat weakly beside her. "Damn. My head hurts," he muttered after a few minutes. Then he looked at the caretaker. "Better call the police. And an ambulance."

"Already did."

Sabrina avoided Dan's eyes, trying to remember the sequence of events. Dan had started the engine, and everything had gotten weird and funny, until he'd wrecked the car. And after that. She didn't want to think about after that.

The caretaker was a merciful interruption.

"You still in one piece, missy?"

Sabrina kept her head bent away from the old man. "I've felt better." The words were punctuated by the wail of a siren. In a matter of moments Dan's car was surrounded by emergency vehicles and personnel.

He got to his feet. "Let's hope they don't ask me to walk a straight line."

"You haven't been drinking. I can vouch for that."

He laughed again sharply. "Sure, we'll be each other's alibis."

Sabrina watched him move off toward the lead police car. He still wasn't quite steady on his feet. But he was tucking in his shirt as he walked. Then he combed his fingers through his hair.

Going up to one of the ambulance attendants, he gestured toward Sabrina. Then he took one of the uniformed officers over to his car.

She wanted to watch Dan, but a young man in a white coat trotted toward her. Squatting down, he began to assess her condition.

"Do you remember the accident?"

"Yes."

"How do you feel?"

"Okay. Except for a little bump on the head."

"Cassidy says you were both gassed with something."

Sabrina nodded.

"I should take you in for evaluation."

The last thing she wanted was to suffer through the rest of the evening being poked and prodded.

"No, really. I'm fine."

"Let's have a look in your eyes."

She waited while he got an ophthalmoscope and went through the standard routine for concussion.

"Guess you're okay," he said.

Sabrina sank her fingers into the dry grass. A few minutes ago, she'd wanted to keep Dan in view. Now she wanted to disappear before he came back and met her eyes. "I see Mr. Cassidy's busy. Is, uh, there any chance of getting a ride back to my car?" she asked as he turned to leave.

"I'll check."

Sabrina wasn't quite sure how she'd been holding herself together. However, as soon as the man left, she started to shake. Leaning back against the granite headstone, she tried to stave off the nausea that threatened to sweep over her. A cold sweat bloomed on her skin. Grimly, she strove to concentrate on some of the relaxation techniques she'd learned. The effort was only partially successful. Behind her closed lids, images of flames danced and flickered, making her shudder.

When she felt a light touch on her arm she jumped and gasped. Eyes snapping open, she found herself staring stupidly at Dan.

He hunkered down beside her and trailed his fingers gently to the cold skin of her forehead. "The medic said you were okay. You're not."

"I'm fine."

"Can you walk?"

"Of course." At least he wasn't bringing up what had happened between them. But why should he? Probably he was as embarrassed as she.

Sabrina struggled to her feet and found she was swaying on rubbery legs.

Taking her arm, Dan waited until she was steadier. "Are you sure?"

"Yes," she snapped.

He didn't reply as he led her toward a police car parked at the bend in the narrow road. "They need a statement from you, too. You don't want to go to the station house, do you?"

"Not if I can avoid it."

When he helped her into the back seat, she found her purse sitting on the vinyl upholstery. Until then, she'd forgotten all about it. Wrapping her arms around the white straw satchel, she hugged it to her chest.

"What exactly did you tell them?"

"That as near as I can figure out, some sort of gas was released in the car. It made me crash into a tree."

Sabrina nodded. That sounded pretty accurate. He must be used to coming up with coherent observations under stress.

"That's all they have to know," he continued. "Although, they'll probably want to try and dredge up some details of how it made you feel."

Some of the tension seeped out of her shoulders.

Dan stared at the purse still clutched in her arms. "I'm sorry. If I hadn't been so damned determined to drag you here, none of this would have happened."

"You couldn't know," she mumbled.

Further discussion was cut off by the arrival of a uniformed officer. Ritz, his name tag said.

Dan glanced questioningly at Sabrina. "Want to go to your house?"

"All right," she murmured and then gave the officer the address. After Ritz started the engine, she sank back against the hard seat and tried to pull together her scattered thoughts. Her relief was almost tangible as they drove through the cemetery gates.

Beside her, Dan was also silent. She slid him a sideways glance, sensing he was far from relaxed. In the dim light from the passing businesses along Route 40, his chiseled profile was silhouetted against the window of the squad car. On the ride out to the cemetery, they'd been casual acquaintances, but the cherry-flavored vapor had changed that irrevocably. All at once she wanted to get away from him so she could think. Probably he was having a similar reaction. Yet he must have a strong sense of obligation, because he was still sitting beside her in the police car.

They turned off the highway, and Sabrina had to give directions, since the city policeman wasn't familiar with the unlighted back roads of Howard County.

The old farmhouse she'd bought in Ilchester was situated on twenty acres, some of which were wooded. Sabrina had turned the fallow meadows near the house into lush fields full of fragrant herbs. But it wasn't garden-club pretty, and she was glad the darkness hid the somewhat straggly effect.

The impact of the accident was catching up with her. She felt sore and bruised, and stifled a wince as she climbed the steps to the porch. Dan was beside her quickly, taking her arm.

"What hurts?"

"What doesn't? How about you?"

He flexed his own leg and grimaced.

The critters inside must have heard the additional footsteps on the porch. Through the glass panel she saw two pusillanimous cats leap for the safety of the basement. At the same time her shelty, Robbie, came running toward the door, barking as if he were prepared to tear any invader limb from limb.

Ritz took a quick step back when Sabrina reached for the knob. She bit back a secret grin. He'd find out Robbie's character defects soon enough.

A woman living alone in the country might want a dog for protection. Robbie was probably about as much good as those recorded barking tapes she'd heard New Yorkers used. Her sense of security came more from the cats. If they rushed out to be fed when she opened the door, she was okay. If they were already hiding in the basement rafters, there might be an interloper in the house.

When Robbie saw her, he changed his tune and began to leap around excitedly, wagging his tail and sniffing the visitors. Dan stooped to scratch him behind the ears and admire his sleek good looks.

After opening some windows and turning on a couple of lights, Sabrina ushered the men into the sitting room and switched on the ceiling fan. It was one of her few extravagances. Most of the profits she'd made over the past few years had been plowed back into the business. There were whole sections of the rambling house that were little more than storerooms. The furnished parts sported a collection of hand-me-downs and thrift-shop purchases that she'd decorated with bright fabrics, dried flowers and whimsical pillows. But she suspected that the haphazard charm was lost on both Dan and Officer Ritz.

Dan surprised her as he looked around at the high ceilings and wood plank floors. "What a great old place. It's got a lot of potential."

"I think the biggest stumbling blocks are time and money, but I'm working on it."

Robbie hopped upon the sofa and looked at her expectantly. Ritz had lowered himself into a mission oak chair with shocking pink and green plaid cushions.

The dog could only hold Sabrina's attention for so long. Finally her gaze swung back to Dan. "Uh, could I get either one of you something cold to drink?"

"You need to rest. I can get something."

"There's a pitcher of herb tea in the refrigerator."

Well, they could still have a normal conversation, Sabrina thought after she'd told him where to find the glasses and he headed off toward the kitchen.

When he'd left, she sat next to the dog. Ritz opened his notebook. "I'd like you to tell me what happened—in your own words." Sabrina felt her palms grow clammy. It was comforting to stroke the shelty's long fur while she gave a brief account of the gas attack.

"Did you see anybody approach Mr. Cassidy's car while you were at the cemetery?" Ritz asked.

"No. But I wasn't looking that way."

"Nobody else was in the vicinity? People visiting graves or anything like that?"

Sabrina hesitated. "Earlier, I thought maybe I saw something in the shadows. Then the caretaker came running when he realized what was going on," Sabrina recounted, vaguely surprised that she sounded so coherent.

"When did the effects of the gas commence?"

Sabrina thought back. "Pretty soon after Mr. Cassidy started the engine."

"What happened?"

"At first everything seemed funny, and distorted. It looked as if the driver's seat had moved far away from me. Then the car started going fast."

"Is there anything else you think is relevant?" Ritz asked just as Dan appeared in the doorway carrying a tray with three glasses of iced tea, some of the flower-print napkins Sabrina had made from fabric remnants, and a tin of the chocolate-chip cookies she liked to pick up at the bakery in Ellicott City.

Robbie got down off the couch and trotted hopefully toward the man with the food.

Sabrina reached for a pillow tassel and ran the silky strands between her fingers. "The rotten-cherry smell, I guess. That was the first thing I noticed."

"You smelled it, too?" Ritz asked Dan.

"Yes. I assume it was the smell of the chemical. What about the trigger mechanism? Was it the starter?"

"Yes. It was wired like a bomb."

"A bomb!" Sabrina glanced from Dan to Ritz. They both looked impassive.

"Whoever it was didn't want to blow up the car," Dan said. "Maybe they were hoping I'd make it to the highway."

Sabrina went rigid, suddenly understanding the implications. If Dan had been going any faster, they might have both been killed.

"You think we can get this wrapped up?" Dan said.

"Just a few more questions." The officer turned back to Sabrina. "How long did the experience last?"

The tightness in Dan's voice had made Sabrina's pulse start to pound. She tried to focus on the question. "I guess not more than fifteen minutes."

"Short-term effect," Ritz remarked as he wrote, "Besides the laughing, what else happened to you?"

Sabrina swallowed and glanced quickly at Dan. "A couple of different things. After the car hit the tree, I thought we were surrounded by fire. Then for a few minutes I hallucinated. I felt as if I were somebody else, in a different place."

"Somebody else?" Dan asked, his expression odd as he studied her face.

"In the Middle Ages or something. There was a crowd around us, jeering and shouting. They wanted me dead." She looked pleadingly at Dan. "I was confused. I wasn't sure whether you were there to save me or—"

"Or what?"

She shrugged. "Well, it was just, you know, a fantasy. I was feeling as if I were a peasant girl and you were the lord of the manor."

Ritz was taking it all down; Dan had stopped eating the cookie he'd been holding.

"Is there anything else you can tell me about the effects? Anything physiological?" the officer asked.

Sabrina could feel tension zinging around the room like an electric hum. Ritz didn't seem to notice. Dan's gaze shot to Sabrina and then back to the officer. "Like what?" he demanded.

Ritz shrugged. "Rapid heartbeat. Distorted judgment. Visual or auditory disturbances."

"All of those," Dan clipped out.

"When we find out what the substance was, we'll let you know. And if you have any flashback, or anything like that, you should notify the department—and you may want to be checked out by your family physician."

"Yes. Thanks."

Ritz took a long pull on the glass of tea and made a face. "I'd better be going," he said as he picked up two of the cookies.

Dan followed the police officer to the door and onto the porch.

Sabrina sighed with relief and slid down against the sofa cushions, feeling her skirt ride up her legs. It didn't matter what she looked like. It was finally over. Scooping up a couple of ice cubes out of her glass, she wrapped them in one of the napkins and pressed the makeshift pack against her forehead. The cold felt soothing, and she closed her eyes.

But her mind wouldn't shut down. Rotten cherries. Impaired judgment. Visual and auditory disturbances. Yes, she'd experienced all that and more.

Her eyes snapped open again when Robbie jumped up and began to bark.

Chapter Five

"I didn't mean to activate your watchdog," Dan said from the doorway.

Robbie had already stopped playing guard dog, woofing softly and wagging his tail. Dan stooped to pet him.

Sensing he had a cooperative human, the dog rolled over, exposing his tummy for a good scratching.

Dan's hand moved across the white fur in long strokes, but his eyes were focused on Sabrina's thigh. From the floor, he had an excellent view. Quickly she pulled her skirt back down.

"I thought you'd left with Officer Ritz. What are you still doing here?"

"They're sending a car back for me." He didn't move from the doorway. "I wanted to make sure you were all right."

"You could have asked on the way out."

"I'm not going to attack you again if that's what you're worried about." His voice was gritty.

She felt her face color and wished she'd stop reacting that way. There was nothing more unattractive than a redhead whose face was on fire. "It wasn't an attack. And I'm not."

"I wanted to apologize. For dragging you there. For almost getting you killed. For grabbing you like a maniac." He looked as if he might be about to say something more; instead his lips pressed into a thin line.

When he'd gotten up to leave, she'd breathed a sigh of relief that they'd escaped the topic of the torrid little scene that had played itself out down the hill from the car. She'd thought it was all her fault. Now he was telling her the sensual madness had been mutual. Pushing herself to a sitting position, she clutched her fingers against the ice. "It wasn't something *you* did. It seems to be something that happened to both of us. And about the accident. If I'd been driving, the results would have been the same. When you started speeding up, I thought it was hilarious."

He nodded tightly.

"Whatever that stuff was, it had us both flying pretty high," she said.

"Yeah." He got to his feet, and she saw him grimace.

"You're worried about tomorrow's headlines?"

"The police department will keep the story under wraps for the time being."

"What else is bothering you?" she asked suddenly.

"What do you mean?"

"I can tell there's something you want to say."

"The experience brought back some bad memories."

"Oh?"

"Let's leave it that tonight wasn't my kind of scene at all," he said.

"Well, don't assume it was my kind of scene, either. What do you think I am, some flower child left over from the sixties?"

"I didn't mean to imply—" he swallowed audibly "—that you were into drugs."

"Maybe my life-style looks weird by your conservative standards," she interrupted him. "Maybe I've even tried stuff you'd rank on the lunatic fringe. But that doesn't include getting high. Because I was never comfortable with—with—polluting my body." Probably that sounded self-righteous. At this point she didn't care.

He held up his palms. "Okay, so we're both virgins. When it comes to controlled substances, anyway."

They laughed uneasily, still wary of each other. "If you say so," she murmured.

He sat down in the chair that Ritz had vacated, and steepled his hands. "What do you mean by my conservative standards?" he demanded.

She pursed her lips. "I don't know. Law and order. The establishment."

"Guilty, I guess," he admitted. "And how do you define lunatic fringe?"

"Tarot cards. Palm reading. Herbal remedies. Harnessing psychic energy. We don't have a lot in common."

"We both like dogs."

He took things so seriously, which she supposed was why she responded so strongly when he let his guard down. Her eyes flicked to Robbie, who was sitting on the floor beside the chair, not the sofa. She felt her lips tugging up in a smile. So did Dan's. Then he caught himself the way he always did.

"Let's stop fencing with each other and get to the point," he said. "I don't particularly want to talk about what happened, but I've got to understand it—for this investigation, if nothing else. We're two adults and we're alone. Anything we say right now is strictly between the two of us."

"You really want to pursue this?"

"No. But we can't just let it go. How about starting with the murder case?"

"Someone tried to kill *you*," Sabrina whispered.

"Or scare me off. Or maybe they didn't know it was me. They could have been after whoever came out to have another look at the murder site."

"Do you believe that?"

"Let's say, I'll watch my back from now on."

Sabrina shivered.

Dan leaned forward. "I want to understand what happened after we hit the tree."

She felt heat creep into her face again.

"You thought we were surrounded by fire," he prompted.

"Yes," she whispered.

"Where do you think the image came from?"

Sabrina shrugged.

"Were you badly burned when you were a child?"

"I don't think so. It's just something that's always terrified me. We lived down by the shore when I was a kid. They'd have bonfires on the beach at night, and everybody would roast hot dogs and marshmallows. Everybody except me."

"You must have gotten burned when you were a baby, and only your subconscious remembers. Did you ever ask your mother about it?"

"She had six other kids to worry about. It wasn't the kind of thing we took time for. Or maybe she didn't know."

"What do you mean?"

"I was the second from the youngest, and I got left with my older brothers and sisters a lot. If one of them was careless and I got hurt, they might not have told anybody."

"You're kidding."

"Not getting in trouble was a big goal in my family." Before he could ask her any more questions about her background, she changed the subject. "Neither one of us was hurt."

"But we're still dancing around what took place." He stood up and turned toward the window. The two cats, who had crept up the basement stairs, scattered again. Sabrina was feeling just as skittish.

Without looking at Dan, she cleared her throat. "We don't know each other very well. That's part of what makes this so difficult."

"Okay. I'll start. First it was kind of a joyride. Then you thought you were surrounded by fire. Then I got the turn-on of my life."

She tried to control the betraying quiver of her lips. "Why do we have to talk about it?"

"I need to know how it affected you."

"My God, couldn't you tell? I was turned on, too."

She heard him let out the breath he'd been holding. "So I didn't force you into something…"

"You didn't force me into anything."

His gaze wouldn't cut her loose. "Are you still feeling it now?"

"Are you?" she whispered, her pulse surging.

He turned back toward her, and she could see honesty and discretion fighting it out on his face. "Yes."

"Maybe we're still under the influence," she whispered.

"Is that what you think?"

"It could be."

"I'd like to know."

She didn't answer, and he sat down on the couch. His

nearness made her pulse race even faster. Slowly he leaned toward her, giving her a chance to pull away. She didn't.

His lips hovered questioningly over hers. She tensed, wondering whether she was afraid of him or herself. Or was it the memory of being out of control? She was still frightened by that. Yet she yearned to know how much had been from the drug and how much had been from the man himself.

His lips touched hers.

This time was very different. A man and a woman who were attracted to each other. A man and a woman agreeing that they wanted to get to know each other better and not in a hurry to force the issue.

This kiss was slow, delicious. Impossible to resist. Not what she would have expected from Dan Cassidy.

He didn't rush her, but when she slid her hands around his waist, she felt him smile. Then slowly, very slowly, he deepened the kiss. His tongue skimmed over the sensitive tissue of her mouth, creating new sensations—sensations they controlled, not ones that controlled them.

There was a thrill of discovery, and for long moments they both enjoyed the exploration. Yet the longer it continued the more she realized that the deeper awareness hadn't gone away. On some subliminal level, the pleasure was tinged with danger. If things went much farther, they'd be back at the primitive level of need they'd both felt before.

Did they both sense it? Was that why it had to stop?

Dan lifted his head. Bemused, Sabrina stared up at him. "I guess that answers the question," he murmured.

Which question? That they were attracted? Or that they had the situation under control? She wasn't about to demand clarification.

His fingers played with her unruly curls. Then he smoothed them back from her face.

"I'm confused," she whispered.

"Are you?"

She flushed.

"I think we're both embarrassed about getting all tangled up together a couple of hours ago. Under normal circumstances, we'd have been governed by the civilized standards of behavior that keep people from acting on their impulses when it's not appropriate. Like now."

She nodded.

"The trouble was, when the cherry bomb hit us, we skipped over the niceties."

"You put that very well."

"Legal training." His fingers moved from her hair to stroke down the side of her face. "We can't pretend it didn't happen."

"We could if we never see each other again."

"Is that what you want?" There was a new tension in his voice.

That would be the safer course, Sabrina thought, but it wasn't what she said. "What do you want?" She held her breath.

He laughed. "To spend the night with you."

A man could admit that. A woman couldn't—shouldn't.

"But I'll settle for dinner tomorrow," he added.

"I can't."

"Oh?"

"I promised two ladies I know that I'd go to a lecture with them."

"Is that what you usually do for excitement?"

"No. But it will probably be an interesting experience. Besides they'll be disappointed if I don't show up."

He looked as if he wasn't sure she was being straight with him. "You could tell me about it at lunch on Thursday."

"All right."

Before he could respond, Robbie jumped up and started barking again.

Sabrina's head swung apprehensively toward the door.

"That's probably my ride." Dan stood quickly and went to the door. Over his shoulder, Sabrina could see another uniformed officer on the porch.

Dan came back to the living room. "I hate leaving you."

Any reserves Sabrina possessed had drained away, and she was past being able to judge the undercurrents of the conversation. Was he referring to his earlier remark about spending the night? Or was he worried that she was going to freak out again?

He must have seen the mixture of emotions that flashed across her face.

"I just want to be sure you're okay."

"I will be," she responded automatically, determined that it was going to be true.

SABRINA SANK BACK into the sofa cushions, grateful that she didn't have to engage in any more sparring—verbal or otherwise—with Dan Cassidy. She was emotionally and physically wrung out, and she might have simply fallen asleep right where she was. But within five minutes after the coast was clear, the two cats came sidling into the living room. Elspeth, a calico with a black-white-and-orange face, settled down on the sofa and began to wash. Malcolm, a ginger tom, initiated a series of piercing wails he knew from experience would propel his mistress toward the pantry.

Sighing, Sabrina pushed herself to her feet and dragged her aching body into the kitchen. When the animals' food and water dishes were full, she stumbled upstairs toward the bedroom. By the time she'd showered and slipped into a light cotton gown, three warm bodies were already waiting for her.

The hot water had revived her somewhat, and she smiled as she thought about Dan's admission that he wanted to spend the night. Probably he wouldn't have liked the crowded conditions in her bed.

Twenty minutes ago, she'd been on the verge of unconsciousness. Now sleep evaded her. Probably she should have taken something for the headache that had begun to develop.

However, it wasn't just pain that was keeping her awake. She shouldn't have pictured Dan Cassidy up here in her bedroom—even as a joke. Because her nerve endings had begun to prickle as she remembered the kiss. Not the one in the living room a little while ago, which had been relatively safe, but the one in the cemetery when they'd devoured each other like long-separated lovers who were finally back in each other's arms.

But they weren't long-lost lovers. They'd only met at lunch at Sabatino's in Little Italy this afternoon.

By a tremendous effort of will she managed to avoid thinking about the images her mind had served up when she'd been under the influence of the drug. But she couldn't turn off the feelings that had flamed between herself and Dan. They were too powerful to handle.

In her twenty-eight years, she'd never felt so wildly out of control in a man's arms before. Never even close to it. Her relationships with the opposite sex were better described as pleasant. She'd hoped that eventually she'd meet someone to settle down with and raise the children she'd like to have. But she'd long since decided that whatever poets romanticized and women's magazines analyzed to death wasn't going to happen to her.

Until she'd found herself twisting against Dan Cassidy, trying desperately to get closer to his hard body.

Her cheeks heated, and every place that wasn't bruised or bumped tingled pleasurably. With a snort of disgust, she sat up and snapped on the light. The cats and dog looked up inquiringly.

"Go back to sleep," she muttered.

A cold shower didn't sound very appealing. But there were other approaches. She'd been putting off making a grocery list. That ought to sober her up.

There was a pad and pencil on the bedside table. After plumping up the pillows, she leaned back and began to write.

carrots
celery
cauliflower
milk
cheese
lentils
tomato sauce...

The familiar room swam and wavered like a scene underwater. Deep underwater where the pressure squeezed the air from her lungs. Sabrina clutched desperately at reality, struggling to breathe even as she passed more easily through the fear and the barrier her mind tried to erect. Once she reached the other side of the divide, she felt a profound sense of homecoming.

...of a powerful horse brought her to the door of the little cottage. She had wrapped a shawl around her shoulders

against the chill wind and stood wiping her hands on her apron as the rider dismounted.

He took off his hat. "Mistress Campbell?"

Sara looked up into startling blue eyes, and the breath whooshed out of her lungs.

"It's the wood sprite," he breathed.

She flushed. "I'm just ordinary Sara Campbell. Who are you?"

"Duncan McReynolds."

They stared at each other. It was two years since the accident out in the mountains. His horse had been nearby. After she'd tended to his wound, he'd climbed back into the saddle and ridden off. Until this moment, she'd never known his name or what had happened to him. But that had not stopped her dreaming about him.

Now here he was, a man grown, standing in front of her. The look in his eyes told her he hadn't forgotten her, either.

Trying hard not to be too obvious, Sara took his measure. His hair was rich and tawny. The promise of power and strength had been fulfilled in wide shoulders that could have moved a mountain, and a stubborn jaw capable of winning an argument with a jut.

"So you survived, did ye?"

"The injury didna kill me, but my sire almost had my hide for laming the destrier." He grinned, bringing a devilish glint to his remarkable blue eyes. Then he seemed to remember what he was doing there.

"I've come to fetch the healer, Elspeth Campbell."

Sara's chest tightened painfully. "My gran."

"Can she ride to the castle?"

"I wish she could." Sara couldn't keep the bitterness out

of her voice. "But she's dead and buried since just before the harvest."

"I'm sorry. For ye." His voice took on a more somber note. "And Ian McReynolds."

"Ian McReynolds?"

"Aye. He's bad off. And the physician canna cure him. Then himself remembered the old woman from the village who saved the Lady Tanya when she came down with child-bed fever."

Sara saw the look of despair on Duncan's face. "My gran taught me well."

"Would ye come then?"

"Tell me what ails him."

"His lungs."

"They're weak?"

"Nay, they were strong. Until he went through the ice and into the pond. A few days later, he started coughing."

"And shaking? Chills? Headache?" she asked.

"Aye."

"And it came on sudden like?"

"Aye."

So it probably wasn't consumption. But peripneumonia was bad enough. Were her skills up to the challenge?

"What did ye do for him?" Sara asked.

"Fergus McGraw bled him and flushed the poison out of his system with a physic."

And made him weaker, Sara thought, her anger rising. Gran had tried to tell the physician a sick body needed blood to fight off illness. As for making him bring up his supper, that was useless unless he'd been poisoned. "I'll come," she said. "Just let me get my supplies."

Duncan tied up his horse and came in out of the cold while she packed a few things for herself and put her med-

*ical supplies into a leather pouch. Now that she was ac-
tually getting ready, her hands began to shake. She'd
learned a lot from Gran, but she hadn't been the one making the decisions. What if she made a fatal mistake now?
And there was another worry. No matter what she did, she
might fail to cure the patient. Even with the best of treatment, peripneumonia could go either way.*

"I'll bank the fire," Duncan said.

*When she turned quickly back a few minutes later, she
almost bumped into him.*

*"Steady, lass." His large hands cupped her shoulders.
For a moment they stood by the hearth. "I never thanked
ye for taking care of my leg."*

"It was my fault in the first place."

"Nay. I should never have been out on that horse."

*She looked up into his blue eyes, longing to admit her
qualms and yet reluctant at the same time. Her only way
of making a living was through her healing abilities. If the
patient died, Fergus McGraw would warn everyone away
from her.*

*"We'd better hurry. Before it's too late and there's
naught I can do."*

*Outside, mist was pouring over the edge of the mountain
and down through the pass.*

*Duncan took a plaid from his saddlebag and wrapped it
around Sara's shoulders. Then he hoisted her into the saddle and climbed up behind her. His strong arms held her
fast as he urged the horse forward. Bravely she settled back
into his embrace, barely feeling the cold. She was glad he
made a wide circle around the Devil's Gorge—a slash
across the land where it was said the evil one's tail had
touched down when he was flying to a witches' conclave.*

Finally she could see the castle in the distance.

The gray stone walls rose tall and forbidding against the winter sky. A refuge or a prison? Sara wondered, as they passed the armed guards at the entrance and plunged into the dark passageway leading to the keep.

Sara felt a tap against her arm and tried to shake the annoyance away. It persisted.

DUNCAN'S ARMS were around her. Why was he hitting her arm? Sabrina looked down in confusion at the orange-and-black paw tapping against her flesh.

It belonged to a cat. Not a man.

Elspeth, who knew she'd finally gotten her mistress's attention, meowed.

Sabrina blinked, her gaze shifting from the cat to the lines of script she'd been writing. As she stared at the paper, a shiver swept over her skin, rippling in waves of fear through her body and her mind. Unable to stop herself from shaking, she sank under the covers, pulling them up around her chin. It had happened again. Like in her office when she'd been brainstorming designs for the baskets. Only this time it was scarier.

Sabrina closed her eyes and forced herself to breathe slowly and evenly as her mind scrambled for solid ground. ''The drug attack at the cemetery. That's why you feel so bad now. Some of that stuff is still in your system. You should have been more careful.'' She chanted the reassuring words over and over. After a while, they had the desired effect.

Sitting up, she looked at what she'd been writing. It started with the grocery list, but after that the narrow sheet of paper was covered with lines of script.

She'd calmed herself. But the fear came zinging back. For long moments, she sat with her shoulders pressed into the pillows and her pulse pounding. Yet even without see-ing the words, she knew what story she'd been writing.

It was the tale of Sara again. But she'd known it would be. Now the young woman had a last name. Sara Campbell. And her grandmother was Elspeth. With a deep sigh, she began to read what else she'd scrawled.

When she was finished, Sabrina sat stroking the cat, will-ing herself back to calm. Elspeth. Well, she knew where she'd gotten that name. All the same, it was weird how the story had just come back again as soon as she'd started writing.

Perhaps the fictional account was a reaction to stress. Was it going to turn into an obsession? She'd even dredged it up when the cherry bomb had hit her. Sabrina's body went rigid. She hadn't wanted to think about the time and place she'd conjured up out of the cherry vapor, but now it was unavoidable. It was the same setting. Except that under the influence of the drug, it had been suffused with danger.

Maybe that was just the way the hallucinogen was sup-posed to work. Maybe it was supposed to terrify you.

Sabrina grabbed that explanation and held on to it for dear life. Slowly a measure of calm returned. As it did, she went back over the details of the story.

The part about the raven being a bad omen. That was an old European superstition. The craggy mountains, the mist and rain could be in any northern country. But the words were more specific. *Laird. Lass. Dinna* instead of *didn't.* They sounded Scottish. And what had that battle horse been called—a destrier? That would be easy enough to check if she wanted more evidence.

It gave her a strange sense of satisfaction to have pin-pointed the locale. Then her eyes narrowed. She was the one making up the story. She could set it anywhere she wanted. But she'd picked Scotland and come up with an awful lot of very specific details.

Well, some of the fine points were things she knew well. Like herbs. Sara's familiarity with the old herbal remedies came straight out of the books she'd read. The Scottish part made some sort of sense, too. She'd always been interested in that country. She'd read a lot about the history and the customs. Back when she'd been a teenager, she'd devoured a slew of historical romances set there. She'd even named her dog Robbie and her cats Elspeth and Malcolm. Good Scottish names.

Sabrina glanced at the clock. Two-thirty. She should finish the grocery list and get some sleep. But she felt a strange reluctance to pick up the pen again while she was alone. Part of her was fascinated with the story. She wanted to find out how Duncan and Ian McReynolds were related. Did Sara cure Ian? Did the obvious attraction between Sara and Duncan develop into anything? And what happened when Sara confronted the doctor? What was his name? Fergus McGraw.

There was a moment of sheer, black fright as she pictured the evil old man. His pinched features were as vivid as if she'd met him on the street in downtown Baltimore. Just as she'd sensed the evil in the cemetery, she knew he was dangerous. Very dangerous. Fergus McGraw wanted to do her harm. If she had any sense, she'd stay as far away from him as possible.

Except that he wasn't real. So there was no way he could hurt her...was there?

Chapter Six

Dan Cassidy wished he'd had the sense to get someone to take his car home. Instead, as the young officer who'd given him a ride downtown pulled up beside the burgundy Olds in the courthouse parking lot, he hesitated. "You okay to drive, sir?"

"I'm not planning to crash into any more trees. And I want to see the report on whatever gassed me and Ms. Barkley as soon as the department has anything."

"Yes, sir."

He didn't linger to chat. In fact, he roared away with a screech of gravel that made it look like the assistant district attorney still had a buzz on. But he didn't care. He was trying to outdistance his conscience. It was bad enough playing mind games with Sabrina instead of explaining about the gold-foil seal in Ian Alastair's pocket. That was only the tip of the iceberg.

In the silence of the car, Dan heard himself swallow. Maybe he couldn't help what had happened in the cemetery, but he shouldn't have kissed her before he'd left her house. Hell, he shouldn't have compounded the infraction by asking her for a date.

He tried to relax his painfully tight muscles. But too

many disturbing things had happened this evening. Until Sabrina had given Ritz her version of the experience, he'd thought he'd understood the effects of the hallucinogen. The drug had sent his mind spinning off into a very strange fantasy.

It hadn't been a good experience for either one of them. Sabrina had been terrified of flames. For a few startled seconds, he'd seen them, too. And he'd assumed her wild cries of fear had suggested the image to him. But what about the other part? She'd said she'd felt as if there were a crowd of people around them jeering and shouting for blood.

He'd sensed the onlookers, too, just at the edge of his vision. Somehow he'd known they weren't after him. They wanted Sabrina, and he was the only one who could save her.

Dan's fingers gripped the wheel more tightly. Again, he felt the terrible urgency to rescue Sabrina. The same urgency that had driven him headlong across the dry grass after her.

His foot pressed down on the accelerator. When he realized suddenly that he was going seventy-five miles an hour, he eased up on the pedal. Behind him, a horn blared just before another car shot past.

Dan vented some of his frustration with a verbal assault that the other driver couldn't hear. It didn't make him feel a damn bit better. Sabrina had said she was a peasant girl, and he was the lord of the manor. Bizarrely enough, that had been part of it for him, too.

How in the world could they have shared that particular fantasy? As he pulled into the garage under his Camden town house, his lawyer's mind tried to come up with an explanation that made sense. He and Sabrina couldn't be replaying anything they'd done together. Perhaps it was a replay of a different type. Could a horror movie or TV program they'd both seen have triggered the fire image? That was certainly easier to buy than some psychic mumbo jumbo. Except that he didn't go to horror movies or remember seeing any scenes like the one he'd lived through tonight. Sabrina might have some clue. If he could bring himself to ask her about it.

He sat without moving in the darkened garage. He'd never been content to let events sweep him along. But how did you take action when you felt as if every step carried you farther and farther onto unstable ground? Which way did you turn when you thought you might crash through the fabric of reality and tumble headlong into—

He didn't dare put a name to what he was feeling. It was too far beyond anything he'd ever experienced—too far from what he considered normal.

All at once, the fear he'd been struggling to suppress boiled over into anger. Someone like Sabrina Barkley had no right to come in and tear his life apart. No, not *someone*. Sabrina.

There was something unnerving about his feelings for Ms. Barkley. Before he'd even met her, he'd felt a compulsion to find out as much as he could about her without letting her know that he was doing it. Then she'd walked into the restaurant and turned toward him. And ever since he'd been fighting a disturbing sensation that her innocent green eyes were going to swallow him up—or that running his hands through her fiery hair would set him on fire. The red-headed witch might as well have cast a spell over him.

Was that why everything was happening so damn fast and making his head spin? Was that why he wanted to protect her and save her so badly? And make love to her until the flames of passion consumed them both?

Dammit, he barely knew the woman. Why did she have such a hold on him? He grimaced, recognizing that he was dangerously close to careering out of control for the second time that evening. And without drugs. For all he still knew, Sabrina Barkley could be the chief sorceress in a diabolical murder ring.

No. That wasn't fair. He had no proof of anything like that. Just a crumpled charm in a dead man's pocket.

SABRINA WAS TENSE all morning. Probably because she was waiting for Dan to call and suspected that it wasn't going to happen. By noon, she'd convinced herself it was for the best. Getting mixed up with each other was all wrong. More, it was dangerous. Instead of hanging around the shop, she drove out to a craft supplier in Towson and picked up two hundred small baskets, plastic bags and ribbons, negotiating a very good price on the bulk order.

Two or three times during the day, she almost decided to call Hilda to say she wasn't feeling well and couldn't attend the lecture after all. But each time she changed her mind. Somehow the prospect of going home to her dog and cats was too depressing.

At seven, Sabrina drove to the Andromeda Institute, a renovated house not far from the Johns Hopkins campus. After stepping through the entrance, she stood looking around at the well-dressed crowd, feeling a bit apprehensive and out of place. Either the faithful were gathered to worship, or a lot of people were curious about Dr. Davenport.

She could see that her presence was being noted. Some of the patrons were her own customers and former customers. Many greeted her with a smile. But a number seemed embarrassed. One, a Mrs. Garrison, who'd been a pretty regular patron until a couple of months ago, wouldn't quite meet Sabrina's eye. Had she done something to alienate her? Or was the lady feeling guilty about not shopping at Sabrina's Fancy?

Well, she wasn't in direct competition with Dr. Davenport, Sabrina assured herself. Or was that the general perception?

The unspoken question did nothing to lessen the tension she'd been feeling since arriving. Nevertheless, when Hilda came rushing over to greet her, she responded with as much enthusiasm as she could muster.

Hilda tugged on Sabrina's arm. "I want to look at the product displays before the lecture. Afterward, the tables are always so crowded."

Others had the same idea. She and Hilda were more or less carried along by the surge of bodies up the stairs into a reception area decorated in what Sabrina could only describe as bastard Greek with Ionic columns and faux marble walls.

Gwynn Frontenac was talking with a slender, tweedy-looking man near an alabaster fountain with a pair of spouting dolphins. A good six inches taller than her companion, she leaned down to catch what he was saying.

Spotting the newcomers, Gwynn waved and gestured. "Sabrina Barkley," she called across the room, "come over here this minute."

As scores of heads turned in Sabrina's direction, she kept a smile plastered on her face. But she wished she hadn't become the center of attention.

"Professor Ashford is very anxious to meet you," Gwynn explained as Sabrina joined the twosome.

She inclined her head toward the man.

"I'm doing an article on alternative medicine, and

Gwynn has been telling me about your shop. Perhaps we could get together for an interview,'' he suggested.

Sabrina glanced quickly at Gwynn, trying not to show her annoyance. She didn't need someone making false advertising claims for her. "I'm not really treating illnesses or anything like that,'' she said in a low but firm voice.

"But you do stock herbal cures, don't you?"

"Only the ones that have been in general use for centuries. And that's not really my focus. Really, I'm more into soaps, dried wreaths and food products.''

"Hmm. Well, perhaps I'll have more luck with Dr. Davenport,'' the professor allowed.

"I was just trying to get you some free publicity,'' Gwynn said when the man had departed.

"Thanks for thinking of me. But it's better if you don't give the impression I'm any kind of healer.''

Gwynn reddened slightly. Sabrina spent five minutes making her feel better and then excused herself. Really, she had come here to see what Davenport was up to. And she'd better get on with it, even though what she really wanted to do was turn and flee. Instead she moved quietly about the room taking note of both the people and the displays. One man in particular caught her eye because he was wearing Western boots, a cowboy shirt and a string tie held in place by an ornate silver clasp. The outfit might have cut it in Santa Fe. In Baltimore, it was odd. But his clothing wasn't the only distinctive thing about him. His skin was flushed, and his eyes were very bright. Was he sick? Or terribly excited about the lecture?

When he caught her staring, Sabrina dropped her gaze to a table piled with relaxation and self-motivation tapes. Surprisingly they were free. Well, that was an expensive advertising approach. Were the cassettes simply disguised promotional material? Or were they genuinely helpful? Sabrina tucked two different ones into her purse for future study. Of course, right beside them were the high-priced pamphlets, all written by the good doctor on topics like curing constipation and insomnia, and fighting cancer.

Sabrina was looking over some expensive protein supplements guaranteed for rapid weight loss when she heard her name spoken again.

"Ah, Ms. Barkley."

Turning, she found herself staring into dark, deep-set eyes, the most remarkable feature in a face that would have stood out in any crowd. The man's swept-back hair was silver. His cheekbones were high and broad. And his nose was an eagle's beak.

Sabrina recognized him from the portrait in the lower lobby but wondered how he'd identified her. "Dr. Davenport."

"My good friend Mrs. Ahern pointed you out to me," he said, clearing up the mystery at once.

She was going to be almost as well known as the good doctor by the end of the evening. And on his turf; he couldn't possibly appreciate that.

"I hope you enjoy the lecture."

"Well, I've been curious about you," Sabrina said, hoping he'd take the statement as a compliment.

He smiled. "We do our best to ease the pain and suffering of the world."

A middle-aged woman wearing a turban and a long black dress hurried toward them. "Oh, Doctor, I was hoping to have a word with you in private," she gurgled.

Davenport nodded to Sabrina. "If you'll excuse me." Then he draped an arm over the woman's shoulder. "I always have time for you, my dear. But it will have to be a quick minute. We're almost ready to start.''

Sabrina took a seat near the middle of the auditorium. No one was talking. Rather, they were sitting in expectant silence, as if the light classical music playing in the background had put them under some kind of spell. Sabrina felt the tension easing out of her body as she listened to the soothing strains.

The peaceful feeling was dispelled when the man in the cowboy outfit plopped into the aisle chair in front of her. As he turned his head, Sabrina saw his skin had gone from flushed to pale. However, her scrutiny was cut off as the lights dimmed and a swell of music heightened the feeling of expectation. As the last notes faded away, an elegantly dressed older woman stepped under the spotlight at the front of the room like a model about to display a stylish outfit. Instead she delivered a brief, laudatory introduction before Luther Davenport materialized onstage. With the lights gleaming off his silver hair, he looked even more impressive than close up as he paused to acknowledge the enthusiastic applause.

After a few inspirational anecdotes, he segued into a description of his philosophy, which seemed to be based on communion with the natural way, whatever that was.

"Friends, I have gone to the source of wisdom. Once a week I leave civilization behind and commune with nature. In the woods. In the mountains. In the hidden cave only I have ever entered.

"There, I listen to the pulses of the earth—the original teacher of mankind. And I feel their rhythms throb within me. The experience brings me back to the laboratory and the consultation room renewed and recharged, free to turn my energies to the innovative diagnostic techniques and specially prepared treatments that have set many a gravely ill patient on the way to recovery.''

That sounded nice. Then Sabrina gave herself a little mental shake and sat up straighter. Nice? More like hogwash.

It was almost a relief when Sabrina was distracted by an abrupt movement in front of her, until she realized that the man in Western garb had doubled over and was sitting with his head cradled in his hands.

''Hoarding wisdom is as unconscionable as hoarding money,'' Davenport was saying. ''Anyone who can help mankind has a responsibility to share. Through classes, through private sessions, and through booklets published by the Andromeda Institute, I—''

His words were interrupted by a sharp groan. As Sabrina watched in horror, the cowboy pitched forward, hit the floor and lay sprawled in the aisle—white-faced and unmoving.

Several things happened simultaneously. The woman in front of Sabrina scrambled up, knocking over her chair as she backed away. Someone else began to shout for help. Dr. Davenport's voice ceased in the middle of a sentence. And the house lights came up.

''What's happened?''

''What is it?''

Sabrina knelt beside the prostrate figure. The man was shaking violently and struggling for breath. As she leaned toward him, his face contorted as if he were in terrible pain. She grasped the man's hand. ''What is it? What's wrong?''

His eyes focused on her. Something in their murky depths made her shudder. Then his jaw clenched, and his body convulsed. With a final shudder, he went perfectly still.

His eyes were closed, his skin had turned gray blue, and

he had the look of death about him. Still, Sabrina's fingers went to his neck, searching for a pulse. She couldn't find one, and his chest had ceased to rise and fall. Pressing her ear against it, she tried to find a heartbeat. As far as she could tell, there wasn't any.

"Get an ambulance," she shouted. "Hurry."

Sabrina had no idea whether anyone responded. She was too busy trying to remember the CPR techniques she'd learned a year ago. But performing on a human—one whose life was in her hands—threatened to overwhelm her.

"Can anybody help?" she begged as she flung aside the heavy silver clasp of the man's string tie.

When no one came forward, she began the procedure, counting as she forced air into his lungs and then expelled it. She was dimly aware of the curious faces watching, but she blocked them out and concentrated on the victim until large hands gripped her by the shoulders.

"Thank you, Ms. Barkley. I'll take over."

It was Dr. Davenport. Sabrina stared up at him, awfully glad he was going to assume the burden. Still on her knees, she moved aside and watched as he leaned over the unconscious man. Instead of continuing the standard rescue procedure, Davenport lifted a lid and looked into a dilated pupil. Then he stroked his hands across the clammy skin of the slack jaw.

"What—what are you doing?"

Ignoring Sabrina, Davenport picked up the man's fingers and began to examine the blue-tinged nails with great interest.

"Please. He needs CPR until the rescue squad—"

"I think I can judge the situation better than you," the doctor murmured.

They had been joined by the woman who'd made the introductions. He barked at her, ''Quickly. Get me—''

Sabrina didn't hear the last part of the sentence, because it was spoken into the assistant's ear.

The woman rushed away. Sabrina was left staring across a lifeless body into Davenport's deep-set eyes. They were challenging and commanding at the same time. She felt as if she'd been thrust into some kind of contest. And the loser was going to be the man on the floor.

Chapter Seven

Sabrina could hear a buzz of voices around her, but nobody interfered.

Of course not. Who else was going to defy the director of the Andromeda Institute?

Precious seconds were ticking away. Without blood and oxygen, the cowboy's brain cells would start to die. Bending down again, Sabrina flexed the rigid neck back and started the CPR procedure again. At least Davenport didn't try to stop her.

All her attention was focused on the unconscious man. She didn't see two large men materialize on either side of her. However, in the middle of a breath, she was rudely lifted out of the way by two sets of very strong arms.

"Wait. No."

The gentlemen ignored her. Although dressed in conservative suits, they could have been bouncers in a nightclub. With a firm hold on her elbows, they moved her several feet from the lifeless man.

"No, please..." Sabrina repeated frantically. "Don't you understand? He's not breathing. His heart..."

"Let the doctor do his stuff," someone growled.

A hush had fallen over the room. With a flourish that

managed to be both calm and theatrical, Davenport pulled the stopper from a small glass vial. Prying the cowboy's lifeless jaw open, he poured a white, grainy powder into his slack mouth.

Sabrina could feel her own heart thumping like a kettle-drum. At the same time, she realized she was holding her breath. For several seconds nothing happened. Then the prostrate figure began to cough.

The breath hissed out of her own lungs. She heard the same sigh repeated many times around her.

The coughing on the floor became louder. The cowboy's jaw muscles twitched. His eyes fluttered open, and he looked around, as if wondering where he was and what had happened.

"The light...the shining light," he whispered.

"My God. Would you look at that," somebody marveled.

There were murmurs of agreement, followed by a babble of excited voices. Sabrina was no less astounded as she stared at the man on the floor who was now struggling to sit up.

Davenport restrained him gently. "Just relax, my friend," he said. "You've been through quite an ordeal. But we've brought you back."

Sabrina couldn't take her eyes off the cowboy. An ordeal, indeed. She'd been sure his heart had stopped. And she knew for certain he hadn't been breathing on his own. What in the world had Davenport given him to revive him like that?

"How do you feel?" the doctor asked.

"D-dizzy...head hurts."

"That's to be expected. Can you tell me your name, my dear fellow?"

"Ed-Edward."

Once again the doctor checked eyes, face and fingernails, this time with a satisfied smile. Then he looked up and appealed to the crowd. "Edward needs air. And privacy. Please move back."

Some of the onlookers obeyed. Others hesitated as if they were afraid they'd miss something.

"What did you give him?" one man asked.

"A special herbal preparation that I keep here at the institute for emergencies," Davenport explained.

"By gosh, I'd like some of that stuff," someone else muttered.

"It can only be used in conjunction with carefully acquired knowledge," Davenport replied smoothly.

"I want to get up," Edward's voice cut into the exchange.

"I wouldn't advise—" Davenport began. But the cowboy was already struggling to his feet. As he tried to right himself, he grabbed on to the front of the director's suit jacket.

A look of distaste formed and was quickly erased from Davenport's face. He glanced meaningfully at the two men who were still silently restraining Sabrina. They dropped her arms, came quickly forward and took hold of the cowboy. A string of curses accompanied his attempts to fight them off. However, in a matter of seconds the bouncers were supporting his weight while hauling him away from the doctor.

"Perhaps we should take him to one of the treatment rooms," Davenport suggested, beginning to move toward the side of the auditorium.

"Wait, Doc," a man in the crowd called out.

"Later. I'll be back later to answer any questions you

might have," the director replied. "I believe this man still needs my attention."

People milled around, still talking excitedly about the unexpected drama. Now that Sabrina was no longer wedged between two burly men, she knelt to pick up her purse. Beside it on the floor was a small circle of rubber about a quarter inch across and half an inch deep. Coarse white grains clung to one flat surface.

Sabrina tensed as she realized she was looking at the stopper to the vial Davenport had been holding. It must have gone flying when the cowboy had clawed at the front of the director's coat.

Pretending to check through her purse, she pulled out a tissue and dropped it on the floor over the stopper. Then she quickly folded the prize into the tissue and tucked it into her bag.

She was straightening up again when Hilda appeared at her side. Tensely she waited for her to ask what she'd been doing. She didn't.

Instead Hilda patted Sabrina's shoulder consolingly. "I'm sure you did your best to help that man. You just don't have access to the same kind of knowledge as Dr. Davenport."

"I guess not," Sabrina muttered. There was no point in trying to defend herself. Probably the best course was to fade into the walls before anything else happened.

"He talked about a light. It's a sure sign of a near-death experience."

"Umm." Sabrina tried to keep her attention focused on Hilda, but out of the corner of her eye she could see people staring at them. Was she imagining the looks of malice on their faces? Did they all hate her? What had she done that was so terrible?

Then, in her mind, it wasn't just looks, it was shouting. Far away and then closer, she heard a crowd jeering, calling for her blood. It was happening again; they were coming after her. Like the hostile crowd she'd conjured up in the cemetery. The crowd long ago.

"Dear? Are you all right, dear?"

Sabrina had been about to cut and run. With an effort, she brought her attention back to Hilda. "What?"

"You look so pale. Are you all right?"

Still too shaken to respond, Sabrina backed toward the stairs.

"I'm sure the doctor will be with us as soon as he makes sure that poor man is comfortable," Hilda said. "Aren't you going to stay for the rest of his talk?"

"No," Sabrina managed.

Turning quickly, she dashed down to the first floor and through the lobby.

Outside, she stood for several moments sucking humid air into her lungs. It didn't help her feel any better. It was hard to shake the illusion that the crowd had been closing in on her, intent on making her pay for her mistake. But she hadn't done anything wrong. Somehow, that was the worst part.

Shoulders hunched, she headed for her car. She was pretty sure what had just happened. She'd been upset and it had all gotten tangled up with the drug experience in the cemetery. That's where the frightening images had come from.

Yet reasoning it out logically didn't help much. All she wanted to do was get away from this place. With a jab of her foot on the gas pedal, she roared out of the parking lot. It wasn't until she reached Roland Avenue that she slowed down. Fingers clutching the steering wheel, she headed for home.

Half an hour later, she turned into the long driveway that led to her house. When she rounded the last curve, her foot lifted with a jerk from the accelerator. Another car was occupying her usual parking space beside the porch.

Sabrina stared at the vehicle. It was almost 10:00 p.m., and she certainly wasn't expecting anyone.

As she debated whether to get out of her car, a figure came around the side of the house from the direction of Robbie's fenced yard.

The dog started to bark, sounding more disappointed than aggressive.

When the visitor stepped into the glare of her headlights, Sabrina saw it was Dan Cassidy, dressed casually in jeans and a striped pullover. He stood with his hands thrust into his pockets, and she couldn't help wondering if she'd conjured up his image.

Then he called out to her, and she knew it was no illusion. "I wasn't expecting company," she tossed out as she exited the car.

Dan would have given a lot to have seen her face. Last night and most of today, he'd been feeling guilty about Ms. Barkley—as much for making her the focus of his misplaced resentment as for anything he'd done. He'd been trying to figure out how he could come clean with her and not drive her away. Then tonight she'd turned up in the middle of another one of his investigations. Ever since the phone had rung an hour ago, he'd been vacillating between astonishment and renewed anger that perhaps the red-headed little witch really had pulled the wool over his eyes. Maybe her nervous act at the cemetery the other night had been part of her plan to confuse him, to throw him off the track. And there were other things that were still hard to explain. Like the hallucination they seemed to have shared. But he chose not to focus on them. It wasn't the important point now. If she'd been making a fool of him all along with her innocent green eyes and her logical explanations, she was going to be damn sorry.

Was she working for Luther Davenport? And did tonight's melodramatic incident somehow tie the two cases together? Or had she simply been in the wrong place at the wrong time once again?

Hating his own confusion, Dan willed his jaw to unclench. It might still be true that Sabrina had been flummoxed by Davenport along with the rest of the crowd. If that was the case, she was undoubtedly feeling pretty bad. But he couldn't keep the other side of the argument from stabbing through his brain like a hot poker. If she'd just earned a tidy performance fee, she was surely cursing her bad luck at finding the assistant district attorney on her doorstep.

Dan's features betrayed none of the turmoil churning in his stomach. The only thing he knew for sure was that since he'd first laid eyes on Sabrina, his judgment had been impaired, his reactions to her had been out of whack, and he hated the accompanying feeling of weakness.

"What are you doing here?" Sabrina demanded in a tone that wasn't exactly friendly.

He turned his hands palm up. Whatever he was struggling with, he'd have to act as if she'd just been through a very traumatic experience. At the same time, he was going to have to be prepared for the consequences of tipping his hand to Davenport if he screwed up. Although maybe things were far enough along that it didn't matter what the old reprobate of a doctor found out. "I thought you might want someone around,'' he said, taking several steps toward her.

''Why?''

''After what happened this evening.''

''You mean at the Institute?''

He nodded.

''Are they broadcasting it on the radio or something?'' Sabrina snapped.

''No. Of course not.''

''Then what's it got to do with you?''

Dan hesitated. ''If I tell you how I found out, you've got to treat it as strictly confidential.''

''Yes?''

''Someone at the lecture tonight is under investigation. I had a man in the audience. He called me from his car phone right after the excitement was over.''

''Who are you investigating?''

''As I said, it's confidential.''

''So the assistant district attorney's not going to tell me anything except that he knows Ms. Barkley made a very public—'' she stopped and fumbled for a word ''—fool of herself.''

Dan closed the space between them and slipped his arm around Sabrina's shoulder. At first she held herself stiffly. Then he felt some of the tension go out of her body. ''I know you're upset,'' he murmured. ''I would be, too. But the way I heard it, you did CPR on the guy. That's hardly making a fool of yourself.''

Sabrina sniffed. ''Explain that to everyone else who saw the miraculous recovery after Dr. Davenport came to the rescue.''

Dan turned Sabrina toward him and folded his arms around her. ''It's okay,'' he soothed.

She stirred in his embrace, her face coming up to search his. For the space of several heartbeats as she gazed up at him, he was sure she was going to tell him something she thought was important.

"What?"

"Nothing. Just thanks for being here," she whispered, the words barely audible. The gratitude was a painful squeeze to his chest. She made a little murmuring sound like birds' wings beating the air and closed her eyes. As she relaxed more fully against him, he began to stroke her back and shoulders.

Moments stretched, and neither one of them moved. "Dan, after everything that happened yesterday, I was kind of assuming you wouldn't call me."

"Why?"

"Because…" She sighed. "I told you. Because the two of us together don't make sense."

"No?" He looked down at her full, sensual lips, trying and failing to come to grips with his own confusion. "I almost went down to 43 Light Street to make sure you weren't going out on a date this evening."

"I wouldn't have lied to you."

He couldn't repress a low, gritty laugh. "In my business, I've learned that people who are afraid often lie their heads off."

"I try not to."

He felt a shiver ripple through her body. Because she was caught in the middle of something illegal and was doing her damnedest to talk her way out of it? Or was it more personal? Did she feel it, too? The invisible force that had wrapped itself around the two of them?

She could have stepped out of his embrace, but she didn't

move. He should have thrust her away. Instead he held her tighter.

"Dan..."

He wanted to keep holding her. He wanted to shift her body so that he could claim her lips, feel their incredible softness, finish what they'd started when they'd been wild and out of control. The hot need was still there, even when he'd come back to her house with suspicion uppermost in his mind. She was looking up at him, waiting. Almost desperately, he distanced himself. "I need to find out why you've turned up in the middle of one of my investigations," he clipped out.

"Oh."

The look of betrayal that flashed briefly across her face made his throat ache. He had to remind himself that she kept turning up like a bad penny. "I need some information from you," he repeated.

"Is this how you usually start an interrogation?"

"It isn't an interrogation."

"What is it?"

Several moments passed before he answered. "If I sounded cold a moment ago, it's because I'm having trouble keeping my cool around you."

"Why?"

His eyes locked with hers. "Don't you know?"

She swallowed. "Yes. It's not exactly easy for me, either."

He wanted to ask her exactly what she meant, what she was feeling. Overwhelming physical attraction? Or something deeper? He didn't dare, because he didn't know if she would tell him the truth. Or if he could handle the truth, whatever it was. "I promise I'll behave myself if you invite me in to talk," he said instead.

"Will you?"

"Do you have any herb tea with saltpeter?"

She laughed. "I don't know. I've never gotten that kind of request before. It's usually the other way around."

He waited while she climbed the steps to the porch.

Robbie had gone back inside through his own door and was in the front hall. He started jumping and whining the moment they stepped across the threshold.

"Down," Sabrina ordered.

The dog gave her a wounded look and moved quietly beside Dan.

Sabrina and Dan stood uncertainly by the door. "You relax. I'll get you a cup of tea," Dan offered. Good cop, bad cop, he thought. Only he was taking both parts.

"You're going to know your way around my kitchen better than I do."

"Yeah, but I've about reached the limit of my culinary skills."

Sabrina headed for the living room, Dan for the kitchen. The dog hesitated for a moment before jumping up on the sofa.

When Dan came back, Robbie was cuddled against his mistress, eyes closed and head lolling as she stroked his silky fur. And one of the cats was bravely peering out from behind the easy chair.

Dan stood gazing down at Sabrina for a moment before putting the tray with the tea on the table and taking the easy chair. She wasn't as relaxed as she looked.

"So what kind of doctor is Luther Davenport?" she asked suddenly. "Does he have a medical degree?"

Dan's brows drew together. "What makes you think I know?"

"I think he's the one you're investigating."

"And how would you feel about that?"

"Good."

"Why?"

"I think he's dangerous."

"Why?" Dan continued to probe.

Sabrina looked back at him, struggling to sum up her feelings. "He seems to have power over people. He's like a guru or something. And I've heard he gets big contributions out of the faithful." She told him a little bit about the reaction of the assemblage to the doctor, both before he'd started to speak and after the lecture had begun.

As she described the evening, Dan's posture became less closed. "He has a Ph.D. from a place in California where you can more or less buy credentials."

"Is that why you're after him?"

"I really shouldn't talk about it. But I appreciate your insights." He sighed.

Sabrina hesitated for a moment, thinking about the stopper of the bottle she'd picked up off the floor. It might provide some more insights. But she wasn't absolutely sure she wanted to share them with Dan—yet.

For a few moments they sipped their tea, but they were each keeping an eye on the other. Sabrina could feel several forces at war in the room. Dan wanted information, but didn't want to compromise himself by telling her anything. She wanted to feel comfortable with him but found it impossible to manage that, under the circumstances.

After a while, Dan set down his mug. "Can I ask you some questions about what happened after Davenport took over with Edward?"

"All right."

"Do you think the performance was staged?" Dan asked.

"Staged? As in faked?"

Dan nodded.

"I'm not a doctor. But as far as I could tell, that guy wasn't breathing and his heart wasn't beating."

"And Davenport had a convenient witness to confirm those facts for the audience. You."

Sabrina sucked in a startled breath. She hadn't thought about her role in those terms, but Dan was right. If the whole thing had been a put-up job and Davenport had needed someone to affirm the gravity of the situation, she'd filled the bill pretty well.

"If that's true, the cowboy was playing a risky game," she whispered.

"Maybe he didn't know he was playing."

"What?"

"There are drugs that can stop the heart that can be administered without the victim knowing what's happening. You know, poisons with no immediate symptoms. And some of them have antidotes."

"Perhaps that was it." Sabrina's fingers played with the dog's silky hair as she debated whether to say anything else. If only she could connect with Dan on a more personal level. Or was it better to keep her mouth shut? The only thing she was sure of was that she didn't want him to leave yet.

"Aren't you going to tell me if anything's developed on the other case?" she asked.

He looked surprised, as if he'd forgotten all about the original reason why they'd gotten together.

"There's nothing new on that front," he said.

"Well, then—"

Just as he stood up, the phone rang.

Dan's gaze shot to the old-fashioned oak clock on the

wall. It was almost twelve. "Expecting someone?" he asked sharply.

Sabrina shook her head. There was an odd feeling in her chest as she crossed to the side table and picked up the phone. It came as much from Dan's wary expression as her own puzzlement over the late call.

After one more ring, she lifted the receiver. "Hello?"

"Ms. Barkley?" The voice was low and whispery and obviously disguised. "I was beginning to think you weren't home."

"Who is this?"

There was no answer. If she'd been alone, she would have hung up.

Dan had come over and put his hand on her shoulder.

"Who is this?" she repeated.

"A friend." There was a familiar quality to the speech pattern, but it was nothing Sabrina could identify.

"What do you want?"

"I saw you tonight at the lecture."

Sabrina felt the hair on the top of her scalp prickle. She'd recognized dozens of acquaintances there. But which one matched the low-pitched voice? Her eyes shot to Dan.

He gestured and she lifted the receiver slightly away from her head. Bending, he brought his ear close so that he could listen in on the conversation.

"You saw what happened at the Institute?" Sabrina asked.

"With the man. Yes." There was a long pause on the other end of the line.

"Are you still there?"

"I'm not calling about that. I'm calling because you're in danger," the voice whispered.

The prickles traveled from Sabrina's scalp down her spine all the way to her toes. "How?"

"Don't you realize how you figure into all this?"

Sabrina's anxious gaze shot to Dan. "No!"

"Somebody's trying to put you out of business—for good."

Beside her, Dan was standing rigidly, his hand covering hers as she clutched the receiver. She felt cold all over. "Wh-who? Dr. Davenport?"

There was an indrawn breath on the other end of the line. "It's dangerous to talk on the phone."

"Then why are you calling?"

"I couldn't just stand by and let it happen."

"Will you meet me?" Dan mouthed.

"Will you meet me?" Sabrina asked.

There was another hesitation on the other end of the wire.

"Please. You can't just tell me I'm in danger. You have to give me more information," Sabrina pleaded.

After several agonizing seconds, she could hear a breath being expelled. "All right. I shouldn't. But I'll meet you at Penn Station. Downstairs where the trains come in."

"When?"

"In an hour."

Dan shook his head vigorously.

"I can't get there that fast. I'm not dressed. And, uh, my hair's wet. Give me an hour and a half," Sabrina said.

"All right. But you have to come alone, or I won't talk to you."

Sabrina swallowed. "How will I—"

"Don't worry. I'll find *you*."

The line went dead.

Chapter Eight

It was Dan who replaced the receiver firmly in the cradle. Sabrina's fingers were so tightly clenched around it that he had to pry them loose.

"My God," she breathed.

He wrapped his arms around her, holding her trembling body against his. "I'm glad I didn't leave five minutes ago."

"Not as glad as I am," she admitted, sinking against his warmth.

"Has anything like this ever happened to you before?" he asked.

"No. Nothing. Do—do—you think it's a crank?"

"I don't know. Let's try to figure it out. Any idea whether it was a man or woman?"

She shrugged. The voice had been high, and whoever it was had been striving for distortion. Yet there was that odd feeling of recognition. "Something…sounded…familiar, but I can't quite place it."

Dan looked thoughtful. She could almost picture wheels turning in his mind. "They mentioned the lecture. Did you spot anyone you recognized?"

Sabrina laughed and then fought for control. "Plenty of

people. The woman who gave me the ticket. Her friend. A lot of my customers and former customers.'' The last observation gave her pause. ''There were a number of people who used to drop by my shop. Regulars who haven't been around in three or four months.'' Then she remembered the way the doctor had come up to her, pretending to act friendly. ''Do you think Davenport has got it in for me?''

''I don't know.'' She could see he was struggling with a decision, weighing evidence, making rapid judgments. ''All right, I'd better put you in the picture.''

''Later, are you going to act like I forced you into it?''

His eyes drilled into hers. ''What makes you think I'd do that?''

''The way you've been acting all along.''

''Stop dissecting my motives,'' he snapped.

''Stop dissecting mine.''

''It's my job.''

She lifted her chin. ''So let's get on with it. What were you about to tell me?''

''It's Davenport we're investigating.''

''I was pretty sure of that. Why are you after him?''

''According to our preliminary information, his name's been linked to a few scams and a suspicious death in Georgia.'' As he spoke, he watched her face carefully. ''But he's been clever enough to keep his hands from getting too dirty. Maybe whoever called you will have something more damaging.''

''Yes. What about his assistant? The woman who introduced him tonight. Could it be her?''

''Not unless she's changed her loyalties. She's been with him since Atlanta, at least.''

''Well, now you—''

Dan cut her off with a wave of his hand. ''Later. I've

got to set things up at the station.'' He reached for the
receiver again and dialed. When the call was answered, he
began to speak rapidly, explaining the situation. ''This is
Assistant District Attorney Cassidy. I want a man in place
on the lower level of Penn Station before 12:45. And alert
Amtrak that we'll be on the premises.'' He continued the
clipped series of orders.

As soon as Dan hung up, he turned back to Sabrina.
''You just sit tight. If we get lucky, we'll bring you down
to headquarters for the identification.''

Sabrina licked her lips. She'd had more than enough difficult situations to cope with in the past couple of days, and
she should feel relief that Dan wasn't dragging her directly
into this one. But she'd heard the urgency in the caller's
voice. First she'd been frightened. Perhaps it was a defense
mechanism, but now her fear had transformed itself into
anger that someone would be trying to wreck her business.
A business she'd poured years of her life into making a
success. She couldn't just sit on the sidelines and watch it
happen. ''I'm going with you.''

''No, you're not. This could be dangerous.''

She turned to face Dan, her expression urgent. ''You
heard the call. Didn't it sound to you like this person wants
to help me? Maybe he's going to warn me about Davenport.
Maybe it's something different, but there's no guarantee
you can pick him out of a crowd of travelers. If I don't
show up, we might never get another chance to find out
what it's all about.''

A flicker of doubt crossed Dan's stern features. ''Okay.
You may be right,'' he allowed. ''But I don't like it. What
if it's a nut with a gun, for instance?''

His words made Sabrina shudder, but she pressed her
lips together to smother the reaction. Her business. Her life.

She had to know. "You're working with the police department. What can they do to protect me?"

"You're really sure you want to go through with this?"

Sabrina took a deep breath. "Yes."

Dan didn't waste any more time arguing. Instead he hurried Sabrina out the door and into his car. When they reached the main road, he turned to her. "Would you have phoned me if you'd been alone when you got that call?"

"I was scared. I would have phoned someone. You or Jo."

"She's a good choice," he said, his expression tightening, "but I'm better."

As a public transportation facility, Penn Station was open twenty-four hours a day. But after midnight there were few trains arriving, few cars in the parking lot and few people about.

A charming place to get shot, Sabrina mused as she stepped through the front door of the massive cast-iron-and-granite structure that had been erected during the glory days of train travel. She felt dwarfed by the two-story lobby with its marble walls and domed skylights.

Dan and several officers had arrived earlier. Sabrina didn't know where they were. She wasn't supposed to know. Her eyes flicked past the bronze candelabra and mahogany benches to the more Spartan room beyond the ticket counter. At the far end were the public stairways leading down to the arrival and departure area, situated two flights below the main waiting room. She checked her watch. Twelve-forty. Time to descend the right-hand flight and wait near the center of the platform.

Was the mysterious caller already on the lower level,

lurking in the shadows? Would he use the public access? Or did he know about some other entrance?

"I'm going down now," she whispered, hoping the transmitter she was wearing really worked.

Sabrina's shoes echoed on the metal stairs. When she reached the tracks, she stopped and looked nervously around. In contrast to the splendor above, the arrival area was done in early Edgar Allen Poe. The floor was grimy, the lighting was dim and the air was heavy with the essence of engine oil and sweat.

A handful of sleepy-looking passengers with luggage waited by the side of the tracks for the southbound 12:55 train. Nearby, a janitor swept the platform with a long-handled broom. His efforts didn't seem to have much effect.

Probably the man or woman she'd come here to meet wouldn't want to join the travelers, so Sabrina moved slowly down the pavement in the other direction. Watching. Listening. Waiting for someone to jump out of the shadows and clamp clammy hands to her body.

She had left the main area and was approaching the boundary of the walkway. Maybe she was at the wrong end. As she turned to go back, she thought she saw a flicker of movement near the next to the last support column.

"Who's there?" Sabrina called out.

There was no answer, but her nerve endings tingled, and she was sure she felt eyes following her. Hesitantly she took a step closer. "I can't see you. Come out of the shadows."

"No. I see you. That's good enough." The voice was low and whispery, like the one over the phone earlier that evening. Now it was also shaky, as if the person were unnerved by this face-to-face encounter.

Sabrina's next step drew a sharp warning. "Don't come any closer!" The voice congealed with dread.

"All right. Anything you want. Why did you contact me?" Sabrina asked.

"The Servant of Darkness is hurting too many people."

Sabrina drew in a quick breath. All at once, she felt the way she had in the cemetery—as if an evil presence were hovering in the shadows, ready to spring out at her. It was all she could do to keep from shifting her position so that her back was pressed against one of the grimy walls. "The Servant of Darkness? What do you mean?"

"Evil. Years of evil."

The hair on the back of her neck stood and prickled. Yes. Evil. Desperately she grasped at an explanation she could understand. "Davenport. Are you talking about Dr. Davenport?"

The only answer was a wheezing cough that echoed hollowly through the underground station. Sabrina cast a quick look over her shoulder. None of the passengers appeared to be paying the conversation any attention, but the janitor was pushing his broom slowly in her direction.

"The evil. What does it have to do with me?" Sabrina forced the question through numb lips.

"The Servant is afraid of…you…" The cough had turned to a frantic choking gasp.

"Are you all right?"

"Stay back. Don't come any closer." Fear mingled with labored breathing.

"Why is this servant afraid of me?" Sabrina pressed.

"You don't know? You really don't know?" The speaker gave a strange imitation of mirth before stopping abruptly and gasping for breath. The raspy, labored sound raised goose bumps on Sabrina's arms.

"No. Please. Tell me."

"You fool. Don't…you…remember what happened…all those years ago? In the fire?"

"What fire?"

"The Burning." The voice gasped with pain, and Sabrina saw a figure slump to the floor, a figure wearing an oversize raincoat and a hat pulled low over the face. She rushed forward to help.

"Are you sick?"

"What's happening to me? Ahhh…"

"Let me help you."

"Oh, Satan! Oh, Saraaa…" The exclamation ended in a groan of pain and terror.

"Help. I need help," Sabrina cried out, but she didn't need to shout to get action.

Seconds later she heard footsteps pounding down the platform. Then Dan was beside her, his face pale and strained in the dim light.

She stared up at him in confusion as two other men rushed past. He slung a protective arm over her shoulder.

"Get an ambulance," one of the policemen ordered into his walkie-talkie. He bent over the person on the floor to check for a pulse. When Sabrina tried to help, Dan pulled her back and prevented her from joining the rescue efforts. "They'll take care of it," he said, turning her toward him.

She held on to his arm for support, and for just a moment she had the odd sensation that he needed bracing as much as she did.

"Are you all right?" he asked.

"I…I guess." She couldn't tell him what she was feeling. It took a great deal of effort to keep her teeth from chattering. "You heard all that?"

"The Servant of Darkness stuff. The evil. Yeah."

"Do you have any idea what it means?"

"No. But it's all on tape, for what it's worth."

Their whispered discussion was interrupted by the sound of feet thumping down the stairs. Two attendants arrived with a stretcher and other equipment.

"How did they get here so fast?" Sabrina asked.

"They were on standby. In case…" The explanation trailed off.

Sabrina was vaguely aware that a couple of uniformed policemen were holding the small crowd of curious passengers back at the end of the platform, but her attention was focused closer by. The rescue team had started CPR, fighting for a life that was inexorably slipping away. As Sabrina watched the tense drama, she lost the battle to stay calm. When she shook, Dan's arm tightened around her, holding her steady.

"That's what I was doing at the Institute," she managed, her eyes glued to the trio on the grimy concrete.

"Yeah. I didn't think of that."

Sabrina was thankful it wasn't her responsibility. A pair of trained paramedics were doing the job. And there was another important variation, as well. It wasn't a man lying still as death on the ground. Sabrina sucked in a shaky breath as she got her first good look at the person under the raincoat and hat. The ill-fitted clothing hid a woman.

Sabrina focused on the contorted face. Again she couldn't hold back an exclamation.

"You know her?" Dan asked urgently.

"Yes. She used to be a customer of mine." Sabrina struggled to keep her voice steady. "She was embarrassed this evening when she saw me at the lecture. At least that's why I assumed she turned away when she spotted me."

"Her name?"

"Mrs. Garrison." Sabrina's numb brain scrambled to come up with the rest of it. "June Garrison."

The ambulance attendants had brought one of those portable electric units used to restart the heart. After ripping away the bodice of the woman's dress, one of them pressed the paddles against her skin.

"Clear," he shouted. Current surged through the wires, and the woman's body jerked.

The other medic had his eyes fixed on the controls. "Nothing."

"Again. Clear."

Once more the body jerked, but the heart didn't start.

"I think we've lost her."

The other medic nodded.

Sabrina felt her heart sink.

A train whistle shattered the air. The 12:55, right on time. In the space of fifteen minutes a woman had tried to warn her and died in the attempt. Whatever information June Garrison had wanted to tell her would be buried with her.

The paramedics transferred the body to the stretcher and covered it with a sheet. One of the detectives picked up a small black purse lying on the floor. Since Sabrina hadn't spotted it earlier, she guessed it must have been tucked under the raincoat.

The detective turned to Dan. "I'll arrange for an autopsy first thing in the morning." Then he nodded to Sabrina. "You did a wonderful job, Miss."

"Thanks," she managed.

Dan introduced them. The plainclothesman was Brian Lowell, who had been in charge of the operation.

Dan kept his arm around Sabrina's sagging shoulders as they climbed back up to the lobby. When they stepped out of the muggy lower level into the air conditioning, she started to shiver again.

Dan's fingers gently rubbed her arms, bringing a warmth that felt like a heat lamp on a January evening. "It's over now. All over. She can't hurt you," he soothed as he led her to one of the wooden benches.

Gratefully Sabrina slid down onto the firm surface. She could feel herself drawing inward, her mind shutting down.

Lowell's voice brought her back. "I've had a quick look at the personal effects. There's not much there. June L. Garrison. Age forty-five. Five feet six inches tall," he read from a driver's license. "She's got the usual credit cards."

"Can I see the purse?" Dan asked.

Lowell handed him the black leather bag, and he began to riffle through the inside pockets. Moments later he pulled out a folded pink slip. "Looks like she withdrew ten thousand dollars from New Court Savings and Loan just this afternoon."

"Ten thousand dollars?" Sabrina repeated. "How much did she have in her wallet?"

"Ten dollars and change," Lowell answered. "Wonder what she did with all that cash."

"She was at the Andromeda Institute earlier in the evening. My...my assistant said that people sometimes make sizable donations to Dr. Davenport."

"I was wondering about that myself," Dan said. "Is there anything else you can tell us about her?"

"When she used to come into my shop, she was friendly but on the quiet side. She was always looking for something to ease her rheumatism. Maybe Davenport was helping her." Sabrina gulped. "And now she's dead."

"A chronic illness would make her an easy mark for a con man like Davenport," Dan pointed out.

"The Servant of Darkness. Do you know what that means?" Lowell broke in.

"Sounds like someone who serves the devil," she guessed.

"Well, if she was ill and on strong medication, she could have dreamed up some sort of conspiracy." The officer's voice didn't hold a lot of conviction.

Sabrina sat on the hard wooden bench, feeling as if a hand had closed around her throat. Through a screen of lashes, she looked up at Dan, wishing he could take her in his arms and hold her the way he had when he'd come to her house earlier this evening. But they weren't supposed to be involved. They were only working together on a case.

"I don't like leaving you. But I have to turn in a report," he muttered.

"I understand."

"A few hours ago I asked if you were going to be all right. How about now?"

That was back when she'd only been worried about making a fool of herself. The plot had thickened considerably.

Sabrina pulled herself up straighter. "I'll survive," she said in a voice that surprised her with its strength.

Dan escorted her to a police car, opened the back door and gave her hand a squeeze. She clung to him for several heartbeats. As she slid onto the seat, he looked as if he was going to say something. Instead he turned away and gave some instructions to the driver. Then she was on her way home.

In the darkness, she leaned back against the vinyl cushions, vaguely glad they were more comfortable than the benches in the station. She didn't want to think about what had just happened. She just wanted to go back to her own house and relax. But when June's words began to echo in her head, she was too tired to fight them off.

The Servant of Darkness. The Burning. Satan. Saraaa.

Sabrina jerked erect as her mind echoed that last urgent syllable. In the exigency of the moment, when she'd been worried about so many other things, it had simply been a strangled sound trickling from the lips of a dying woman. In the silence of the police car, it took on meaning.

It wasn't just a sound. It was a name. Sara. The name of the woman in her story.

A bead of perspiration formed at Sabrina's hairline and slid down the back of her neck.

Was she really getting this right? Or had her mind conjured up the connection?

Her story. Reality. She'd convinced herself they were like two sets of train tracks running beside each other. But she could feel them converging. Her story. The fire she'd imagined at the cemetery. The Servant of Darkness. June Garrison. In some mysterious way, they were connected.

More droplets of moisture trickled down the back of her neck, and she reached to wipe them aside. Her palm came away slick and clammy.

Chapter Nine

For the remainder of the ride home, Sabrina sat tensely in the back seat of the police car. Then she waited with her heart thumping against her ribs while her escort walked around checking the house and making sure the doors and windows were locked.

He gave her an appraising look as he rejoined her in the living room.

"It's all right. The house is secure."

"Yes. Thanks," Sabrina managed, hanging on to the appearance of normalcy as she ushered him out. Let him assume she was worried about the house. Better to have him put that in his report than what was really making her feel as if a coil of barbed wire were twisting in her stomach. She watched to make sure he was actually leaving. When she saw his headlights cutting through the darkness down the driveway, she rushed into the little room she used as an office and snatched up a pen and pad of paper.

The story she was writing. It was her only clue to what was going on. She had to go back to it. Tonight. Before it was too late.

Still, when she settled herself on the sofa and took the pen in her hand, she felt a surge of panic as if someone had just dropped a dark, suffocating shroud over her head and started to secure the covering with heavy ropes.

She fought the feeling of claustrophobia. Was she crazy? Or possessed? Was some strange outside power exerting an influence over her?

Shuddering, she tried to loosen her grip on the pen. But her fingers were locked in a death grip.

Her eyes squeezed closed. Then she saw an image. Sara. So like herself. Yet different. Standing on the battlement of a castle, the wind blowing her wild red hair.

She beckoned. And suddenly it was all right. Swiftly and surely, the pen began to move across the page.

Thin morning sunlight slanted in through the narrow windows in the stone wall of the castle. Sara was half dozing in the chair when a flicker of movement made her jerk to wakefulness. She hadn't heard anyone come in, but Duncan was leaning over the bed, looking down into the patient's face.

"He seems much better."

"Aye. I think he's going to be all right." She laid a hand against the sleeping man's cheek. The fever had broken several hours earlier, and his skin was dry and cool.

"Ye must be exhausted, lass," Duncan said.

She stretched and winced slightly.

"You do yourself ill spending the night in a chair like that."

"The serving girl was weary. She'd been with me for hours, so I sent her away."

"How long has it been since you've left this room?"

Sara didn't answer. Days, she thought. But she'd felt a kind of safety in here—after the terrible confrontation with Fergus McGraw. He'd been furious that someone else had been brought to tend his patient, and he'd predicted dire consequences for the man who lay coughing on the bed.

Sara had turned away to tend him. Duncan and several other men had removed the physician forcibly from the room.

Duncan must have seen the expression that crossed her face as she remembered the scene. "You're brave—as well as skilled."

"Not so brave. Is Dr. McGraw still about?"

"He's gone."

"Thank the Lord. I dinna want to face that fierce stare of his again."

"He won't harm ye. I'll see to that." Duncan came around to stand in back of Sara. She felt him behind her, heard the breath stirring in his lungs. There was a long moment of anticipation when she imagined she felt his hands hovering above her. Then he lifted her hair from her neck.

"What are ye doing?"

"You've given so much to Ian. Let me ease the stiffness in your shoulders." His large hands began to knead her tired muscles. It wasn't proper for a man to touch a woman like that, but when she opened her mouth to protest, no words came out. Instead she closed her eyes and sighed. The massage felt good.

"What did ye do for him?" he murmured.

Sara had been drifting with the physical sensations. It took a moment for her mind to focus on the question. "There wasn't so much I could do. Force him to take fluids, keep him quiet, bind his chest, give him something for the pain."

"That sounds like quite a bit, to me. Your gran taught you all that?"

"Aye."

They were silent again. The hands on her shoulders moved to her neck and then into her hair.

"Don't. You shouldn't."

"Your locks are like fire. I've been wanting to touch them," he murmured.

There was a knock at the door. Duncan quickly moved back and dropped his hands.

"Come in," Sara called out, her voice a bit shaky.

The maid she'd sent away after Ian's fever had broken came in. *"I'll take over. Go on. Get up for a stretch,"* she said.

Sara checked the patient's breathing and tucked the covers up around him. *"If he wakes, give him some water. And if he's in pain, come and fetch me,"* she said.

"Aye."

She'd been sitting for so long that she was unsteady on her feet. Duncan grasped her elbow, and for just a moment she sagged against him. Then she straightened. But he kept hold of her as he ushered her down the hallway and out onto the parapet that circled the castle. After the close quarters of the sickroom, the cool morning air felt wonderful, and Sara drank in a long draft as she looked out over the countryside. The valley below them was hidden in the mist, creating the fancy that the rest of the world had gone away, leaving only this high mountain stronghold.

The cold began to make her shiver. Duncan was behind her again. This time, his arms circled her waist. She should move away. Instead she eased back against him, enjoying the warmth and the supple strength of his body. Neither one of them spoke.

"Some wanted to call in Lillias."

Sara had heard dark whisperings about the old woman

who lived on the other side of the mountain from the village. "They say she's a witch."

"Aye. But Calder and some of the others were for it. I argued against her."

"Ye did?"

"Aye. I dinna want her working her spells on Ian. Now I'm doubly glad."

Did she feel his lips in her hair, or was that her imagination?

Nay, not imagination.

She moved her head and felt him sigh as he pulled her closer. Now she was inviting his attentions like a wanton woman.

"Duncan." *Knowing she'd made a mistake, she tried to draw away, but he held her in place.*

"Shhh. I mean ye no harm. I haven't been able to get ye out of my mind all this time, lass. When I saw you at the door of the cottage, it was like a bolt of lightning shooting through me." *His mouth moved over her hair. His hands slid up and down her arms, stroking her, drawing her back into his heat. She closed her eyes, unable to resist the seductive pull. Pleasurable sensations curled through her body.*

When he turned her in his arms, she could only stare up at him, her eyes heavy-lidded. Then reason stabbed at her sharply like a knife in her breast.

This was wrong. It could lead nowhere. Not between a girl from the village and a laird.

"Duncan. Nay."

He ignored her plea as his lips descended to hers. Her hands pushed against his chest. Her body tried to twist out of his arms. But he held her tight—tight. And there was only one place she could escape.

SABRINA GASPED air into her lungs with the desperation of a drowning swimmer who finally breaks the surface of the water. The room had no reality. It was too warm. Too comfortable. Too modern.

The wrong place. In the wrong time.

Then, as if a burlap sack had been roughly turned inside out to reveal a quilted lining, reality reversed itself.

Sabrina's breath was coming in little puffs, and her whole body was drenched in sweat. With a trembling hand, she picked up the hem of her dress and wiped it across her face. She was sitting on the sofa in the living room with a clipboard and a pad of lined paper in her lap.

Robbie slept on a nearby cushion. But across the room, a frightened cat peered at her from behind a chair.

"You probably think I'm going nuts," she said.

As if answering the question, the cat bounded away, and Sabrina was left with nothing but her own doubts. At first she'd felt a warm surge of relief as if she were coming home to Duncan's welcoming arms. But in the end, it had been no refuge. She'd felt a terrible, driving need to escape from the story. From Duncan. From the sweetness of his kiss. Because it had been wrong. And dangerous.

Sabrina pressed her palms against her forehead, feeling as if she were wandering in a cruel maze where every path led to disaster. Was there nowhere she could find refuge from danger? She'd taken up pen and paper to find out what June Garrison had been trying to tell her when she'd died. Fleeing to her Scottish story hadn't given her any answers. Just more questions.

Feeling a pulse pound in her temple, she looked around her cheery living room. In the train station she'd felt a terrifying presence hovering in the shadows. Just like at the cemetery, she acknowledged with a shudder. It had followed her home, and it was hiding in the dark corners where she never dusted, waiting to pounce. If she didn't somehow outdistance the unseen menace, it was going to spring like a hungry tiger and tear her to bits.

THE CLARENCE MITCHELL Courthouse was empty, save for the few clerks who worked the night shift. The assistant district attorney's office was dark, except for the old-fashioned brass lamp, which cast a pool of yellow illumination on the desk blotter. A tape recorder hummed in the center of the lighted circle. As the last words faded from the minicassette, Dan reached out and pressed the stop button. Then he rewound the tape.

He felt the hairs on the top of his scalp prickle as June Garrison's dying words seemed to echo in the small room. The Servant of Darkness. The Burning. Satan. Saraaa. It might have been the long, drawn-out gasp of a woman in pain. When you listened to the tape, you could interpret it that way.

But as soon as he'd heard it, he'd known it was a name. Sara. And he couldn't explain why it had come from June Garrison's lips.

He'd lain awake at night, hearing that name in his head. It was the same name he'd spoken in the graveyard when he'd gone racing after Sabrina. When she'd been terrified and he'd been trying to save her. At least, that was what his drugged mind had thought he was doing.

Tonight, at the station, he'd felt the same desperate need to shield her from danger. When that apparition in the raincoat had popped out of the shadows and lurched toward her, he'd almost gone rushing down the platform to save her again. Somehow, he'd forced himself to hold back until the drama had played itself out.

Cupping his face in his hands, he pressed his palms hard against his eyelids. It didn't help. In his mind he saw a woman's countenance, hauntingly delicate and framed by a wreath of long red curls. Oddly, he seemed to see it surrounded by a crystal sphere. It was Sara.

As he stared at her, the features blurred and changed subtly. When the face reformed, the skin became clear and translucent. The hazel eyes altered to sea green. The straggly brows were almost tamed.

Now it was Sabrina.

Dan's eyes snapped open, and he jumped up from the chair as if the seat had suddenly become red hot.

Then he went dead still. Sara. Sabrina. Terrified of the fire.

Panic gnawed at his vitals. By an act of will, he brought the fear down to a level he could manage. He knew what was happening to him. What had to be happening. Because there was no other explanation he could accept. He was having a flashback from the cherry bomb.

He let out the aching breath he'd been holding in his lungs. A flashback. Yeah. That was it. He'd never thought he'd be glad someone had drugged him. Now he clasped it to himself. Because if he didn't believe that theory, he'd have to believe...

He stopped, unable to complete the thought.

SABRINA OPENED sleepy eyes and glanced at the clock. She was shocked to find that it was almost eight-thirty. That was very late by her standards. But at least she'd gotten a good night's sleep.

For long moments she lay in bed staring at the crack that jagged like a lightning bolt across the middle of the ceiling, trying to figure out how she felt. In the morning sunlight, it was difficult to recapture the dread and the crazy speculations of the night before. Thank goodness.

After a quick cup of tea and a cookie, she took a shower. While she was washing her hair, she remembered something that had completely slipped her mind with everything else that was going on. She still had the stopper from the bottle that Davenport had used to revive Edward.

Quickly she washed away the shampoo and dried off. In her bathrobe, she ran downstairs, fished the prize out of her pocketbook and clenched it in her fist. It wasn't out of a story or part of a whispered warning over the phone. It was solid and concrete. And maybe it would yield its secrets.

She could turn it over to Dan. Then she thought about explaining to the police lab how she'd acquired it. Was it stolen property? Maybe they couldn't even accept something like that. Instead of calling the assistant district attorney's office, she got out her phone book and looked up the number for Medizone Labs, where Dr. Katie Martin McQuade had recently assumed the position of director of research.

"Can I hire you to analyze a magic elixir I picked up last night?" she asked when she was put through to her friend.

"Sounds interesting. What does it do?"

Sabrina fingered the plastic bag that now held the tissue-wrapped stopper. "It appears to bring the dead back to life."

"Sounds even more interesting. Bring it right over."

Before Sabrina left, she made a quick call to the shop to tell Erin she'd be late.

"Not to worry," her assistant told her. "I'm just getting out some new stock. And you had a call. From Mr. Cassidy.

He wants to take you to lunch again. I said it would be fine.''

"Maybe you should have checked with me first."

"Don't you want to go?"

Sabrina reconsidered her response. "Yes. I'm sorry. I'm just kind of uptight."

"After last night, you're entitled."

Sabrina gulped. "You know about last night?"

"Well, Hilda called with a report."

"About the man at the Institute?"

"Yes. She told me to look after you," Erin continued.

"Sweet of her," Sabrina murmured, wondering who else her wacky customer had called. Still, it could be worse. The Institute was bad enough. What she really dreaded was getting into a discussion about the train station. "Do me a favor. When I come in, pretend this is just a normal day."

She could hear Erin take in a breath and let it out. "Sabrina, everybody comes to you with their troubles. You're always there for us. You ought to know it's all right to ask for help with—with problems."

"If I thought it would do any good, I'd take you up on it."

"Well, I'm here to listen, if you need me."

"Thanks."

After hanging up, Sabrina reached down to stroke the cat that had plopped into her lap. She was pretty sure that talking about her present problems wouldn't help. No, that wasn't exactly true. There had always been a part of herself that she didn't feel comfortable sharing. If she started talking about witches and spells and evil eyes, she was going to feel too exposed and vulnerable.

Twenty minutes later, Sabrina pulled into one of the spaces reserved for visitors in the crowded Medizone parking lot. Marcia, the executive secretary, knew Sabrina was expected and ushered her right into Katie's spacious office. Katie's husband, Mac, was leaning against the desk, a mug of coffee gripped casually in his left hand—the one made of stainless steel. The metal fingers had saved his and Katie's life when they'd been in a tight situation six months earlier.

Perhaps Mac hadn't entirely come to terms with the prosthesis. But it was apparent marriage to Katie had changed him. Once he'd avoided people. Now he was comfortable meeting the public. Still, Sabrina was flattered that the company president had taken time off his busy schedule for her.

"Katie told me about your find. I'm always interested in turning up wonder drugs," he explained.

Sabrina knew that before he and Katie had gotten back together, he'd spent his life traveling around the world looking for exotic antitoxins.

"Maybe you don't have to go any farther than Baltimore." Sabrina took out the plastic bag and set it on the desk. Along with it, she gave her friends a capsule summary of the amazing revival and a warning that the analysis of the white powder clinging to the stopper might have impact on a police investigation.

"Can you be more specific?" Mac asked.

"If you don't want to get involved, I und—"

Mac cut her off. "We'll do it. I just want to make sure you're not into something you can't handle."

"I'm just on the fringes," Sabrina assured him, still anxious not to open herself up for a discussion. Besides, going into detail would only worry her friends.

But Katie had been watching the nervous twists Sabrina gave to the silver ring on her right hand. "I know what it's like to be sitting on information you're afraid to trust to the authorities. If you need us for more than lab work, we're here," she said.

"I appreciate that."

Katie took out a notebook. "Even if you don't want to say more about the case, I do need some information about exactly what happened. Are you sure the victim wasn't breathing when the doctor gave him the stuff?"

"I took a pretty complete first-aid course last year. I couldn't detect either breath or heartbeat."

"Tell me everything you can about his symptoms."

Sabrina complied. When she finished, she saw Katie give her husband a quick, pointed look. He nodded almost imperceptibly and picked up the plastic bag. "I'll take this down to the lab. We'll have to run a number of different kinds of tests, so I'm not sure how long before we get the results. Check back with us this afternoon."

When he'd departed, Katie put down her pen. "Sabrina, you're more upset than you're letting on. Are you sure there isn't something you want to tell me?"

"You didn't have to get rid of Mac. I'm worried about business stuff."

Katie looked dubious. "You're sure?"

Sabrina forced a smile. "Everything will work out."

However, as she drove downtown, she felt her thoughts and her stomach starting to churn again. After pulling into the parking garage, she sat gripping the steering wheel with white-knuckled hands.

She'd sat like this in the car the morning it had all started. Then she'd just had a vague sense that something bad was going to happen. This morning she was smack in the middle of it.

She'd thought it was all tied in with the account she was

writing of Sara and Duncan. When she'd gotten home from the terrible scene at the train station, she'd hoped she could get some answers from the story. Now that seemed like grasping at straws. This wasn't about fiction. It was about the here and now.

If somebody wanted to hurt her, all they had to do was wait until she got out of the car and walked across the street. They could come roaring around the corner and mow her down. Except that wasn't the way anything had happened so far. Moisture beaded on her upper lip as she pictured a witch leaning over a boiling caldron, chanting sinister incantations against her.

Deep down, she'd always wondered if she really believed in the power of evil spells. Was that what had killed June Garrison? And what about the star stone at the cemetery? Even when she'd told Dan it was cursed, she hadn't quite believed it. That was before so many other things had happened.

An echo of the painful shock she'd felt when she'd held that innocent-looking oval in her hand reverberated through her body. It left her breathing shallowly and feeling as if fire ants were crawling on her skin. Scrambling out of the car, she began to run her hands up and down her arms. A man who'd just gotten out of his own vehicle gave her an odd look, and she turned away, embarrassed.

Reaching across the front seat she snatched up her purse and slammed the door with a loud thunk. She remembered what she'd told Dan about magic and witches' curses. If you thought they were going to make you sick or kill you, they probably would. Undoubtedly that was what had happened to her at the cemetery. She'd started worrying that something bad was going to happen even before Dan had driven through the gates. So it had.

Quickly she crossed the street. After entering the building, she stood looking across at her shop. She'd worked hard to make Sabrina's Fancy a success. And she wasn't going to toss it all away. Maybe that was the real threat. Someone was trying to frighten her into self-destructing. But why? She'd been worried that Davenport was out to ruin her, but that didn't exactly make sense. Not when her yearly profit was peanuts compared to what he must be taking in at the Institute. Was he so greedy that he wanted to be the only one selling herb products in Baltimore? Or was the threat from somewhere else?

Had she inadvertently done something to hurt someone?

She couldn't think of anything. Certainly nothing deliberate.

"Planning a new window display?" a soft voice asked.

Sabrina whirled toward the door.

"Sorry. I didn't mean to sneak up on you," Noel Emery, the paralegal who worked for Laura Roswell, apologized as she came into the lobby carrying a heavy briefcase.

"That's okay. I was just thinking about something," Sabrina said. "What do you think about featuring some of that silver jewelry I've been getting from the Eastern Shore?" she improvised.

"Good idea." Noel tipped her head consideringly. "I used to help my uncle in his jewelry shop so I know a good buy when I see it. I've had my eye on a pair of your earrings for a couple of weeks. Maybe I should buy them before I lose out."

After they'd chatted for a few minutes, Noel walked to the elevator. Sabrina crossed to the shop. Although the door was open, Erin was nowhere in sight. Then she heard her assistant bustling around in the back room.

Sabrina checked the cash register to make sure there was

enough change, but she was still thinking about threats. Davenport was the only one she could identify. If he saw her as a business rival and wanted to discredit her, he'd gotten a wonderful start last night. However, to be prepared, he would have had to know she was going to show up at the lecture. Had he been the one who'd urged Hilda to invite her?

Sabrina pulled a phone book from under the counter and found the number. When she picked up the receiver, she realized Erin was on the phone, talking to someone in a low voice.

"Oh, sorry."

"Sabrina? I'll be off in a jiffy."

Her assistant came out of the back room a few minutes later carrying a box full of decorative metal tea canisters. Sabrina tried Hilda again. But there was no answer. Maybe she was out having a tennis lesson, or was it golf? She'd have to try later.

Sabrina was conscious that Erin was hovering around her. "Are you sure you don't want to sit down for a cup of tea and a chat?" her assistant finally asked.

"No. I need to work. Why don't we change the window display. Let's use those canisters, and some of our silver jewelry, too."

"Yes. Maybe that's what we both need," Erin agreed.

At twelve-thirty, Dan found Sabrina in the lobby staring at the shop window. Her hair stood out in a red cloud around her face, a smudge of dirt tinged her cheek, and a satisfied smile quirked her lips.

Turning to Dan, she felt a rush of pleasure. He gazed back at her expectantly, yet there was a tension around his eyes. She'd seen that look before in her customers—when there was some personal problem they wanted to discuss but didn't know how to bring up. The mixed signals made her heart start to beat faster.

"Hi" was all she said.

"Hi, yourself."

She'd thought he'd be dressed for the office. Instead he was wearing jeans and a turquoise knit top that was wonderful with his blond hair and tanned complexion.

"Where are we going?" she blurted.

"I'm planning to kidnap you."

"Isn't that a federal offense?"

A small smile played around his lips. "I think I'm immune from prosecution."

He reached out to lay his hand lightly on her arm, and both of them stood very still, gazing at each other. For a moment, she felt something very warm and open between them. Then the guarded look was back behind his eyes.

"What is it?"

There was a five-second pause. "Not that I care, but probably you want to wash your face and comb your hair."

Sabrina had forgotten Erin was in the doorway. Now she turned accusingly to her friend. "Why didn't you warn me I was a mess?"

"I think he's telling the truth. He doesn't care," Erin seconded the observation.

Nevertheless, Sabrina made a quick trip to the bathroom to put herself back together. After washing her face and brushing her hair, she snatched up a green-and-yellow scarf from the new stock she'd gotten in recently and slipped it around her neck.

But once she and Dan were alone, neither one of them seemed to be able to dredge up any casual conversation. As Sabrina buckled her seat belt, she slid Dan a quick glance. His expression was grim.

"You didn't have to take me to lunch."

"I wanted to."

"Are you going to tell me what's making you so uptight?" she asked.

He didn't answer.

"Is it about the case? Has something happened that I should know about?"

"It's my problem, not yours," he said cryptically as he started the car.

Dan kept his eyes glued to the noontime traffic. He had a lot to worry about. Unaccountably he was thinking about something that should be at the bottom of the list. His ridiculously out-of-proportion reaction to the June Garrison tape last night.

Maybe it had really been from a drug flashback. On the other hand, now that he was thinking more clearly, he'd decided it was just as likely that he was feeling the effects of extreme stress. He'd seen it happen to other guys. When you were under a lot of pressure and not getting any sleep, your mind played all kinds of stupid tricks. Either you had to find a way to cope, or you quit the department and went in for something tamer, like commodities trading.

He wasn't ready to bail out. But unfortunately none of his problems had vaporized during the night. They'd only gotten worse. After a couple of hours of restless sleep, he'd come back to the office to confront a whole set of unpleasant realities. Starting with the June Garrison preliminary autopsy report and how it affected the Graveyard Murder case.

The chief of police had had something to say about that one, and it hadn't been a very enjoyable conversation. Dan had been angry and frustrated, and he hadn't even been able to say, "I told you so."

He'd come away from the meeting needing to feel that there was *something* effective he could do. Getting Sabrina out of the city had been the most constructive alternative he could conjure up. He hadn't even let himself think about how much he simply wanted to be with her.

So he'd called up her assistant and made the arrangements. Then, instead of sitting behind his desk stewing over the ineffectiveness of the system, he'd played hooky and spent the rest of the morning getting ready. But as soon as he'd seen Sabrina standing there with that mixture of innocence and mystery he found so appealing, he'd realized it would have been smarter to let Brian Lowell handle this particular part of the job.

Which made him a coward. And an underhanded coward, at that. Even if he didn't plan to talk about the weird feeling he'd gotten while he was listening to the tape last night, he owed it to Sabrina to share the information he'd acquired from the police department.

His jaw clenched, and the cords of his neck tightened. He didn't want to start a conversation about the police report on June Garrison. Or about the way he'd brought Sabrina into the Graveyard Murder case in the first place. From a personal point of view, that was the worst part of all.

However, sooner or later he'd have to come clean with her. On all counts. But please, God, not yet.

Chapter Ten

Sabrina pretended to watch the crowds of office workers and tourists enjoying the summer weather, but from the corner of her eye she continued to study Dan's tense features. You didn't have to be a psychic to read his clenched jaw and evasive eyes. Whatever he was worried about might be his problem, but she'd bet the next month's receipts from her shop that it involved her.

Last night when she'd wanted to be in on the action at Penn Station, she'd made it clear that she wouldn't take no for an answer, even when he'd warned her she might be walking into danger. Today she didn't feel on such solid ground. And as she sat with one hand wedged under her leg, she started to worry about something else. She was concealing a piece of information she was pretty sure Dan would be interested in. It hadn't started off as concealment. But Dan might think that's what it had turned into. She didn't know how to bring it up, because when she did, he'd assume she hadn't completely trusted him.

Sabrina saw Dan sigh. "Sorry. I'm being selfish. I just want to enjoy a couple of hours with you before I have to start thinking about business again."

Relieved, Sabrina grabbed on to that. In a very funda-
mental way, it was what she wanted, too. "Okay."

His tension went down several levels, and she was glad
she hadn't pushed.

Dan headed toward the Science Center, and Sabrina
guessed they were going to eat at the Rusty Scupper, several blocks farther on. Instead he pulled up at the entrance
to the marina directly across the harbor from the World
Trade Center. After cutting the engine, he got out and unlocked the trunk. Inside was a plastic cooler, a shopping
bag and a wicker hamper.

"What's all that?"

"Lunch. If you take the hamper, I'll take the rest."

She tested the weight of the basket. "You must have an
enormous appetite."

"Yeah." He led her toward one of the small piers. She
followed him to a tidy cabin cruiser named *Legal Eagles*.

The name brought a smile to her lips. She'd thought of
the Redford movie as soon as she'd met him.

"Yours?" she asked, eyeing the well-cared-for craft.

"Four of us down at the office pitched in and bought her
at one of those sales the police department holds twice a
year. She belonged to a drug dealer who stretched his luck
too thin. Craig uses her the most. But the rest of us get in
enough weekends to make the investment worthwhile."

Dan climbed aboard and set the cooler on the deck.
When he turned to help Sabrina across the gunwale, he
found her already standing on the varnished planking.

"I told you I grew up at the shore. Some of my friends'
parents had boats, so you don't have to worry about my
going overboard or anything like that."

"Good."

It seemed they'd both made a silent agreement to act like two people out for a day of sun and fun.

"Listen, I was thinking, let's head down to the bay before we eat," Dan said when he returned from stowing the gear.

"All the way?"

"I can do it in forty minutes."

Why not? She'd decided to drop her problems until after lunch. It was even more effective to leave them far behind in Baltimore. Or cast them upon the water, as it were. "Okay. Can I do anything to help?"

"You can untie the ropes."

"Will do."

While Dan climbed up to the the pilot's seat, Sabrina attended to the lines. Then she opened one of the low folding beach chairs and tried to relax as Dan maneuvered the boat out of the marina. But she was too restless to sit still for long.

They cruised past Fort McHenry where Francis Scott Key had watched the bombs bursting in air during the War of 1812, then past Sparrows Point and Gibson Island, the posh enclave at the mouth of the Patapsco River.

As the boat reached open water, the green-and-yellow scarf Sabrina was wearing began to blow around her face. Taking it off, she wound it around the handle of the wicker hamper. Then, curious about what Dan had brought, she began poking through the contents of the ice chest. He had obviously gone overboard at the Harborplace food stalls. Among other things, she found spiced shrimp, crab-claw cocktail, potato salad, marinated vegetables, hot peppers, "buffalo" wings, cheese bread, blueberry cheesecake, cola and raspberry soda.

"I repeat, this is *lunch?*" she asked as she set out containers on the square table in the cockpit.

Dan anchored the boat and sat down in one of the low chairs. "I was working off nervous energy shopping."

"Oh?"

Looking a bit sheepish, he began filling his plate. "Did I get some things you like?" he asked.

Sabrina nodded and dipped a peeled crab claw into the cocktail sauce. "This will do for starters."

Dan leaned back in his seat, looking like a man trying to loaf, but his muscles were too tightly coiled for that.

Sabrina nibbled on a cheese cube, but she pushed more food around her plate than she conveyed to her mouth as she watched Dan watching her. Even if they both wanted to act as if this were a normal outing, it wasn't working. They weren't being honest with each other. She'd tried to get him to tell her what was wrong. He was being evasive. On the other hand, so was she. She hadn't wanted to talk to anyone about what was worrying her. But here she was sitting with the one person who didn't need a two-hour briefing to understand why she was uptight. Perhaps if she took the risk of making the fist move, he'd be candid with her.

Sabrina took a sip of soda to wet her throat. "I'd feel more comfortable if I told you something," she said before she lost her nerve.

"Oh?"

"It has to do with what happened last night at the Institute."

Dan put the chicken wing he was holding back on his plate. "About Davenport? Something you've remembered?"

"It's about the stuff Davenport gave Edward. He had it

in a little bottle. And when Edward lurched against him, the stopper must have gone flying. It landed on the floor beside my purse. I found it and picked it up.''

''That's withholding evidence. You had an obligation to turn it over to me. Why the hell didn't you?'' The question exploded out of him, belying the relaxed pose he'd been cultivating.

Sabrina shrank back. ''Did I? You didn't even want to tell me you were investigating him, remember?''

''It could be important. If we can get an analysis.''

Sabrina knit her fingers together in her lap.

Dan stared at her. Then he climbed out of his seat and came over beside her, reaching for her. She held herself stiffly as she felt his hands on her shoulders. ''Sabrina, I'm sorry,'' he muttered. ''You didn't deserve that.''

She didn't, couldn't respond.

His hands tightened on her shoulders. Then they dropped to his sides, and he returned to his chair. ''I've been trying to keep my problems to myself. Maybe that was a stupid idea,'' he said in a gritty voice.

''I think that's true for both of us.''

''You know, I've had a man in custody for the Graveyard Murders. Raul Simmons. I never thought the case against him was very strong. It was blown to hell in a hand bucket this morning.''

''Why is that?''

''Because the graveyard victims died of exactly the same poison that killed June Garrison.''

Sabrina felt a wave of cold sweep across her body. ''Murder? Another murder?''

''That's the one conclusive report I do have on my desk. It's definitely a homicide, unless Ms. Garrison injected her-

self with a lethal dose of poison before she went to meet
with you at the station.''

Sabrina wrapped her hands around the chair arms.

Dan plowed on. ''The only difference is that the other
two were killed quickly. However, as I told you, I don't
put much faith in coincidences. The poison isn't something
you can go buy at the drugstore. You have to grow it.''

''A herbal extract?''

''Yes.''

Sabrina studied the tense planes of Dan's face.

''I was wondering this morning if Edward had been
given the same thing,'' he said tightly. ''Only in a lesser
dose. Enough to stop the heart unless an antidote was given.
If I had an analysis of the drug Davenport gave him, I might
be able to tell.''

Sabrina understood what he'd been thinking and why
he'd reacted so strongly. ''That would tie Davenport to the
murders,'' she breathed.

''The stopper should go to the police lab.''

''I already gave it to a friend who's in the medical research business. She's doing an analysis for me.''

He looked as if he were mentally counting to ten.
''You're sure you can trust her?''

''Of course. She's very reliable. And she knows how to
keep things confidential.''

Dan seemed somewhat mollified. ''When are you supposed to get the results?''

''Later today.''

''I hope you're planning to share them with me.''

''At this point, it would be stupid not to. Not telling you
in the first place was probably stupid.''

''You didn't have any reason to trust *me*,'' he said in a
low voice.

She reached out and covered his hand with hers. "I do now. And...and...there's something else I have from the Institute."

"What?"

Sabrina pulled her purse over, retrieved the two cassettes and handed them to Dan. He read the titles. "'Tapping Every One of Your Inner Resources' and 'The Uses of Imagination.' You bought these? What's he asking for them, ten dollars apiece?"

"No. That's the funny part. Everything else is for sale at inflated prices. These are free."

"It sounds as if he wants people to take them home. Do you think it's an advertising pitch?"

"I don't know. Let me tell you how I was feeling— before the lecture and while the good doctor was talking. A lot of people I know are wildly enthusiastic about Davenport. It's like he has some magic secret for inspiring confidence. Well, rave notices like that make me skeptical. So I was in a questioning frame of mind when I went to the Institute."

Sabrina was gratified to see that Dan was listening intently. "I didn't like the place. In fact, I was on edge the whole time I was there, until I sat in the auditorium and started listening to the soft music. It had a strangely calming effect on me. And on everybody else who was listening. Then Davenport began the lecture, and it was almost as if Moses had come down from Mount Sinai. After a while, I don't know, I started being in a, uh, receptive mood, ready to give him more than the benefit of the doubt. By the time he was halfway through his lecture, I was beginning to agree with what he was saying. I had to give myself a mental shake to remind myself it was hogwash."

Dan's eyes narrowed. "You're suggesting there was

some factor—some hidden factor, that helped influence you and everybody else favorably toward him?''

''Uh-huh.''

He looked thoughtful. ''On-the-spot motivation. Like subliminal persuasion, maybe? I've heard about grocery and department stores doing that kind of thing.''

''Maybe that's why he wants people to take his tapes home. Suppose when you do, you can get a hidden message along with the free lecture.''

''It's an interesting theory.''

Sabrina gestured toward the tapes. ''Maybe you should send *those* to the police lab.''

He turned the boxes over in his hand. ''One's got a little silver dot in the corner. I wonder what that means.''

Sabrina shrugged.

Dan stood up. ''Maybe only the ones with the markings have the hidden messages. Since you brought it along, I'd like to have a listen.''

''You've got a recorder on the boat?''

''In the cabin.''

''I wish you had a phone so I could call my friend and see if she's got that lab report,'' Sabrina mused.

''Actually, I do. A portable. It and the recorder are both stored where the salt air won't ruin the electronics.'' Dan descended the short flight of steps to the boat's interior. Sabrina followed.

''You'll probably get better reception up on the deck,'' Dan said as he set the recorder and the phone on the table.

''Before I call, could I ask what you found out about June Garrison?''

Dan sighed. ''I was trying to stay away from that.''

''I noticed. Why?''

''There's hardly anything else of consequence to tell, but

I can bring you up to speed on Brian Lowell's investigation. Garrison was in the process of getting a divorce. Her ex-husband moved out of town, and the department hasn't been able to get in touch with him. The people in the neighborhood where she lived say she was a conventional sort of housewife. She liked to garden. She took an exercise class at a health club on Liberty Road. Her taste in furnishings ran to Early American rock maple."

"You're right," Sabrina murmured, the disappointment apparent in her voice. "There's really nothing that gives us a clue about what she wanted to tell me."

"I wish there was more. I've brought you a summary of the report. You can look over it later and see if anything strikes you."

Dan searched through one of the bags he'd brought and handed Sabrina several sheets of paper, which she folded and tucked into her purse.

He slipped his arm across her shoulders. "I know you were hoping we'd figure out how she fit in to all this. It's going to take some more digging."

"So I'm supposed to go back to my herbs and teas and pretend that everything is just peachy?"

"The police will find out more."

"But I'm just small potatoes. What do they care about weird, unsubstantiated threats?"

"I care." Dan's hand shot out and covered hers. "And I can't take any more of this."

"Any more of what?" she whispered.

"Pretending this conversation is only business."

"You're saying it isn't?"

"It would be, if you were simply another witness who had stumbled into a police investigation."

"What am I?" Sabrina whispered.

He still couldn't spell it out any clearer in words. Sabrina had half turned, ready to take the phone up on deck. He pulled her against him, her back to his front. His hands went to her shoulders, kneading and stroking as if he were starving for the contact. And he was. Greedily his fingers tangled in her hair. When he lifted the heavy tresses to stroke her neck, he felt a shiver go through her body. "Duncan did that to Sara," she murmured.

"Who the hell is Duncan? And Sara?" Even as he said the names, he felt a dangerous ripple of sensation sweep over his body. Then he turned her to face him, searching her eyes as if they held the answers to all the questions he didn't want to ask. The mixture of confusion and certainty in their depth knocked the breath from his lungs. Later, she was going to hate him. He couldn't tell her that. But he had this moment with her. Now. And he wanted her to remember how it had felt to be in his arms.

"I'm not going to let you go," he muttered. Then he pulled her tightly into his embrace, unable to hold back the surge of primitive emotion that swept over him.

Dan could feel her surprise, and then her panic as his lips moved urgently, potently over hers, demanding a response. He sensed that she was clinging to safety like an overturned white-water rafter clinging to an outcropping of rock.

He deepened the kiss with deliberate ruthlessness, holding nothing of himself back. He knew the instant that she surrendered. Relief and triumph took him as he felt a shudder sweep over her.

"Hold on to me," he growled against her mouth.

Her hands climbed his arms, anchored to his shoulders and stayed put.

"Yes," he grated as his mouth took deeper, fuller possession of hers.

His fingers stroked up and down her arms, then found the sides of her breasts. The tiny moan of surrender was like a shock wave zinging through him.

Deep inside, Sabrina knew she'd been waiting for something like this since he'd walked through the door of her shop this morning. No, since their eyes had locked that first time at lunch.

She was his. Her body tuned itself to the wordless vibration rumbling deep in Dan's throat, a vibration that resonated to the core of her soul.

One of his muscular hands tangled urgently in her hair, angling her head so that he could plunder her mouth from a new angle. The other hand slid to the swell of her breast, kneading and stroking. When his fingers found the hard point of her nipple, pleasure shot downward through her body.

She knew he felt her response as he shifted her in his arms, pulling her more tightly into his heat and hardness.

Her body had never answered a man's with such passion. No. Perhaps it had—once. Long, long ago. Blood rushed hotly through her veins. Desire uncurled deep in the pit of her stomach.

He held her close, close for several moments longer. Then he eased his body away from hers.

She heard him cursing softly. "I had to do that," he murmured. "I'm sorry.

She'd been lost in a world where only two of them existed. Her eyes blinked open. Light-headed, she tried to get a grip on reality.

"I'm taking advantage of you again," he confessed.

"Are you?"

"You may think so later."

"Dan?"

"Go make that call," he said thickly. "Before I forget we *do* have business to take care of."

He'd started it. And stopped. And made it very clear he wasn't going to discuss his reasons. Confused, Sabrina picked up the phone and climbed the stairs to the deck.

Behind her she could hear Luther Davenport introducing himself again. Dan was playing the tape. Maybe it would mellow him out.

At the gunwale, she stood for a moment looking out at the water and taking in large drafts of the salt air. The wind had risen slightly, and waves rocked the boat, so that she had to steady herself with a knee braced against the wooden bench that ran around the side of the deck.

Dan had held her against him the same way Duncan had held Sara. It had felt so right. And so scary. The way it had a long, long time ago.

She didn't understand it. And there was no way to get in touch with something so outlandish. The easier course was to focus on the phone in her hand. After a moment's hesitation, she began to dial. The Medizone switchboard put her right through to Katie.

"I've got the information you want," the physician informed her.

"Great."

Downstairs in the cabin, Sabrina thought she heard Dan make some kind of exclamation above the sound of Davenport's voice. Glancing in his direction, she saw his back was turned to her, making it impossible to catch his eye.

"I'm sorry we took so long," Katie said. "We were looking for something beyond the obvious. But as far as we can tell, there's nothing very startling about this sample.

It's a very common stimulant.'' She named a compound that Sabrina had heard of.

"Um."

"Is that what you expected?"

"I don't know. So it's not a specific antidote for any poison," Sabrina mused, feeling a stab of disappointment. Probably they'd hit another dead end. She looked at Dan again. He stood up quickly and walked toward the counter in the galley area. Was he getting something to eat while he listened to the tape?

"Is the use of a stimulant consistent with the kind of dramatic revival I described?" she asked Katie.

"It could be. Depending on what caused the man's problem in the first place."

"Which we don't know." Sabrina's mind was only half on the conversation now. A wisp of odor drifted toward her. Fruit.

"I've got a written analysis for you," Katie said. "Should I mail it?"

"Umm…hold it at the lab, and I'll pick it up later."

"Will do. And keep me posted on how the case is going," Katie said.

"Yes. And thanks." Sabrina was barely paying attention to her friend as she replaced the receiver. With a strange sense of urgency, she set the phone down on the padded bench along the gunwale. As she started toward the stairway to the cabin, the fruity aroma she'd noticed a few moments ago became stronger, and she realized what she was smelling.

The frighteningly familiar odor of rotten cherries.

Chapter Eleven

Oh God, the drug that had hit them in the car. Somehow, here it was on the boat.

Pulse pounding, Sabrina peered into the cabin. Dan was still standing with his back toward her at the galley counter. She heard him curse, saw him bang his fist against the table. The epithet was followed by a low moan that sent tremors rocketing up and down her spine.

"Dan?"

He didn't answer, didn't react as if he'd heard her at all.

As wisps of cherry vapor snaked toward Sabrina, she coughed, swayed and backed up until her legs bumped against the bench that hugged the gunwale. She knew she was catching the faint scent of the hallucinogen. Even outside, in the fresh air, with the wind blowing, the poison was making her slightly dizzy. She sat down heavily on the bench, feeling fear gather in the pit of her stomach. The terror expanded, oozing through every pore of her body, turning her skin to ice.

For a moment, it held her in its grip. Then she turned her head into the wind and forced herself to breathe deeply, dragging in lungfuls of the salt air. She didn't realize how

tightly her hands were clenched until she felt the stabs of
pain where her nails dug into her palms.

Her eyes darted to the cabin. Dan was leaning over the
tape recorder, breathing raggedly. Her eyes went from his
rapt face to the machine on the table and back again. In
the background, she could still hear Davenport's voice.

The only conclusion she could draw was that the drug
was coming from the cassette. But why? How? She
couldn't answer the questions. She only knew the tape had
been in her pocketbook. *She* had brought it here. And given
it to Dan.

Panic, sickness, guilt rose in her throat. Dan was still
leaning over the machine, dragging in deep breaths. When
he lifted his head again, he was smiling dreamily.

God, no. It really had him. Now he was courting the
effect.

Dan wove toward the counter in the galley again and
cradled his head in his hands. When he started to cough,
Sabrina felt the painful spasms in her own chest. Then she
thought she heard a metallic noise as he rummaged in one
of the drawers.

She wanted to rush into the cabin and pull him out of
the drugging vapor. What if she held her breath? Would
that work?

No. He might struggle. Or more likely, grab on to her
and hold her down. If she had to take a breath, she'd be in
the same fix. The boat gave a little pitching motion, and
Sabrina reached to steady herself against the gunwale. Her
frantic gaze darted around the deck and lighted on the
phone she'd put down a few moments earlier. If she called
the Shock Trauma Unit in Baltimore they could have a
helicopter here in minutes. But then what? The copter
couldn't land on the deck. And what about the loud whir

of the blades overhead? Sabrina shuddered as she remembered her own terror when she'd been under the spell of the drug. What would Dan's mind do with the frightening noise overhead?

Her speculation was cut off as she saw Dan turn toward the stairway and squint into the brighter light outside. "You're out there, aren't you?" He growled in a voice that scraped along her nerve endings like fingernails being drawn across a blackboard.

"Dan?"

On unsteady feet, he moved toward the short flight of stairs that led to the deck. His hand was pressed against his side, concealing something. His expression was cruel and crafty. Instinctively Sabrina took a step back.

Dan reached the top of the stairs and stood swaying with the motion of the boat. Sabrina started toward him. She was stopped by the scent of rotten cherries wafting from the interior—and by the harsh look on his face. For a terrible moment she thought he would pitch backward into the cabin again. Then his right hand wrapped itself around the railing, and he shook his head as if trying to clear away the drugging mist.

"Dan?" Sabrina called again.

He took a very deliberate step toward her and then another. The spark of madness gleamed in the blue depths of his eyes as he advanced, breathing heavily. But at least he was taking in fresh air now. The effects of the drug hadn't lasted too long when they'd gotten out of the car. How many minutes before it wore off now?

She shuddered. Or were the effects cumulative?

"Old witch. What have ye done, old witch?" Dan cried out.

"What?"

"Witch!"

He was advancing purposefully on her now, his right hand raised. Something metallic glinted in the afternoon sunlight, and she saw an eight-inch-long knife that must have come from the galley.

"Dan, what are you doing? It's me, Sabrina."

"No more of your tricks!"

His face a mask of hatred, he kept advancing on her, still swaying slightly so that she alternated between fear of what he might do to her and fear that he would be the one to get hurt.

"Dan," she tried again, her voice rising unsteadily. "I'm not the witch. I'm Sabrina"

"Ye lie," he shouted as he lunged toward her. The knife swung down in an arc. Sabrina dodged aside, her foot thumping against the wicker hamper.

Cursing, Dan came at her again. Snatching up one of the cushions from the bench, she held it up like a shield. The blade slashed through the plastic and into the cotton batting. Dan cursed.

Sabrina dropped the cushion, leaving it skewered on the knife. Dan was forced to grab it with his free hand in order to try and work the weapon free.

He succeeded all too quickly.

"Dan. It's Sabrina. Dan!" she shouted again, praying that the drug was wearing off, praying that she could get through to him.

Thoughts came to her in disjointed snatches. In desperation, she looked around at the sky and the water. Nothing had changed. There was no coast-guard launch speeding miraculously toward her. She was still on her own with a man who was totally out of control.

She was trying to snatch up the phone when Dan whirled

on her again. As he turned, she dodged aside. There was nowhere to run except toward the poison gas wafting from the interior. When she reached the stairs, the vapor hit her—along with a wave of dizziness.

Coughing, she dropped the phone. It landed with a splash in the water as she wrapped her fingers around a rung of the ladder that led to the flying bridge.

Behind her Dan was panting, taking in more salt air. Soon he'd be okay. He had to be okay. Because all communication was cut off, and the only thing she could do was keep away from Dan until he came to his senses.

Lips set in a grim line, Sabrina began to scramble up the ladder. The knife slashed at her skirt, ripping through the fabric. With a little sob, she climbed faster.

He hurled a curse, and his fingers scrabbled for her foot, caught her heel. Grimly she wrenched away and the shoe came off in his hand.

"Ye won't get far," he shouted after her. "I'll get ye. For Sara."

Sabrina reached the top of the ladder and scrambled across the flying bridge. Then she was sliding down the windshield at the front of the boat. With only one shoe, she landed unevenly on the foredeck, twisting the ankle of the foot that was still shod. On a grunt of pain, she kicked the shoe off and began to hobble out of range.

Dan leaped to the deck right behind her. As she tried to dodge away, he caught her legs and brought her down in a flying tackle that knocked the breath out of her chest in a painful blow.

Half gasping, half sobbing, she fought to wriggle out of Dan's clutches. They rolled together on the deck, both breathing heavily.

Sabrina tried to pull away. When that didn't work, she

beat at him with her fists. But she might as well have been pounding at Mount Rushmore. He was far stronger than she under ordinary circumstances, and the fury of drug-induced madness fueled his vitality.

He pinned her to the deck, straddling her body and clamping her arms against her sides with his knees. She could see the knife sticking in his belt. The terrible look on his face turned her blood to ice. She was frozen, unable to move. Unable to save herself.

The motion of his hand as he reached for the knife released her. She began shouting and kicking wildly with her legs, making him work to subdue her again.

"Dan, no. Please, Dan."

The struggle to get away scooted her a few inches toward the edge of the boat so that her head and shoulders jutted over the deck, and she was half hanging above the water. But she couldn't move any farther.

The look of satisfaction on his face made the breath trickle from her lungs. Now he held on to her with one hand while he bent to retrieve the knife from his belt.

Staring down at Sabrina, he raised the weapon above his head. The blade was pointed at her throat.

"Dan! No!"

For the first time since the nightmare had begun, he paused. Uncertainty warred with fury in the depths of his eyes.

"Dan. Please. It's Sabrina."

"Tricks! You've made yourself look like her."

Yet despite the fierce words, the hesitancy lengthened, and his grip on her body loosened.

It was now or never. Sabrina wrenched herself away and felt her dress rip as Dan made another grab for her.

His fingers grazed her leg as she plunged over the side of the rub rail.

She heard a string of expletives above her as she hit the water. Then she was below the surface. Swimming underwater, she didn't come up until she was half a dozen yards from her original position.

Dan was peering over the side, but his back was toward her. Making for the side of the craft, she shook the wet hair out of her face.

Dan turned, spotted her and shouted—part order to halt, part curse. She ducked under the water again, coming up on the other side of the bow.

"Gotta get a gun. That's it. Get a gun and shoot her. I'll shoot the old witch," he muttered.

His heavy footfalls clumped off along the narrow side deck.

Sabrina held her breath, half expecting him to slip and plunge over the side. She didn't want to think about what might happen if he went into the water in his present condition.

Somehow he kept his footing and disappeared into the cabin, where she could hear him rummaging around in the storage boxes. Did he really have a gun? Or was that part of the illusion his drugged brain had conjured up? Afraid to stay where she was and find out, Sabrina swam toward the stern. But her ruined dress hampered her movements. Struggling out of the garment, she tossed it away and watched it fan out across the top of the water like a woman with her arms spread wide.

A noise from the deck brought her attention back to Dan. She could see him again. He was on the catwalk, heading toward the front of the boat.

She froze when she saw that he was indeed clutching a

flare gun in his right hand. Oh God, what if he spotted her? She was about to duck under the surface again when a loud report made her body jerk in reaction. Twisting around, she saw a flaming hole open in the middle of the dress where it floated about thirty feet from the boat.

"Got ya! I finally got ya," Dan shouted, his voice a mixture of rage and triumph. "For Sara."

Heart slamming against her ribs, Sabrina hugged the side of the craft, trying to make herself invisible as the flames quickly sputtered out. Dan thought the dress was the witch, and he'd shot it with the flare gun. What would happen if he saw her?

In the next moment, she heard a moan of agony from the deck.

All sorts of terrible images flashed into her head. He'd hurt himself. He was sick. Unless it was a trick to get her back on board. No. He thought the witch was dead.

Grabbing the mooring rope where it was attached to one of the metal holders, she began to haul herself up the side of the boat, bracing her feet against the transom for leverage.

"I killed her. Oh, God, I killed her."

A moment ago that had been the man's primary goal. Had the shots startled him to partial sanity?

With a surge of strength, Sabrina pulled herself toward the gunwale. Her body was shivering, and she had to clamp her teeth together to keep them from chattering. From where she huddled below the level of the deck, she couldn't see Dan. But she could hear him.

"Sabrina. Oh, please. No. Sabrina. I did it all over again, didn't I?"

There was another groan of agony. Dan was still hidden

from view, but she saw the gun as it went sailing through the air into the cabin, where it crashed against the bulkhead.

"Oh, God, Sabrina."

Suddenly she understood the source of Dan's torment. He'd shot a hole through the middle of the dress. But he thought he'd killed her. Not the witch. *Her.* Sabrina.

Panting from the exertion, Sabrina pulled herself high enough to peer into the boat. As she craned her neck over the gunwale, she saw Dan. He was on his knees a few yards from her, swaying almost imperceptibly back and forth, his face cupped in his hands. "I couldn't even play it straight with her, and now she's dead," he moaned.

The words made no more sense than anything else he'd been saying. In fact, anything could still happen. But Sabrina was willing to bet her life that some measure of sanity had returned. Throwing herself into the boat, she landed in a wet heap on the bench. There were no cushions to soften her fall. They'd been scattered in the struggle across the deck when she'd been trying to fend off the knife.

Dan's head snapped up. Dull blue eyes blinked and finally focused. For a moment Sabrina saw hope bloom. Then he shook his head, and his shoulders sagged as if he wasn't able to credit what he was seeing. But then why should he? He thought she was dead. He knew he still might not be in possession of his faculties—that reality and illusion might be cruelly twisted.

"Dan, it's me. It's Sabrina," she said, clambering toward him. He didn't move. He didn't breathe.

"See? I'm all right." As she spoke, she took him in her arms, holding him, rocking him, marveling at the warmth of his body against her wet skin. "Oh, Dan. I'm so sorry," she whispered.

"Sorry?"

''The tape—''

''Why are you so cold?''

''I'm all right,'' she repeated.

He ran trembling hands over her shoulders and water-slick back. ''It's really you. It's not a dream.''

''It's really me.'' His large frame began to shake, and it was several moments before he got back some measure of control. ''Where are your clothes?'' he asked.

A flush bloomed on her skin as she focused on the state of her undress. ''In the water. Don't worry about that.''

His hand skimmed over her warming skin and winnowed her dripping hair. ''You're alive. You're really alive. I didn't shoot you.''

''No.''

''Thank the Lord.''

His touch became more possessive, more urgent as if the contact were the only way to assure himself that she was really unhurt, that she wasn't one more illusion conjured up by the cherry mist that had filled the cabin. His lips moved over her face, coming back again and again to her mouth. His hands found her breasts, playing over the hardened nipples through her bra.

A little moan escaped from her lips and she clung to him. They were both kneeling on the deck, swaying slightly with the motion of the waves, their bodies molded together by arousal.

Then his grip on her shoulders changed, tightened painfully. All at once his fingers were digging into her flesh.

When he groaned, the sound was harsh and tinged with pain. Sabrina's eyes fluttered open, and she struggled to focus. Dan's face was deathly pale and slick with a fine sheen of perspiration.

''Dan. What's wrong?''

He slumped backward against the wooden bench and sprawled there, breathing heavily.

"Dan?"

"I'm okay."

She knew he wasn't. She glanced at the cabin, wanting to help him inside to one of the bunks. But it wasn't safe to go in there yet. Instead she collected the cushions where they'd been scattered around the deck and arranged them as best she could. Then she eased him down until he was supine.

He lay with his eyes closed and his arm across his forehead. His breathing was labored. When a large wave rocked the boat, he gritted his teeth.

"Does your head hurt?" she asked.

"Yeah."

Sabrina sat down on the deck and reached for his wrist.

"What are you doing?" He tried to jerk away, but she held him.

"Taking your pulse."

It was rapid but steady. Even as she counted the beats, she felt the rate slowing. And some of the color had come back to his ashen face.

"The drug. Like in the car," Dan finally whispered.

"Yes."

"How?"

Sabrina's features contorted. "The tape I gave you," she said in a low voice. "Somehow the cassette must have been fixed to give off the vapor when it was played."

She felt his fingers close around her wrist. "It's not your fault."

She swallowed.

"Davenport," Dan muttered, his eyes still closed.

"It's hard to believe he'd go that far to affect people's

minds. I mean, do you think there was some kind of mistake? An experiment that wasn't supposed to be distributed?"

His eyes blinked open. "How come it didn't get you?"

"I was up on deck calling my friend, remember?"

"So this time I'm the only one who wigged out," he said in a deadly dull voice.

"It's strong stuff. I started to feel it, too. Even up here in the fresh air. But I could get away. You couldn't."

"Lucky you." His voice was still thick. He started to push himself up and winced.

Sabrina laid a gentle hand on his shoulder, unnerved by how easy it was to hold him in place.

"Now I remember." He spoke slowly and deliberately. "You went outside to make the phone call, and I wanted to play the cassette and see if it had the effect you talked about. Then everything went out of focus." A look of horror took over his face. "I...I tried to kill the witch. With the knife. We were fighting."

His eyes bored into her, and she was suddenly very conscious that she was wearing nothing more than a soaked bra and panties.

"It wasn't the witch. It was you."

"Dan, you're not responsible for what happened. It was the drug. You couldn't help yourself. You didn't know what you were doing."

His rough curse made her grip his shoulder more tightly.

"As if the rest of it isn't bad enough, I end up trying to murder you." His voice was raw now.

The rest of it? She wasn't sure what he was talking about. But it didn't matter. All she wanted was to give him whatever warmth and comfort she could. "Oh, Dan."

Bending down beside him, she folded him into her embrace.

He buried his face against her neck as his arms came up to circle her shoulders. He clung tightly for several seconds. Then he eased away. "I brought some extra clothes. In the bag. Put something on."

Sabrina got up and crossed to the tote he'd set on the deck. Inside she found a yellow knit shirt. After dragging it over her head, she pulled her wet hair out of the collar. The tails covered her thighs. Technically she was decent. When she turned back to Dan, she saw that his state of mind hadn't improved. If anything, he looked more upset.

"The drug. Right. I couldn't help myself when I tried to kill you." His voice dripped with sarcasm. "I was under the influence. That's what they always say."

Sabrina sat back down beside him, stroking her hand against his forehead. "In this case, it's true."

She felt the tension radiating through his body. "Why is it," he said in a voice barely above a whisper, "that so many of the best things and the worst things that have ever happened to me all involve you?"

"The best?"

Pushing himself to a sitting position, he brought his lips to hers and kissed her very gently. It was warm and sweet, but it had a flavor that sent a tremor of fear through her body. "Sabrina, you're a very giving, very caring person. But you've got to take care of yourself, too," he murmured. "Do you know how to pilot this launch?"

"Yes."

"Good. Because the best thing for you to do right now is to take this boat back to Baltimore so you can get off and walk away from me."

It took a moment for Sabrina to realize what she was

hearing. "Dan, don't you understand? What happened a few minutes ago isn't your fault."

He leaned back against the bench glaring at her. "Stop patronizing me. It's taken a couple minutes to clear my head. But I sure as hell remember what I was doing down in that cabin after you left. I was leaning over that tape recorder sucking as much of that stuff as I could get into my lungs. *Trying* to get higher."

"I know you're upset. That's natural," Sabrina soothed. "But you really aren't thinking clearly. The drug had you under its influence. It was making you want more."

Sabrina was riveted by the look of mixed disgust and dread on his face. "Dan, what's wrong? Did you ever—" She fumbled for the right words. "Are drugs a problem for you?"

He laughed mirthlessly. "Not the way you think. It wasn't me. It was my best friend in middle school. He was into LSD." The sentences came out in jerky bursts. "We were roommates on a trip to Ocean City. He jumped off the roof of the hotel."

"Oh, Dan, no."

"That was enough to scare me off dope for good. And somewhere along the line, I turned into a self-righteous bastard when it came to drugs." He winced. "In college, if someone was smoking pot at a party, I got up and left. I was never going to get near anything mind-altering—because until Jerry got mixed up with acid he was a perfectly normal kid, just like me. And if it could happen to him…"

"So that was behind your war on drugs?"

"Yeah."

"And I'll bet you already have a report on—" she gestured toward the cabin "—that stuff. What is it?"

He sighed. "I called the lab this morning. They couldn't

tell me much. The drug is a hallucinogen, which we already know. It's designed to be inhaled. The effects are potent but relatively short-term.''

As he spoke, his voice had gotten stronger. Undoubtedly it was far easier for him to focus on lab reports than on himself. "Designed?" she questioned.

"Right. There's nothing with a similar chemical makeup on the street, as far as we know. This was produced in a private lab. Somebody tailor-made the stuff.''

An idea suddenly hit Sabrina. "Dan, Davenport is selling medical advice. Suppose people who use the tapes have a crazy, terrifying experience they can't explain? Wouldn't that and the hidden message send them running to him for treatment?''

Dan looked doubtful. "It sounds pretty risky. And I'm not going to use it as an excuse for myself.''

Sabrina tried another approach. "Why are you so angry with yourself? This is my fault. *I'm* the one who brought the drug on board.''

"It doesn't matter how it got here. The important point is what it did to me just now.'' His face turned hard and bleak. "Do you want to know what I was feeling? Fury. It took me over. I went berserk. Everything was swept away except raw violence. I had to strike out against anyone who was nearby. And you were it.''

She saw the horror on his face as he tried to come to grips with what had happened to him.

"How do I know I'm not going to do it again?" he asked in a low voice.

"Dan, if you were thinking clearly, you'd stop doing this to yourself. You told me the hallucinogen is very powerful. Everyone has a violent component. The drug blew it out of proportion, that's all.''

He gave her a considering look. As the silence stretched, she felt her nerves grow taut.

"All right, so getting involved with a guy who should have been in the locked ward at Springfield State Hospital doesn't scare you away. What if I tell you I've been lying to you since you walked into our luncheon appointment?"

"What are you talking about?"

"I didn't ask to meet you because I wanted your help. I asked because I thought you might be a murderer."

Chapter Twelve

Unable to move, Sabrina stared at Dan.

"What? What are you talking about?" she finally managed.

He swallowed sharply. "The police found one of the gold-foil charms from your shop in Alastair's pocket. The ones you put in with packages. That's why I was interested in them and your bracelet."

Sabrina could literally feel the blood draining from her face as she pushed herself away and stared into Dan's piercing blue eyes.

"You're making this up," she gasped. But even as she cried out the denial, there was a strange ringing in her ears and for a moment the scene around them wavered and flickered as if it might slip out of existence and replace itself with something that had happened a long time ago. Yet the past was too dangerous a place for her to flee.

"I'm not making it up. It's the truth." His voice was flat and dead. Dan's face was as pale as hers. "I didn't know how you fit in. You could have been the technical adviser, supplying the witchcraft know-how. You proved to me you had a pretty good background in the subject."

Bits and pieces of the previous few days came flying

back at her, each one as sharp and piercing as a broken shard of glass. Finally the one that stuck painfully in her psyche was the evening she'd come home from the Andromeda Institute and seen Dan spotlighted in the headlights of her car. "That night, after Davenport suckered me into trying to help Edward... My God, you weren't at my house waiting to comfort me. You were there to pump me for information."

"Yes."

"No wonder you didn't want to tell me who was under investigation." She gave a harsh little laugh. "You thought I was working for Davenport. Didn't you?"

"Yes. That night I did. Until you got that phone call from June Garrison. Then—"

He didn't finish the sentence. But it didn't matter. Sickness swept over Sabrina. When she felt her hands begin to shake, she tucked them under her legs and pressed them against the deck. She had to hold on to something. She'd been so dumb, letting herself care about Dan, letting herself lean on his strength. And he'd just been playing with her. Unwilling to let him see the tears gathering in her eyes, she swung her body away.

They sat in frozen silence as Sabrina listened to her heart pound. Finally she was able to push herself off the deck. Then, with lurching steps, she started for the front of the boat. At first all she wanted to do was get as far away from him as she could. As she raised the anchor and climbed the steps to the pilot's station, she tried to concentrate on what she had to do to get out of here. That was better than letting the pain swallow her up.

Savagely she twisted the key in the ignition. The engine sprang to life. Dan hadn't taken the boat very far from the mouth of the Patapsco. It wasn't going to be all that difficult to get back to Baltimore. The minute her feet touched the pier, she could walk away from everything she'd dared to hope for with him and never look back.

At first Sabrina kept her attention glued to the shoreline. She shouldn't give a damn about Dan Cassidy's welfare, yet she couldn't stop herself from worrying about the effects of the drug. Dan had gotten another heavy dose just a couple of days after the first one. This time there had been more physical effects, like the headache. Was he really okay? For several minutes Sabrina succeeded in keeping herself from glancing back at the place where he'd been sitting on the deck. Then she couldn't stop herself from looking.

Dan sat immobile, staring into space, his arms clasped around his knees. The wind was blowing, and the scarf Sabrina had been wearing when she'd come on board had worked its way off the handle of the hamper. With a fluttering motion, it started to blow across the deck. The sudden movement caught Dan's attention. Scrambling up, he reached out and snagged the length of fabric before it could flap over the side of the boat and into the water.

Then, as if the exertion had been too much for him, he sat down heavily again. As Sabrina silently watched, he wrapped the long rectangle of silk around one large fist. After staring at it for several seconds, he closed his eyes and pressed it against his mouth, moving the soft material back and forth across his lips. Long moments passed before he carefully tucked the scarf into her purse.

The breath had stopped moving in and out of Sabrina's lungs as she'd peered down from the pilot's station at Dan. While she watched, he swiped at the corners of his eyes with his hand.

But he'd told her—

She'd assumed—

Sabrina stopped short. What *exactly* had he said? Nothing at all about his feelings for her. In fact, now that she thought about it, she realized that he'd focused on the one thing that he knew would cut her to the very soul. His duplicity. He knew it was the only thing that would drive her away. And the technique had worked quite well.

Why? To protect her? Sabrina closed her eyes, trying to come to grips with what she'd been feeling for days. Since the moment she and Dan Cassidy had set eyes on each other in Sabatino's dining room, there'd been something strange going on below the surface of reality. The feeling of disorientation. The feeling that she knew him well. The feeling that her destiny was wound up with his. She couldn't explain any of that, and she'd been afraid to probe too deeply.

Yet, ignoring the sensations hadn't made them go away. She'd been on edge for days. And it wasn't just because of the Graveyard Murders, or Dr. Davenport, or June Garrison. The wariness tingling at the ends of her nerves had as much to do with her reaction to Dan and the strange story she'd been writing as anything else.

Dan and Sara.

Duncan and Sabrina.

She made a strangled exclamation when she realized she'd mixed up the names of the couples.

With a silent stab of shame, she admitted that a few minutes ago her anger and hurt had been tinged with relief that she wouldn't have to dig any further into the conundrum of how past and present intersected.

Did she have the guts to toss away the safety line Dan had offered her?

She had to. For her peace of mind, if nothing else.

Moving with deliberate swiftness, Sabrina cut the engine.

As the motor sputtered and then stopped, Dan's head jerked up, and he stared at her.

"What are you doing?"

Without answering, she descended the ladder, walked to the anchor and sent it splashing into the water. For several seconds, she stood with her back to Dan, gathering her courage together.

Then she turned. "All right, Cassidy, I was going to run away just like you wanted. But I've changed my mind. I think you owe me the truth."

"I've told you the truth."

"Part of it. The part you wanted me to know. But you've left something out. *Why* did you tell me you arranged our first meeting because you thought I was involved in the murders?"

"Isn't it obvious? I felt guilty."

"I saw you holding my scarf."

He looked away, and Sabrina realized she wasn't ready to tackle that part yet. "Okay, let's talk about something else."

"What?" His voice was angry.

She didn't mince any words. "About the fantasy you conjured up when you were under the influence of the cherry stuff a little while ago. About your violent reaction to it."

A muscle twitched in his cheek and his jaw clenched.

"You said the violence was directed at me because I was convenient. But that isn't true. You were trying to kill the witch. Is it because of the Graveyard Murders?"

"No."

"Then what?"

His expression was closed.

"All right, don't tell me about the witch. Tell me about Sara. Who is she?"

"I don't know. It's just a name I picked up at the station. From June Garrison."

She could see from his face that he was lying. It had meant something to him. "I don't think that's all you know about her."

He sat with his lips pressed together.

"Dan, tell me."

"The rest is just my imagination. Can't we drop it?"

"No."

He slapped a fist against the deck and winced. "Dammit. All right. She…she looks something like you. But that's not so surprising. She lives in a little cottage near the mountains. She cures people with her herbs. The doctor doesn't like it. Neither does the witch. It's not too hard to figure out where I got any of that, either."

The hair on the back of Sabrina's neck felt as if someone had touched them with an electric cattle prod. "And Ian? Is he in the story, too?"

"Sure. Why not?"

"You know a lot of details about this fantasy of yours, don't you? A lot for a quick drug trip."

He shrugged.

"What did the witch do to Sara?"

"There was a trial. The old woman tried to save herself by giving evidence against Sabrina—" He stopped abruptly. "I mean Sara. She told the judges that Sara was in league with the devil."

Sabrina sucked in a piercing breath. So that was where the story was leading. Crossing to her purse, which still lay on the deck, she opened the bag and pulled out several sheets of folded paper. "Maybe you'd better read this," she said.

Reluctantly Dan took the offered pages. Sabrina submitted no explanation. So, after one more questioning glance, he began to read.

Sabrina wasn't able to wrench her gaze away from his face. She was completely absorbed by the changing panorama of emotions as his eyes moved down the page.

"Where in the hell did you get this?" he asked, his voice gritty.

"At first I thought I made it up. I used to tell myself tales about another time and another place when I was a kid. But this experience is different." Sabrina gestured toward the pages. "I started writing the story in my office when I was supposed to be working on a plan for some bath-herb-and-soap baskets for the Harbor Court Hotel. You can't get much farther from the Harbor Court Hotel than that."

She continued with her explanation, deliberately including all the details she'd been afraid to confide to anyone else. "The really scary part is that it's not anything I knew I was going to put on paper. Every time I'm alone and I pick up a pen to write a grocery list or make notes on something to do with my business, I sort of go into a trance. Then when I snap out of it, there's more of the narrative down in black and white.

"At first it skipped big chunks of time. Sara met Duncan when she was out gathering herbs a couple of years before that episode you have there. Then he came to get her grandmother to cure Ian of peripneumonia. But the grandmother was dead, so he took Sara back to the castle. He keeps coming on to her, but she's afraid of getting sexually involved. She knows someone of his class can't marry a girl from a cottage in the mountains.''

With a dark look, Dan crumpled the pages in his fist. Afraid he was going to toss the balled-up mass into the water, Sabrina scrambled up, rushed across the deck and pried his fingers open. ''I'd like to keep the evidence, if you don't mind.''

''What evidence? I don't know what you think this proves. Under the influence of drugs, sometimes two people share an experience.''

''How can they, unless they plan it first, or agree beforehand to communicate the images of whatever it is they're experiencing?''

Dan shrugged again, his expression closed.

''Besides, I started writing this before either one of us got cherry-bombed. Before we'd even met, for that matter.''

''So what conclusions do you draw?'' He didn't sound as if he particularly wanted to hear the answer.

Sabrina laced her fingers together. ''I've been too... scared to draw any conclusions. I know you think I'm into weird stuff. But nothing like this has ever happened to me before. If it had, I might be coping better.''

Dan nodded tightly.

''Are you going to tell me you haven't sensed something strange between us?'' Her hands gestured helplessly. ''Some feeling that we already knew each other before I walked into Sabatino's? That if we just open our minds, we'll discover something extraordinary?''

''This is crazy.''

''Is it?'' Sabrina clenched her fists to help steady herself before plunging ahead with the thoughts that had been worming their way around the barriers she'd tried to erect

in her mind. "I suppose you've never entertained the idea
of reincarnation."

"That's bunk."

"A man and a woman with unfinished business between
them. So they come back to work things out."

"Oh, come on. Have you ever heard of anything like
that? I mean, besides in the movies?"

"People have written about their experiences. You know,
like Shirley MacLaine."

"And you believe it?"

"I wasn't ever sure." Sabrina laid her hand lightly over
Dan's, feeling his muscles jump at the contact. "Okay, we
don't have to talk about reincarnation. We don't have to
try and explain why you and I are independently coming
up with pieces of what looks like the same historical
story."

"The same fantasy, for all we know," Dan interrupted,
but his voice didn't hold the ring of conviction.

"Where is it set?" Sabrina asked suddenly.

He shrugged. "Middle Earth?"

"How about Scotland? Does that sound right?"

"If you say so."

"I can see that my bringing up the subject hasn't exactly
elevated your opinion of me."

"Sabrina, I'm sorry. I admit something odd is going on.
But I'm just too conventional for an off-the-wall explanation like that."

She sighed. "It's pretty clear I don't have anything left
to lose with you, so I might as well keep digging myself
in deeper. A while ago when you tried to make sure you
were getting rid of me, one of the things I felt was relieved.
Dan, since I met you, I've felt as if I were—" she flapped
her arms helplessly as if trying to get her balance "—stand-

ing on unstable ground. And it's slipping away from under my feet.''

Sabrina saw the sharp look that disappeared almost as soon as it flashed across his face. ''Isn't that how you felt, too?'' she asked. ''Wasn't part of your confession motivated by fear of getting involved with me—because you couldn't deal with what was happening between us? Is that part of why you'd like to think of me as a nut?''

''No! Dammit.'' The blue of Dan's irises had deepened to something resembling the sea at twilight. ''You want the truth? I'll give you the truth. The first time I started breathing that drug, it made me want you the way I've never wanted any other woman. This time, it opened up the top of my head like the lid being peeled back from a can.''

The image made Sabrina shudder.

Dan's gaze was riveted to her face. ''My brain was all tender and exposed, and I felt as if icy cold air was pouring over the tissues, seeping down into my skull and through my body. And what I knew when the lid snapped back into place was that if I kept on trying to get close to you, I was going to hurt you. I don't mean I was going to break your heart or anything. Nothing quite so relatable. I mean I knew that I was bad for you, that getting close to me was the worst, the very worst thing that could happen to you. This time I was trying to kill the witch. The next time—''

Sabrina cut him off before he could finish. ''Oh, Dan. No. You wouldn't hurt me.'' When she reached for him, his arms came up stiffly to prevent her from getting any closer.

''You say there's unfinished business between us. Your tale about Duncan and Sara? How does it turn out?'' he demanded.

"I don't know."

"Well, since you're assuming it's the same story, I seem to have supplied some critical details. The old hag clinched Sara's witchcraft conviction. I'll bet her boyfriend Duncan didn't save her from burning."

Sabrina shuddered, remembering the flames she'd imagined engulfing the car. Then she lifted her chin. "Dan, you can't argue it both ways. First you tell me that even though we're both independently coming up with details of Sara and Duncan's lives, they have nothing to do with you and me. Then you turn around and try to use the same facts as an argument for why you're going to hurt me."

He slapped his fist against his hand. "Okay, you've got your feelings, and I've got mine. But I'm used to dealing with facts. Evidence. Unfortunately there's nothing here that either one of us can prove."

Sabrina moistened her lips. "There's something we can try."

"What?"

"What if you could talk to Sara, ask her some questions?"

"Oh, come on."

"Dan, when I start writing the story, I…I sort of turn into her. I mean when I come out of it, I feel like her."

His arms were folded tightly across his chest, and his shoulders were hunched. "I've never been to a séance. I'm not going to let you drag me into something equally ridiculous."

Sabrina raised her eyes to his. "Dan, the—the violence you were so worried about was directed at the witch. Don't you think it's worth trying something a little bizarre to find out why you hate her so much? If it doesn't work, all you've lost is a few minutes of your time."

Dan looked away from her, staring out at the rise and swell of the waves. The sun was low in the west, painting the hills and troughs with shifting splashes of pink and orange. The shifting colors flickered in his vision like flames.

He closed his eyes, but that didn't dispel the image—or dissipate the raw tension gathering in his body. In his life, there'd been plenty of times when he'd been afraid. Nothing came close to what he was feeling now. He could picture himself diving into the water and striking out toward shore. He was a strong swimmer. Probably the boat was close enough so he could make it.

Except that he wasn't going to bail out now. Deep down, he'd already been playing with some of the crazy theories she'd been spouting just now. But he'd been afraid to face them, so he'd lied to Sabrina about his reasons for getting together with her. He'd also used her for bait at the train station. He'd almost killed her this afternoon. The only way to get back a little of his self-respect was to do what she'd asked.

"If you want to try the experiment, I guess I owe you that much," he said in a low voice.

"Not just me. Yourself. And *us,*" she added in a whisper. But he heard.

HE GAVE HER a little time to get started. As he peered down into the cabin, he could see her sitting at the table writing. She didn't look up when he came inside, nor did the pen pause in its trip along the paper.

"Sabrina?" he whispered.

She didn't answer.

"Sara?" The name trembled on his lips.

His heart was thumping as he came up behind her and

bent to read what she'd been writing. As his eyes skimmed the words, his hand moved to her shoulder, pressing, establishing a physical connection that had suddenly become as necessary as breathing.

The morning air was cool and crisp with the promise of an early fall. Sara knew that she had only a few more weeks to gather enough plants to see her through the winter. Basket in hand, she made her way to the cliffs where many of the healing herbs grew. Her feet knew the path, leaving her mind free to wander.

So much had happened in the past year. Ian McReynolds had recovered fully from the bout of peripneumonia, and news of her healing had spread across the glen. Now even clansmen from beyond the mountains sought out her little cottage to buy potions for coughs and rashes. She liked helping people. She also liked the tidy nest egg in silver coins hidden under the floor of the cottage—and the chickens and sheep she'd collected for her services.

But the more success she had, the more malicious the physician Fergus McGraw grew. Aye, she was sure he'd been behind the rumors she'd heard floating around the village. Mistress Campbell was associating with Lillias, the witch. Next they'd have her dancing naked in the moonlight. Or worse.

So far, people still sought her out. But she'd detected a number of speculating glances, and her customers seemed much more interested in making their purchases than in chatting with her. Maybe Duncan could do something to squelch the gossip.

Duncan. Just thinking about him made her heart skip to a sprightly highland tune. She reached down and picked a handful of wintergreen and brought the fragrant leaves to her nose. There was something about the fresh minty scent that reminded her of Duncan. He'd been away for over a fortnight on business for his father, and she'd missed him with an ache that told her she cared too deeply. He'd come to her almost a dozen times since she'd returned from the castle last winter, all on the pretense of buying remedies for members of his family. After the purchases were made, he always lingered, wanting to talk and touch, and bring a blush of rose to her cheeks with his stirring kisses.

Sara sighed. She knew where things were leading, and it wasn't to the church. Duncan, Duncan, what am I gonna do with ye, lad?

She rounded the path to the mountain pass where she'd first met him. As if by some magic summons, there he was riding through the clearing on a spirited black horse. Sara blinked, sure she'd conjured up the image. But it was really him. She knew she should hold herself back. Instead she waved joyfully as she ran to meet him.

He dismounted and gathered her into his large embrace. "Sara! I was on my way to see ye when I thought I spied a red-haired wood sprite climbing down from the crag."

"So you came up to investigate, dinna ye? I think you're a wee disappointed to find a lass instead of the sprite," she teased, giving him a little hug back. It felt so good to be in his arms again.

The corners of his lips twitched in a roguish grin. "And I think the lass is searching for a compliment."

"Nay. It's not your fine words I'm looking for."

"A kiss then?"

"Nay. Not that either," Sara tossed back, thrilling to the light bantering between them and the way Duncan's eyes had turned a deep-water blue.

"Oh, the lass is in a bartering mood then, is she?"

"It depends on what ye have to barter."

Duncan swung her around and sat her on a flat rock. He removed a pouch from his horse and pulled a fine gold necklace from its depths.

"A trinket for a kiss." He opened her hand and placed the gift in her palm.

"Oh, Duncan. It's beautiful." Sara's fingers brushed over the intricate sunburst design on the gold medallion. "It's the prettiest thing I've ever had."

"Then wear it next to your heart and think kindly of the lad who brought it, will ye?"

"Aye."

Duncan took the necklace from her hands and slipped it over Sara's curly red hair. Then he pulled her to her feet. With a feather-soft touch, he traced over the necklace, stroking where the gold nestled between her breasts. Through the fabric of her dress, she felt his touch like a brand and trembled. Why was she so weak to want a man she could never wed? But when she was with him, that argument had no more weight than lamb's fleece.

His hands left her neck to comb through her thick hair, and her own arms anchored around his waist. Then his blond head was bending to hers, and she was letting him take the kiss she'd earlier denied. It was sweet, sweet. And arousing.

And soon she was letting him do more. Letting his hands mold and shape her breasts. Letting his fingers pull open the laces that held her bodice.

HE DIDN'T KNOW when he'd stopped reading. Or when she'd stopping writing. When it had simply started happening. To both of them.

"Duncan. Dan. Don't stop. Not this time. Oh, please, don't stop."

The frantic entreaty came from the woman he held in his arms. The woman whose body moved and twisted against his with the same urgency he felt.

Chapter Thirteen

Present and past merged, wavered, tried to stabilize, and finally came to an uneasy accord.

But time and place were of little importance now. Not when this man and woman were finally in each other's arms, bound together by ties stronger than the forces that would tear them apart.

She had been born for him. Reborn for him.

A muffled sound of craving came from her throat. He drank it in like a man who'd somehow survived a long, parched season of need. In that instant, the terrible years of waiting were swept away. Banished.

"Duncan. Dan."

At the words she'd spoken, her eyes blinked open, colliding with his, held and locked. There was a new light— a new understanding—shining in their blue depths.

"Sara. I lost you once," he rasped. "I won't lose you again, Sabrina."

"You didn't believe me."

"Shh—I can't explain it. I only know I can't let you go." His voice was deep, urgent, persuasive.

The confusion of place and time persisted, tantalized,

made them both dizzy. All the more reason to cling to the
one solid reference point in the universe—each other.

Slowly the confusion gave way to abiding certainty as
hands touched and lips brushed, giving and taking pleasure.
Time was precious. And they had squandered far too much
of it already.

Suddenly, by silent, mutual consent, they both tossed
aside all restraint. Sabrina tugged at the oversize shirt she
wore, pulling it over her head. Dan's shirt joined it on the
floor. Then her hands were sliding across his chest, glorying
in the sight of his magnificent physique and the feel of his
hard muscles and crisp hair. Her fingers found the gold
chain around his neck, drawing her eyes to the medallion.

She gasped and stared at the golden circle. ''The sunburst. It's the same one.''

''We can talk about it later.'' As he pulled her back into
his arms, the chain slipped from her fingers. For a moment,
she was vividly aware of the burnished medallion pressed
tightly between their flushed bodies, the metal heating and
sizzling from their desire. Yet almost immediately the mystery of the necklace was eclipsed by the sensations of Dan's
lips moving questingly over hers.

A sigh of pleasure flowed from him even as his fingers
went to her back, unfastening the clasp of her bra, sending
it quickly to join the unwanted shirts. His hands moved
over her breasts, inflaming her. When his thumbs and fingers found her hardened nipples, liquid heat shot through
her body to her very core. One of his hands followed the
hot trail downward, flattened against the soft skin of her
abdomen, teased the margin of her navel, glided even lower
to slip inside the waistband of her panties and drag them
down her hips.

When Sabrina was naked, Dan's hand slid back up her

thigh to tangle in the springy curls at the juncture of her legs.

On a little sob, she arched into the caress, inviting more, melting as he found her most sensitive flesh.

Sabrina was so weak with pleasure that her knees gave way, and for breathless moments she clung to Dan. Then he swung her into his arms and carried her toward the tiny bedroom cabin. He laid her gently on the bunk and stood gazing down at her, his face suffused with passion.

"So beautiful." The deepened texture of his voice was like a caress.

"So are you. What I can see."

His eyes locked with hers, he reached for the snap of his jeans, shedding the remainder of his clothes in one quick motion.

She was torn between wanting to admire him and needing to feel his naked skin against hers. Need won, and she held out her arms imploringly. He came down beside her on the bunk, and she knew by the way he clasped her body against his that their need had been the same.

He let out a long sigh of relief, and Sabrina turned toward him, stroking his cheek. "I've wanted this for so long." It might have been a strange thing for a woman to say to a man she'd only met a few days before. Yet the look in his dark eyes told her he understood perfectly. It had been an eternity since they'd held each other intimately.

Dan nodded gravely, reaching up to press her fingers. "When I...when he made love to her, he didn't take her virginity. He didn't think that was right."

"I know."

"This is the first time. The first real time."

"Yes."

Their lips brushed, nibbled, held, opened for a long, deep kiss of affirmation.

Sabrina had known the instant she'd wakened from her trance and found herself in Dan's arms that something amazing and splendid was happening. It was still happening, moment by moment—to both of them. Strong forces had worked to keep them apart. But they were together. The wonder of it made the breath trickle from her lungs. Later, they could puzzle it out. Later.

They lay on their sides, facing each other on the narrow bunk. Touching. Kissing. Stroking. Exploring. Loving.

Neither one of them wanted to hurry. They drew out the pleasure, letting the power of their feelings build slowly, beautifully, until it was impossible to postpone the joining a moment longer.

He was inside her, then. Hard and deep and throbbing.

She looked up into his face, touched his cheek, murmured wordless syllables that both welcomed him and proclaimed her pleasure at their joining.

The slow pace was over almost as soon as he began to move, and her hips answered his. Now it was all blinding heat and urgency. A man and a woman giving and taking everything, seeking and finding mutual joy.

Climax took her, spreading out from the point of greatest pleasure in a series of shock waves that brought a cry of ecstasy to her lips. Then she felt him follow her into euphoria and her own rapture was complete.

It had begun slowly. It ended slowly. With kisses and murmurs and sighs.

"Perfect. That was so perfect."

"Yes."

Sabrina snuggled closer, wishing that nothing would intrude. But now that her body was returning to normal, her mind struggled to make sense of what had happened. "The witch tried to keep it from happening. This time, we won." Sabrina didn't know she'd spoken aloud until she felt Dan's body stiffen. Raising her head, she saw the shock of recognition in his eyes.

He nodded slowly, as though trying to deal with a totally alien concept that had come to hold the ring of undeniable truth.

"Dan, what's going on?"

"I don't know."

"But you believe me? That it was us, all those years ago? That we've come back to finish something?" she asked, holding her breath as she waited for his answer.

"Making love with you was like the fulfillment of a promise someone made a long time ago."

"Yes," she breathed.

"But when I try to think about us, I still have trouble with the logic of it."

She could feel her mouth drawing down.

He touched his fingers to her lips, pushing at the corners as if he could turn them upward. "It's hard for someone like me to cope with the paranormal."

"The paranormal," she repeated.

He looked surprised that he'd even said the word. "I've always taken things at face value. Something like this isn't *supposed* to happen. If you can't trust the version of reality you've always thought you knew, what can you trust?"

Sympathy welled inside her. Yes, for someone like him all of this must be terrifying. It was bad enough for her. "We both fought against it. We couldn't fight the truth. Or wanting to make love with each other. I think that's why in the car the drug had that effect on us. As soon as our minds were…freed from normal constraints, we wanted this.''

He pressed her face into his chest, kissed her fiery hair. When she heard him laughing softly, she raised her head inquiringly.

''At least it wasn't yohimbine bark,'' he said.

''What's that?''

''A drug with aphrodisiac qualities. Some members of the counterculture experimented with it in the sixties. The users got about an hour of heavy-duty fun out of it. Then they were violently sick for hours afterward.''

Sabrina made a face. ''Why would anybody want to take something like that?''

''I guess they thought the pleasure was worth the pain.''

''How do you know about it?''

''I've read a heck of a lot about drugs—the common garden variety as well as the exotic. That one struck me as plenty odd.''

''And in all your reading, you never came across anything like the cherry-bomb stuff?''

''No. Nothing.''

She rested her head against his chest again, feeling his heart thump against her cheek and knowing his tension hadn't gone away. ''What are you thinking about?''

His fingers stroked through her wavy tresses, as if that could dissipate his anxiety. ''God, I love your hair.''

''I'd feel better if you'd be open with me,'' she murmured.

He sighed. ''I owe you that, don't I? After what I've already done.''

She tried to make herself breathe normally and couldn't manage the effort.

''Unfortunately what I told you out on the deck is still

true," he said with deadly calm. "Sabrina, getting mixed up with me is dangerous for you. Like getting involved with Duncan was dangerous for Sara. When he took her to the castle, that started the rivalry between her and the doctor, maybe between her and the witch, too."

Sabrina swallowed. "You could be right about Sara and Duncan, but how do you know about us?"

"I can't give you any facts. I just *know*. In my bones. And the hell of it is I know we're going to find out."

"Dan, why is this happening? Who are we, really?" she asked in a small, frightened voice.

"A man and a woman who've loved each other for a long time."

She drew in a startled breath, hardly able to believe he'd said what was in her heart.

"There is that," she whispered, turning to brush her lips against his. "Somehow we've got a second chance to make it come out right."

When he stroked her cheek, there was a touch of regret in the gesture. "If we can."

"Dan—"

"Even without the paranormal, there's enough going on now to make me plenty nervous. The Graveyard Murders. Edward. June Garrison. After what she told you, I was worried about making sure you stayed safe. I brought you out here where I could keep an eye on you while—"

"While what?"

"When you get back to the city, there will be a number of protective mechanisms in place."

"Like what?"

"Like a surveillance team assigned to Davenport so we'll know if he makes a move on you. Like somebody keeping an eye on 43 Light Street."

"Is that why you called the shop to find out my plans this morning?"

"Yes. And I checked back with Erin."

So that's who her assistant had been talking to when she'd been so nervous on the phone.

"I didn't want you to start worrying—before we got a chance to talk," Dan continued.

"And now it's all right."

"You know what I mean." He held her close, and they lay silently in each other's arms.

"I tried to tell myself June was just talking about someone who wanted to put me out of business. But I couldn't stop thinking about witches and spells and evil eyes." She shuddered. "You can't protect me against something like that."

"You think the supernatural could hurt you?"

"I wish I didn't. But that's the problem. If I think so, maybe it could."

Dan looked as if he wished she hadn't brought the subject up. "I'd give a lot to know how this all fits together," he grated.

"Maybe we can figure it out."

When Sabrina started to sit up, Dan's eyes went to her breasts, and she felt her nipples tighten.

"Maybe it would be less distracting if we got dressed before we talked," he said thickly. "Because what I want to do instead of talking is pull you back down on the bed again."

"Yes."

Their eyes locked and held for wild heartbeats.

"Making love to you isn't going to keep you safe," Dan said as he got up and opened the drawers under the bunk. After digging through the clothes inside, he handed Sabrina another shirt and a pair of shorts. When they'd both gotten dressed, he pointed toward the ice chest and hamper they'd stowed in the galley. "I can offer you dinner, though."

She nodded, remembering the quantity of food he'd brought. "Was dinner part of your plans?"

"I guess it was in the back of my mind."

It was almost dark when they came back up on deck. Dan turned on the running lights, and they pulled their chairs close to each other, getting out food and drinks in the semidarkness. Sabrina wasn't very hungry, but there was something comforting about the normality of the shared activity.

After a few minutes, it became obvious that Dan's appetite wasn't much better than hers. He reached for her hand. "Tell me about your story. The parts I haven't read."

Sabrina began to fill in details, knitting her fingers through his as she spoke. There'd been no one she thought would understand. It was a wonderful relief to simply let the tale pour out.

When there was nothing more to tell, they sat in silence, hands clasped.

"The thing I'm thinking," she whispered, "is that it's not just us who came back."

"You're talking about the other two major characters— the doctor and the witch?"

"Do you think that's crazy?"

"It's spooky. But once your mind admits the possibility of reincarnation, then you have to start asking yourself why. It's pretty self-centered to think it's for our personal gratification."

"I like the gratification part," Sabrina whispered.

Dan squeezed her hand. "So do I."

"Do you think it's arrogant to wonder if we came back to stop some evil that's survived the centuries?"

"The witch's evil," Dan muttered.

"I wish...I wish we could just live our lives in peace, but it's not that simple."

"You've convinced me," Dan sighed.

"I keep trying to figure out how the past and present are related. This time, some things are different. I'm interested in herbs, but I don't claim to be any kind of healer."

Dan nodded.

"And then there are the other players. In the twentieth-century version of the story, it looks as if the doctor and the sorcerer are the same person," Sabrina continued. "Is there any evidence to link Davenport to witchcraft?"

"I told you we were investigating him because of fraudulent medical practices in Georgia. I haven't run across any specific witchcraft allegations."

"June obviously knew more than we do," Sabrina said slowly. "I mean, about how the past and the present are connected."

"Damn. That makes sense. But where did she get her information?"

"Maybe she was Davenport's confidante."

"Why would he tell anyone what was going on?"

Sabrina shook her head. "Maybe she worked for him and they had a falling out."

"That could be." Dan cleared his throat. "What about the sample you took to the lab? I, uh, didn't get to hear the report."

"The white powder wasn't any kind of antidote. More like a general-purpose stimulant—which means we have no idea what Davenport gave Edward in the first place."

"Mmm."

"Let's try to tie it into the old story. You…you said the witch framed Sara."

"The way Davenport left one of your foil seals in Ian Alastair's pocket," Dan grated, his countenance darkening and his hand jerking away from hers. "And I fell for it."

Sabrina went very still, remembering vividly how she'd felt when he'd told her he'd suspected she was involved in the murders. "You were *supposed* to think I did it," she murmured, finding his hand again.

His fingers remained rigid, and Sabrina went on speaking almost desperately, hardly aware of what she was saying. "It wasn't your fault. You were trapped in this situation, the same way I was. Davenport has a big advantage over the two of us. He manipulated you, just the way he got me to help him show everybody who came to the lecture the other night that he can work miracles. He *knows* how we'll react. Don't you get it? We're working in the dark, but somehow he's figured out the whole story." She stopped, breathless, realizing what she had said.

Dan's gaze was riveted to her face. "Why are we floundering around like this if *he* has inside information?"

"Maybe he has access to old records. Maybe he—" she gestured helplessly "—has some supernatural advantage. Maybe the story came back to him, the way it did to me. Only earlier."

"The more we find out, the less I like it."

Sabrina sat forward in her seat. "But we have to know more. Would you mind…what about if I try writing it again?"

"So you can find out if Duncan betrayed Sara?"

Sabrina took her bottom lip between her teeth. "If he did, we need that information," she said in a voice that was barely above a whisper.

"Yeah."

"Dan, I'm sorry. I don't know what else to do. Maybe we'll find that Duncan saved Sara."

"I wouldn't count on it," Dan grated. "But if you're going to do it, I'm going to stay with you."

"Maybe it won't work if you're looking over my shoulder."

"I think it will. Now." Unconsciously they drew closer together. "If it doesn't, I'll leave while you get started."

Sabrina was afraid of what she might find out. But even if it was bad, she wanted Dan there with her, in the worst way.

Neither one of them spoke as they stored the food and went back into the cabin. Trying to look purposeful, Sabrina set the pad of paper and the pen on the table. She was about to sit when she felt Dan's hands on her shoulders.

"Not yet." Turning her quickly, he brought her body tightly against his. "It was getting cold in Scotland the last time you were there. I want you to take something with you to keep you warm."

His lips molded themselves to hers. His fingers combed through wild red hair.

Her wordless little murmurs were lost in his kiss as her hands slid up and down his strong arms.

When he finally lifted his head, they were both trembling.

"I'd better start," Sabrina whispered.

Dan's hands dropped away from her body, and it was all she could do to keep from pulling them back. Instead she sat down. This had been her idea. Why did she dread it so much?

She looked up at Dan uncertainly, and he slid onto the

bench beside her. She didn't have to do this, she told herself frantically. She could just forget about going back.

He said nothing. She picked up the pen. For a moment it felt alien in her fingers. "This will work," she said as she began to write, feeling Dan watching over her shoulder. "Because we need to know what happened to Sara and Duncan...."

...Bam. Bam. Bam! The pounding on the door was loud enough to wake the dead. But it was more fear than aggravation that captured Sara Campbell as she moved away from the warmth of the fire and went to answer the urgent call. She'd had the feeling all day that something bad was going to happen. And she'd thought about fleeing to the secret cave in the mountains she'd discovered on one of her herb-gathering expeditions. She and Duncan had lain there in each other's arms more than once. If she left a slip of paper with an ax head on the table, he'd know where to find her, because the way to the cave was marked with a stone resembling that shape.

"Who is it and what do ye want?"

"Murray Frye to see the healer."

She opened the door a bit and held the candle up to illuminate Frye's face. He was a tall, bulky lad of perhaps twenty.

"Mistress Campbell. The lass Megan has taken a turn for the worse. We dinna think she'll make it through till morning. I've come to fetch you to town."

Sara looked at the anxious countenance of the lad on her doorstep. Was he only worried about Megan? Or was it also the rumors he'd heard.

The whispers behind her back had frightened Sara right enough. And she had half a mind not to go with him, even though she knew him to be a cousin of the young girl she'd treated over a fortnight ago. "Megan seemed to be much improved when last I saw her."

"Aye, she was. But this afternoon, she collapsed again," Frye explained, not quite meeting her eyes. "You'll come?"

Sara thought of the wee lass and found it impossible to refuse. "Let me get my medicine."

Frye stepped into the cottage. When Sabrina turned back from getting her supplies, she found him hunched near her bed. He straightened quickly.

"Let's go."

The ride into town was cold and dark and nothing like the time she'd been cradled in Duncan's strong arms. But she hadn't seen Duncan in over a fortnight. When he'd told her he was being sent south to settle some of the laird's business, she'd begged him not to leave. He'd told her he didn't have a choice. But he'd done what he could to quiet the wagging tongues before he left.

Frye's touch was rougher than Duncan's. Perhaps that was the way he treated all women. But she couldn't shake the feeling that something more than Megan's illness was troubling him.

The family's greeting was tense as they ushered her into their small stone abode on the outskirts of the village. A crackling fire burned in the hearth. Not far away, Megan lay tossing and moaning in her cot.

Sara dropped to her side and laid a hand on her forehead. The child's skin was cold and clammy. Her pupils were dilated, and from her tortured utterings, a wild dream must be haunting her sleep. "I dinna think she has the fever. She's too cool to the touch. It must be something else. Help me loosen her dress."

The light wool slid from the girl's shoulders, revealing a series of ugly red patches. Behind her, family members gasped in horror.

"The mark of a witch!" Murray exclaimed.

"No. No. The work of poison, I think," Sara said as she straightened and turned toward the family. "We need to get a strong emetic down her immediately. I've something in my bag. But we need to steep it in boiling water."

No one moved to the kettle. Instead the elder Frye stepped forward. "Then Fergus McGraw was right. You're a witch just like Lillias, and you've doomed the lass with your evil potions."

"That's poppycock and you well know it," Sara responded, struggling to keep her voice from quavering. But the glowering look in their eyes brought a wave of panic to her own. She had to get out of here. Now.

Sara took a step toward the door. But she wasn't quick enough. In an instant, she was grabbed from behind and held tightly between the two large men.

"Your daughter's certain to die if you don't wash the poison out of her system. Let me help her."

"I'll not have a witch touching me bairn again," Mrs. Frye declared, taking a protective step toward the cot. "Or in my house as bold as brass."

Sara's own palms were clammy cold as the men pushed her outside into the bitter cold. After her hands were securely tied with coarse rope, they left her under Murray's guard. "Please let me go. I'll do you no harm."

"Too late for that now. I was at the castle today and heard there will be a reward out for your capture by tomorrow morning. I've got you now, and I'm meaning to collect the gold," the young man sneered.

"Reward? I've done nothing wrong. There must be some mistake. Duncan McReynolds will vouch for me."

"He's not here to vouch for you, my girl. You'll have to tell it to the judges at your trial, now won't you? But when they find the evil-eye symbol under your bed, that will clinch it."

Sara stared at him in horror. "But I don't—"

"Oh, no? I think ye lie, lass."

Sara struggled to break free, but his burly grasp held her prisoner. Tears stung her eyes as he pulled her down the street like a common thief. Someone had put a price on her head. But it was all a terrible mistake. Would anyone believe her?

SHE WAS COLD, so cold. As if icy fingers had wrapped themselves around her very bones. She tried to speak. All she could manage was a shaky exclamation.

"Sabrina. Come back. It's all right. You're here. With me."

"Dan. Oh, Dan." All she wanted to do was cling to his strength, burrow into his warmth. He held her, rocked her, murmured reassuring words.

"It's like…at the Institute," Sabrina groped for words. "She was tricked into treating someone.…"

"It was the other way around at the Institute," Dan said, the grating sound of his voice telling her how much he'd just been shaken.

Sabrina tipped her face toward his. "It's all right. It's going to be all right."

"I don't think so. I didn't keep you warm, did I? He wasn't there to help her when she needed him, either."

"Dan, you don't know. Maybe Duncan came back."

"I wouldn't count on it."

"What happened to you when I started writing?" she asked, determined to change the subject.

Sabrina felt him shudder. "It was strange. First I was reading over your shoulder, seeing the words you were writing. Then it changed, and I was—" he stopped and looked perplexed "—seeing it in some kind of old-fashioned print. In an old book or something."

"You kept reading?"

"For a while. Then it was like I was there somehow. With you. Watching from the shadows. I kept shouting at you. I mean Sara...."

She squeezed his arm, telling him she understood the confusion.

"...trying to warn you to get away. I—I saw him drop the evil-eye symbol under your bed. But you couldn't hear me. There was nothing I could do to save you."

"Oh, Dan. It must have been terrible. Frustrating. I'm sorry."

"I think it was worse for you." He didn't seem to want to talk about it. Instead he tugged on her hand, and she followed him up on deck. The cool breeze blowing off the water helped clear her head.

"The book you saw. Maybe it exists. Maybe there's a record of what happened."

"Yeah."

"We should go back to Baltimore and try to find it."

"I wish...we could just stay here. Or take this boat down the coast where no one can find *us*."

Sabrina pressed her lips together, sensing what he hadn't put into words. Out here on the water they were isolated in a little world of their own. A safe little world. Back in the city lay uncertainty and danger.

"We've got enough food for days. I guess that's what I was really thinking," Dan admitted.

"I wish it was that simple. Running away, I mean. But we've got to go back and face whatever is going to happen."

Dan slipped a protective arm around her shoulder. "You don't have to sleep at your house."

"I have to feed the animals."

"We could do that first."

"The cats don't mind being alone so much. They've got each other. But Robbie…"

"Then we can both stay at your place, unless you're trying to get rid of me."

"I wouldn't do that."

Dan gave Sabrina a quick, fierce hug before they climbed up to the pilot's station together. She didn't want to talk about the case on the way back to the city.

"It's so strange to feel you've known someone for a long time, but you don't know much about their life now," she said.

"Yes. I was wondering, did you have any, uh, special affinity for Scotland?"

"I read historical novels about it all the time, and I used to get all wrapped up in the locale and the characters. And I told you about the stories I wrote. They must have been set there."

"Did you write about Sara?"

"I think so. At least, a girl and her grandmother who lived in a cottage. What about you? Did you have any special interest in Scotland?"

"Not really." He stopped. "I only had the medallion. *It* was from Scotland." In the darkness, Sabrina heard him draw in a deep breath and let it out slowly. "But the minute your name came up in connection with the case, I felt as if I had to get close to you. And I was afraid you'd slip through my fingers if I just went about a straightforward investigation. You were a compulsion, and I couldn't understand why I was making decisions that were so out of character.''

"That day at lunch. I was afraid of you. And drawn to you at the same time.''

"Afraid. Yes. That's what I'm worried about.''

"We'll handle it,'' she said, wishing her voice conveyed more conviction. She reached up to touch the gold charm that still hung around his neck.

"It's yours, I think,'' Dan said in a husky voice, taking it off and slipping the chain quickly over her head. "I guess my family's been keeping it for you all these years. I guess that can't be a coincidence.''

Sabrina looked down at the gold circle. "I shouldn't take it. It's too valuable.''

"I want you to have it.'' She might have protested. Yet it felt so right hanging around her neck that she couldn't give it back.

They rode in silence for several moments. "Why did you get divorced?'' Sabrina asked suddenly, and then was shocked she'd blurted such a blatant question.

"I blamed my wife for a lot of things. Maybe the real problem was that I didn't care enough. Maybe I couldn't care about anyone but you.''

"Oh, Dan.'' Sabrina pressed her shoulder against his, hardly able to believe he was being so open. "That's how it's always been for me,'' she agreed. "I wanted to get married. Have a family. But I just couldn't picture myself spending the rest of my life with any of the guys I met.''

"I'm selfish enough to be glad.''

Sabrina let her head drop to Dan's shoulder. She was consumed with the need to know this man. To know all about him. Raising her head again, she gently reached up and touched the scar on his chin. "Where did you get this?"

"In a fight in high school. When a bunch of tough guys called me a chicken for not trying pot."

"Oh, Dan."

"I came out of it a bit worse for wear. But I guess I did enough damage so they didn't mess with me again."

The lights of the city twinkled in the distance, beckoning them closer. It should have been beautiful sailing into the harbor. Yet Sabrina felt her stomach tightening more and more the closer they got to the dock.

It seemed as if they'd been gone for years. But it was only a little after ten when Dan cut the engine and maneuvered the launch toward the slip.

For a summer evening, the pier area looked strangely deserted, Sabrina thought as she climbed out and began to secure the mooring line. As soon as she'd finished, she was surrounded by several men who had come rushing out of the shadows. Two wore business suits. Two were uniformed police officers.

Dan had told her he'd arranged for protection. But this sudden flurry of activity wasn't what she'd been expecting. Something must have happened.

Sabrina took a step back.

"Don't move. Raise your hands above your head," one of the men shouted.

It was then Sabrina saw they all had guns drawn. And they were all pointed at her.

She couldn't have moved if her life had depended on it.

All at once she realized the speaker was Brian Lowell, the man who had directed the operation at the train station.

"Ms. Sabrina Barkley?"

"Yes. Of course. We…we…know each other."

"I said raise your hands above your head."

"Wh-what?" Sabrina stammered through her confusion, making an effort to comply.

Behind her she heard a curse, just before Dan's feet hit the deck.

"Stay where you are, Cassidy," Lowell called out.

"What the hell's going on?" Dan demanded, his chin raised in anger toward the man in charge. Both detectives boarded the boat.

"Ms. Barkley is under arrest for the murder of Luther Davenport."

Chapter Fourteen

"Luther Davenport?" Sabrina gasped.

"Yes."

"I don't understand." She stared at Lowell, struggling to take in what he was saying. The police were supposed to be protecting her from Davenport. And now—

With a tremendous effort, she forced herself to abandon every painfully arrived-at conclusion she and Dan had recently made.

"On what evidence?" she asked.

"I can't discuss that here. You have the right to remain silent..." Lowell began the phrase Sabrina had heard in countless movies and TV programs.

Sabrina swung back to Dan, who was having a whispered conversation with the other detective. He glanced at her, but his face was as blank as it had been that first day at lunch when she'd told him she wouldn't go to the cemetery.

"Dan..."

"I'm sorry. You've got to go with Lowell."

"Aren't you coming with me?"

His fists were clenched at his sides as he shook his head.

The detective moved Sabrina toward the cabin. "Face the wall."

Sabrina complied and cringed as she felt the man's hands moving over her body, searching for weapons. She was all too conscious she was wearing nothing besides her sandals and the borrowed shirt and shorts. God, what if he went inside the cabin to search for weapons or other evidence? Her wet underwear was down there, and the bunk where she and Dan...

She turned to Dan one more time as Lowell cuffed her hands. He wasn't looking at her now.

Pride kept her from calling out to him again. It was almost a relief when the detective hustled her away. Almost, except that she felt utterly alone and betrayed as she collapsed against the plastic seat in the back of the police car and tried to keep her body from shaking. At the station she held herself stiffly while she was photographed and fingerprinted, trying to distance herself from the abrupt orders and clipped demands for basic information.

Finally she was allowed to make a phone call. It was to Laura Roswell, the only lawyer Sabrina knew. Laura and her assistant, Noel Emery, arrived at the station in less than half an hour. Noel came right in to see Sabrina. Laura went to find out what she could about the case.

Sabrina and Noel stared at each other across the dank, dirty little room set aside for interviews. That morning they'd been laughing and talking about jewelry and show-window displays. How could everything have changed so quickly?

"Oh, honey, I'm sorry you're in this mess," the paralegal sympathized as she gave Sabrina a supportive hug.

"Me, too." For several moments Sabrina clung to her friend. She'd put up a good front since Lowell had taken her off the boat. Inside, she'd felt so afraid and alone.

Half an hour later, Laura joined them around the scarred

metal table. When Sabrina saw the look on the lawyer's face, a ball of tension formed in the pit of her stomach. Laura squeezed her hand. "It's going to be okay."

Sabrina clung to the reassurance as Laura extracted a slim file from her briefcase. Noel pulled out a steno pad.

"Is there anything you want to tell me?" Laura asked gently.

Sabrina tried to gather her thoughts. "I—I—thought Davenport was trying to kill me. Now I don't understand what's going on." To her chagrin, she found that tears had gathered in her eyes and begun to slide down her cheeks. Noel silently handed her a tissue and gave her time to collect herself.

"I was able to find out some things upstairs," Laura told her. "Davenport died very early Friday morning. But since he was supposed to be off on a trip, his assistant didn't find him until just before lunch. A ten-thousand-dollar donation from June Garrison is also reported missing."

"But how could they think I was responsible for any of that?" Sabrina asked.

"There's a lot of circumstantial evidence. Last night at the Andromeda Institute, several witnesses saw Davenport humiliate you during the medical emergency."

Sabrina felt the ball of tension in her stomach start to grow. "I felt like he did it on purpose. But surely that's not a motive for murder and robbery."

"They also found another one of your gold charms in Davenport's office."

"And they think I'm stupid enough to commit a bunch of murders and leave such an obvious calling card?" Sabrina asked through gritted teeth. "Are they charging me with the Graveyard Murders, too?"

"For the time being, it's just this one." Laura pressed

her hand again. "I know how hard this is for you," she murmured. "It happened to me, remember?"

Sabrina nodded. A year ago Laura had been accused of murder. But she'd proved her innocence. It gave Sabrina a glimmer of hope.

"You've got to hear the rest of it before we can start to put together your case," Laura said.

Sabrina braced for more bad news. "Okay. What else do they have?"

"The police got a search warrant for your house."

"But they couldn't possibly find anything there," she exclaimed in disbelief.

Noel nodded sympathetically.

"They did. Ten thousand dollars in cash in June Garrison's original bank envelope stuffed into the back of your desk drawer."

"But I don't know anything about the money."

"Someone obviously planted it there," Noel put in. "I guess it was whoever really killed Davenport."

"Is there anything else?" Sabrina asked.

Laura sighed. "After they found the money, they went tramping around your property and discovered a stand of lily of the valley growing out back."

"Since when is it against the law to grow them?" Sabrina asked.

"The preliminary results are in from Davenport's autopsy. Lily of the valley poisoning was the cause of death."

Sabrina leaned her elbows on the table and cupped her head in her hands.

"I know you feel like a ton of bricks has fallen on you," Laura murmured. "Whoever did this to you *wants* you to feel that way."

Sabrina raised her head.

"So they've won the first round. Now, is there anything we can start building your defense on?" Laura asked.

"I—it's all going to sound so crazy. It already does."

"If Noel and I are going to help you, we've got to have some facts."

Sabrina pressed her lips together. "Facts? Are you going to believe I'm the reincarnation of a woman who lived in Scotland two or three hundred years ago and that a witch living at the same time is also back and trying to do me in? Are you going to believe Dan Cassidy was there, too? Or are you going to try to get me off by reason of insanity?"

"Tell us about it," Laura encouraged.

At first it was difficult for Sabrina to keep her voice steady. But as she went through the sequence of events, it became easier and easier to talk.

When she finished, she anxiously scanned her friends' faces.

"You're right. The authorities are going to have trouble dealing with it," the lawyer predicted.

"What about you?" Sabrina whispered.

"You're talking to a woman who had a run-in with a ghost not that long ago."

Sabrina nodded.

"Unfortunately I don't think we can count on a judge to be as open to the paranormal."

"If it helps, I do have all the Scotland episodes I wrote down."

"They don't really prove anything. They could be something you made up."

Dan had said that, too. Before…he let them take her away. Sabrina clamped off that line of thought. "I swear, I didn't make it up."

"I just want you to know what the opposition will say."
Laura put the folder back in her briefcase. "Do you think
the assistant district attorney will corroborate your story?"

"I don't know," Sabrina answered honestly.

"Well, I'll try to contact him immediately. And as soon
as I can arrange your bail hearing, I'll let you know when
it's scheduled."

"Is there anything else you can think of?" Noel asked.
"Anything that would help you?"

"Ask the police to check the free tapes Davenport was
giving out. It can't hurt if they find the subliminal messages
or the ones that are drugged."

They talked about a number of other details and parted
with another heartfelt round of hugs. But once Sabrina had
been taken back to her cell, she felt worse than before
Laura and Noel had come. Now that she was alone, she
couldn't imagine how she was going to get out of this trap
someone had lured her into and sprung so neatly. The case
against her was simply too hopeless. And she wasn't sure
which was worse—her arrest or the feeling of hurt and
betrayal that surged over her every time she thought about
Dan Cassidy. He'd as much as told her he was going to
turn on her when it came to crunch time. She felt something
inside her shrivel and die. She hadn't believed he would
let her down. Not when she'd come out of the story and
found him holding her so tightly. Not when they'd been
making love.

She should have listened to him when he'd told her to
take the boat back to Baltimore and walk away.

WITH A SENSE of unreality, Sabrina tried to pull herself
together for the bail hearing Monday morning. Noel had
brought one of her most conservative dresses, she noticed,

as she changed out of the jailhouse coveralls she'd been issued.

As the guards led her to the hearing room, Sabrina scanned the faces of the crowd in the hall. It was almost a shock to see how many of her friends from 43 Light Street had come down to support her. But the one face she wanted most desperately to see wasn't there. Of course not. Dan had thrown her to the wolves.

"As soon as you get some rest, we're going to start working on the case," Laura said after Sabrina had been released on five-hundred-thousand-dollar bond guaranteed by Jo O'Malley's husband, Cameron Randolph, CEO of Randolph Electronics. "I have a friend who's a very sought-after criminal lawyer who has agreed to be part of the defense team."

"Yes. Thanks. Have you found out anything we can use? What about Davenport's tapes?"

"The police lab has checked several of them. They do have subliminal messages. But none of them is drugged."

Sabrina had hoped for more.

"I also talked to Dan Cassidy's office."

Sabrina flinched.

"He's been ordered off the case. And ordered to stay away from you. Apparently the department is furious about the way he handled things."

"Too bad for him," Sabrina muttered.

Jo, who had been standing a little to the side, came up and joined the conversation. "I guess I got you into this, by asking you to go to lunch with Cassidy," she said in a low voice.

"It's not your fault," Sabrina told her. "He could have used anyone for the contact."

Jo looked a bit relieved. "But I should have figured out

that you weren't just writing a story that day when I came in, shouldn't I?''

Sabrina shook her head. ''I didn't *want* you to know. I put on a pretty good act, if I do say so myself.''

Noel had parked her car where she could avoid the reporters out front. Half an hour later, she walked into her own house, closed the door behind her, and stood leaning thankfully against it. Katie had been stopping by to take care of the animals. But the warm greeting Sabrina received from her dog and cats made her eyes mist.

After washing off the jailhouse stench under an almost scalding hot shower, Sabrina came back downstairs. Physically she felt better. But she was still all torn up inside. When she thought about Dan, tears gathered in her eyes. But she had to stop thinking about him. That was over. Now she had to figure out how to save herself.

As she sat at the table, she felt as if the kitchen walls were closing in around her. It was all coming together again. She'd assumed that this time around Davenport and the witch were one and the same. Now the only conclusion she could come to was that the witch was alive and well and had set her up again. She had no idea how she was going to confront the overwhelming evidence in the present case. But she still had another avenue of attack. She could try to find out what had happened before.

Hope leaped in her breast as she ran to get a pad of paper from her desk. She didn't know how the story ended. Maybe Duncan had come back in time to save Sara. Maybe that meant Dan was…was…

Sabrina closed her eyes for a moment, willing herself not to hope for anything from Dan. It was better not to think about the man and his motives.

Taking a pad of paper from her desk, she grabbed a pen and sat at the kitchen table.

Each time it got easier.

Elspeth meowed plaintively.

"I'll be back in a little while," Sabrina told her. Then she began to write.

"Please, let me find another clue to what's going on. Something that will help me…"

It had been weeks since she'd bathed. Weeks since she'd changed her clothes or had a decent meal. Weeks since she'd felt the wind on her face.

Sara raised her eyes to the tiny slit of light that came in through the window high up in the wall of the cell where she was being held. Sometimes she could catch a glimpse of blue sky. More often, there had been nothing to see but dull gray.

In the days before her trial she'd undergone the humiliation of being stripped and examined by several clergymen for a witch's mark. The brown mole she'd had on her bottom since she was born was judged to be conclusive. Even after that terrible experience, she'd clung to the hope that Duncan would come back and pluck her from the mess she was in.

But the committee of judges had been selected, and she'd been brought before them to answer to a dozen charges of witchcraft. People she'd treated and ones she'd never even met came forward to testify against her. The most damning words came from the physician Fergus McGraw, who blamed her for the death of three children. Her words of denial fell on deaf ears.

Lillias Weir was in the prisoner's dock, too. Sara had

stared in disbelief as she'd begun to defend herself by heaping all the blame on Mistress Campbell.

But there'd been witnesses against Lillias, too, with plenty of ghastly tales to tell. In the end, Sara suspected, nothing she nor Lillias said or did would have made any difference. After less than an hour of deliberation, the court had found them both guilty and sentenced them to a public burning in seven days.

"No," Sara shouted. "I dinna do the devil's work."

"Be silent, girl," the chief judge warned. "Or it will go worse with ye. Be glad we don't have to get a confession from ye before we burn ye."

Sara shuddered, remembering the instruments of torture she'd been shown. But she hadn't confessed, and mercifully she was not tortured.

With a silent scream, she was dragged away and thrown back in her cell where she huddled shivering on the pile of dirty straw they'd allowed her for a bed. For the first few evenings, she couldn't eat the crusts of bread they brought her for dinner, and the rats carried the food away. Then her mind slipped into a desperate fantasy. Duncan would come. He'd find some new evidence that would save her. Or he'd storm the jail and rescue her, and the two of them would ride away on the destrier. They could go to the cave in the mountains that she'd showed him. That was safe. He could hunt with his sling and throwing stone the way she'd seen him bring down rabbits. And when the search for them was over, they could leave the country and go somewhere else where no one would pursue them. But in her moments of despair, she knew it would never happen. Then she wished she had a leaf of monkshood to swallow. It would provide a quicker, less painful death than the one she knew awaited her.

At noon on the seventh day, they came for her. As she was hustled toward the town square, flanked by guards on either side, she held her head up high. She had done nothing wrong. Let them remember later that she'd gone to her death with dignity.

The crowd was large and jeering. Their cruel shouts echoed in her ears as the burly men led her to the stake. Then Lillias was brought forward. This was the first time Sara had seen her since the trial. The woman appeared to have aged ten years. Lines were etched in her face, and her eyes shone with a hatred so strong that even the guards cowered.

Coarse hemp bit into Sara's wrists as she was pulled against the stake and tightly bound. Then her tormenters stepped away, leaving her back-to-back with the older woman. At the edge of her vision, she saw men standing with torches and cringed, forcing herself not to look at them.

"I see your fine lover from the castle dinna come and rescue ye," the witch hissed.

Sara closed her eyes for a moment. "Why do ye hate me so much?"

"You've brought this on us both by challenging Mc-Graw."

"Aye, it may be I brought it on myself. Your own mischief damned you."

The bailiff was reading the decree.

"...for consorting with the devil, they will be consumed by the fires of hell forever. Let it be done."

Sara couldn't hold back a frightened cry as the men with the torches came forward and the acrid smoke drifted toward her. The evil smell grew worse as they touched the burning tips to the tinder-dry straw. For heart-stopping mo-

ments, the red flames danced playfully along the edges of the straw. Then they suddenly leaped up and raced toward her.

She screamed in terror and then in pain, twisting against her bonds, trying with all her strength to get away from the flames licking at her clothes and her skin. The smoke scorched her lungs. The terrible crackling sound surrounded her. Closing in tighter and tighter.

Then the only thing she could hear above the roar of the fire was Lillias's shrill voice. It seemed to build in power. Like the flames.

"I curse the lot of ye in this foul town. And I fix an entail on the spirits of Sara Campbell and Fergus McGraw. Ye will not escape me. This is not the end. It is but a pause. The circle will not be complete until the Servant of Darkness prevails."

SABRINA WAS CHOKING, gasping for breath, huddling down with her hands flung over her head as if that could protect her from the flames. With a frightened cry, she staggered to the living room, and sank onto the sofa cushions. For long moments she simply lay there shaking.

She'd be writing no more stories of Sara Campbell. Sara was dead. Burned at the stake. Sabrina was too stunned to do more than drag in shaky breaths of air.

She tried to block out the scene. But she could still see the flames racing toward her and then shooting up around her so that every avenue of escape was blocked. Now she knew for certain where her fear of fire had come from.

The terror threatened to envelop her again, the way it had at the cemetery. But she fought against the hideous vision, gradually bringing it down to manageable proportions. As she did, she grasped one stunning fact she hadn't known before. The witch had gone to the stake with Sara. The witch had died, too. Sara had lost everything. But so had Lillias. Or it seemed that way until she'd evoked some sort of curse.

Had it worked? Had she given herself a second chance?

Sabrina sat with her chin in her hands, trying to puzzle it out. The witch had only called back Sara, the doctor and herself. What about Duncan? What was he doing here?

She clenched her fists, feeling her nails dig into her palms. What did it matter? Duncan had abandoned Sara to her fate. Dan had done the same thing. On orders from the district attorney's office. Perhaps Duncan had been following orders from the laird.

Tears were threatening her again, and she pulled her purse off the floor to get a tissue. As she dug through the contents, her fingers encountered several folded sheets of paper—and a circle of metal. She pulled them both out.

The metal was the medallion Dan had given her. The police had taken it away, along with her other personal possessions when she'd been processed. But they'd given it back when she'd been released on bail. As she stared at the sun carved into the surface, the tears began to roll down her cheeks. Tears for what she'd felt when Dan had placed it around her neck. Tears for what might have been.

Acting on an impulse she couldn't justify in any logical way, Sabrina slipped the chain around her neck and tucked the medallion out of sight inside her blouse. The weight of the emblem against her chest was somehow very reassuring.

But she should certainly give it back to its owner. Sabrina reached to remove the chain again and stopped, fighting the feeling of dread that swept over her when she thought about taking off the medallion. All at once she remembered when Laura had come into her shop last fall with a charm she'd wanted put on a chain. She'd worn it around her neck when she'd been in danger, and it had saved her life.

Sabrina sat with her eyes closed for several minutes, her hand pressed against the metal that had warmed to the temperature of her own skin. She couldn't explain why, but it made her feel safer. And she needed all the reassurance she could get. Perhaps it was only a tangible link to the past. Perhaps it did hold some protective qualities, although it hadn't saved Sara. Still, she wanted to wear it for the time being.

Finally her hand dropped to her lap, rustling the papers that she'd forgotten about.

What were they? Sabrina spread the forms open and stared at them. They were the report on June Garrison that Dan had given her.

So far, June was the one person she'd encountered who admitted she knew something about all this. But it was pretty unlikely that the witch had simply told her the story. So where had she gotten her information?

Sabrina's eyes zeroed in on the address. The police had searched her house, but perhaps they hadn't known what they were looking for. Certainly they wouldn't have been after anything that would help *her*. What if she could get in there and have a look for herself?

The idea was compelling. Now all she needed was an expert at breaking and entering.

"YOU *LIKE* DOING THIS," Sabrina accused as she and Jo O'Malley slowly drove around the block off Cold Spring Lane where the modest Garrison house was located.

"Don't tell my husband."

"Cam probably knows."

Sabrina was feeling better than she had in a long time. For days she'd been swept along by events out of her control. Finally she was doing something on her own behalf.

Jo made short work of the basement lock. Then they were hurrying through the silent house. On the way over, they'd discussed strategy. It would have been quicker to split up and each investigate different floors. But Sabrina felt she was the only one who really knew what they were looking for. So Jo had given her a crash course in search procedures. She and the detective moved through the rooms together in an orderly pattern, carefully checking drawers and cabinets, under sofa cushions and rugs, and behind heating vents. At first it was a disappointing effort. Then, in the master bedroom, Sabrina happened to glance at the books piled on the window seat.

One was an old volume with a torn leather binding. She felt her throat close as she read the title *History of the Scottish Inquisition*. She'd wondered if the facts were written down in a book somewhere.

With trembling fingers, Sabrina extracted the volume from the pile, skimmed the table of contents and thumbed through the pages. It became apparent very quickly that the book was a documented account of witchcraft persecution in Scotland.

"Scotland is surpassed only by Germany in the zealousness of its witch trials. Secular courts shared prosecution duties with the clergy who acted the part of inquisitors."

Following was a partial record of Scottish trials beginning with a man named John Fian in 1590 and ending in 1704 with a group called the Pittenweem witches.

When Sabrina got three-fourths of the way down the list, she felt chills run up her spine.

In 1682, in the village of Killearn, two women, Sara Campbell and Lillias Weir, were tried and burned as witches. Sara Campbell had been brought up on a dozen charges, including killing three children by witchcraft. The most damaging accusations came from a physician named Fergus McGraw.

Sabrina didn't realize she'd made a strangled sound until she found Jo standing anxiously beside her.

"What have you got?" Jo asked, staring at the open page.

"It's all here," she croaked. "The names. The charges. The trial. Just like I've been writing about." She thrust the book at her friend, stabbing her finger at the page and feeling a surge of triumph.

UNFORTUNATELY Harry Rosenberg, the attorney who'd agreed to help with Sabrina's case, didn't think the book was going to be much help. And his defense strategy seemed to revolve around finding who had framed Sabrina.

Good luck, she thought as Erin drove her home from his office. Tired and dispirited by the four-hour meeting, she flaked out on the couch. Since there was hardly anything to eat in the refrigerator, Erin volunteered to go out and get some groceries.

A while later, Sabrina's eyes blinked open. She'd hardly slept the night before, but under the circumstances, she hadn't expected to fall asleep.

"Feeling better?" Erin asked in a voice that sounded artificially chipper as she set down several plastic bags on the kitchen counter.

"A little." Sabrina glanced at her watch. Had Erin really been gone almost two hours? It couldn't have taken that long to get the groceries.

Sabrina sat up and stretched. "I guess you thought I needed a rest."

"And some food. Let me fix some sandwiches. Is sliced turkey okay?"

"Yes," Sabrina murmured, wondering if she could force a sandwich down.

Erin was putting the milk in the refrigerator when the phone rang. "I'll get it."

"Who is it?" Sabrina asked as she came into the kitchen.

Erin jumped. "Oh, I didn't know you were standing there. "It's...it's Gwynn Frontenac."

"Gwynn?" The woman could be so trying. She didn't have the energy to cope with her now. Shaking her head, she whispered to Erin, "Tell her I'm asleep."

"She says it's important."

Sabrina sighed and reached for the phone. Erin handed her the receiver and then busied herself with putting groceries away. "Yes?"

"Oh, Sabrina, I read about you in the papers. I want to tell you how sorry I was to hear that you'd been falsely accused."

"Yes, well, thanks..." Since the story had hit the news, customers had been calling to express similar sentiments. Each time, Sabrina felt her chest squeeze. Now the deep, booming quality of Gwynn's voice made the pressure worse.

"My dear, I know you must be trying to marshal your defenses," Gwynn intoned.

"Yes."

There was a pause during which Sabrina felt her fingers tighten painfully on the receiver.

''I think I might have some information that would be helpful.''

''About what?''

''The Servant of Darkness.''

Chapter Fifteen

The sky was overcast, and a few raindrops were just starting to sprinkle across Sabrina's windshield as she turned onto the long, tree-lined drive that led to Gwynn Frontenac's house. The three-story stone mansion was set far back from the street and hidden by a screen of pines. Ancient rhododendrons clustered around it, obscuring the gray walls, as if hiding secrets.

Sabrina, who had never been there before, stared in fascination at the structure. It was one of those monstrosities the newly rich sometimes built in order to make a statement. Was this Gwynn's taste? Or her late husband's? As Sabrina peered up at the long, thin windows, round tower and crenellated roofline, she decided the residence looked like a cross between a fortress and a castle. If she went inside, would she ever come out?

She drew in a deep breath and released it slowly, pretty sure her own melancholy mood was responsible for the out-of-proportion reaction. Although the house was ugly, that didn't make it sinister. Still, she was glad she wasn't going in there alone. While she'd gotten ready, Erin had called Noel, who had agreed to meet her. But she hadn't shown up yet. Sabrina tapped her fingers nervously on the steering wheel as she waited for her friend. A curtain stirred at one of the windows. Was Gwynn looking out, wondering why she was sitting in her car? Sighing, Sabrina got out and rang the bell. Gwynn, who opened the door herself, was dressed in a bright orange-and-green silk dress accented with heavy gold jewelry. As always, the effect maximized her height and her girth.

A mixture of relief and anticipation flashed across her features. "Sabrina, I'm so glad you could make it."

"I'm anxious to hear whatever you know that might help my case."

"Yes. I'm sure you are. Come inside and we'll have a nice cup of your herb tea while I tell you all about it."

"Noel Emery is supposed to be meeting me here," Sabrina said uncertainly as she turned and looked back down the driveway.

"Yes. She just phoned. She's running a bit late and said for us to go ahead and get started. Come make yourself comfortable."

With a grimace, Sabrina stepped across the threshold.

Gwynn locked the door and pocketed the key before leading the way down a hall into a formal living room.

Sabrina shivered as a cold draft of air hit her face. The place looked uncomfortably like a museum, filled with heavy Tudor furniture and decorated with paintings in dark colors and themes. Wishing Noel would arrive, Sabrina perched on the edge of an overstuffed brocade love seat. Gwynn took the chair opposite her and began to pour from an antique silver teapot.

"Sugar and milk?"

"Just sugar. You—uh—you said you know something about the Servant of Darkness?"

Gwynn passed her a cup. "I need to give you some background first. You know Hilda was the one who got me interested in Dr. Davenport.''

"Yes." Sabrina took a sip from her cup. The blend was familiar, yet it had a slightly odd, heavy taste.

Gwynn looked uncomfortable. ''I don't want to tell tales about a friend. But I think she was somehow emotionally involved with the man.''

Earlier, the chill of the house had enfolded Sabrina. As she sipped her tea, she realized she was starting to feel warm and a little light-headed. She loosened the button at her neck.

''Are you okay?'' Gwynn asked.

"Yes. I think so. What do you mean by 'emotionally involved'?''

''I'm afraid Hilda might have developed a romantic interest in the doctor. She hung on to everything he said, wrote him letters, even asked my opinion about some of the notes he sent her.''

''He wrote her letters?''

Gwynn nodded. ''But I could tell he was leading her on. I suspect he was only interested in getting her to make a big contribution to the Andromeda Institute. Perhaps she found out.''

''You're not trying to say you think she killed him, are you?''

''Well, he may have been playing this game with other women, too. But when you finish your tea you ought to take a look at some of the letters she sent him. They're upstairs in my workroom.''

''Why do you have them?''

''They're copies. Hilda often asked my opinion about phrasing and grammar and such.''

Sabrina drained the hot drink and tried to concentrate on

Gwynn's words. Her mind was starting to fog up. "It's hard to believe that Hilda could do something like that."

"You remember how excited she was about his lecture. She was the one who convinced you to attend. I also saw her taking a handful of your pretty gold esses one time when we were in your shop."

Her words seemed to echo softly around the room, making it hard to catch on to them. Sabrina leaned forward trying to get closer to the source. Suddenly the large woman was beside her, laying a hand on her arm. "I know all this must be making you feel confused."

"Yes, confused." Sabrina tried to shake the haziness that was stealing over her. "What does this have to do with—" She stopped abruptly wondering what she had been going to say.

"You will rely on my advice, won't you?"

"I—"

"Let's go upstairs. I think you'll get a better understanding of what's really happening."

Sabrina let herself be guided to the stairs and began to climb with Gwynn at her elbow. Her legs felt heavy as if she were wearing lead boots. Something didn't make sense. Why would Hilda leave her love letters with Gwynn? But she didn't have the mental energy to pursue the thought. They gained the second floor and walked down another hall. It was dark with a slight sickly-sweet smell.

Gwynn's fingers dug into her arm.

They rounded a corner and came face-to-face with an old picture in a gilt frame. It was a print of Hieronymus Bosch's *Garden of Earthly Delights* depicting the wild, out-of-control cavorting of naked men and women—many in very nasty poses.

Repelled, Sabrina drew back.

"Bosch is so good at depicting the pleasures of the flesh, don't you think?" Gwynn murmured. "But his devils are a bit off-putting."

Sabrina wasn't sure how to respond.

"The letters are in here," her guide said, stepping aside so that Sabrina could precede her into a room a little farther down the hall.

It was a workroom, the source of the sickly-sweet odor in the hall. As Sabrina stepped inside, she could see the walls were lined with shelves of glass jars. Some contained familiar leaves. Others held molds and fungi and things she didn't want to examine too closely.

"I think you'll find the design on my floor quite interesting," Gwynn whispered, giving Sabrina a little push into the room.

She looked down, seeing a familiar pattern of stars painted on the polished boards. They were like an hourglass. But it was the hunter, Orion, the giant whose boasting had offended the ancient gods. And she was standing right in the middle of the pattern.

Sabrina felt a web of power stronger than any mortal hands grip her, hold her.

"There are a lot of advantages to being a rich widow," Gwynn murmured. "I'm not an ignorant country bumpkin this time. So I have more weapons at my disposal to defeat those who defy me. Now, turn around and submit to me."

In slow motion, every movement a terrible effort as her muscles fought the command, Sabrina turned to face the large woman.

Gwynn looked completely transformed. The slightly dotty widow had vanished. In her place was someone who knew she wielded power. She was holding up a wide velvet cord emblazoned with the evil-eye symbol. The malevolent image seared into Sabrina's brain, branding through flesh and bone.

"Don't move. I have you now. Soon we will be going upstairs to complete the ceremony," Gwynn ordered, her voice high and piercing.

Fear welled up from deep in Sabrina's soul. *Run. Get away. You, you're the one,* her mind screamed. *You're the witch. It was you all along. And I never suspected.*

Gwynn smiled as if she knew very well what was going through Sabrina's mind.

The witch began to advance toward her, holding up the cord. Sabrina cowered back, unable to break the hypnotic spell holding her immobile.

Then a loud thumping noise from above made her body jerk. In that one desperate moment, Sabrina wrenched her gaze away from the eye.

"Obey me," Gwynn shrieked.

Summoning every ounce of strength she could muster, Sabrina staggered toward the side of the room. When she stepped outside the pattern of stars, it was as if a terrible crushing weight had been lifted from her body.

"No. Stay there," Gwynn railed.

Sabrina's hip hit the workbench. Her hand groped behind her for a weapon, found only a glass bottle and hurled it with all her strength.

It hit Gwynn in the chest. Air groaned out of the large woman's lungs. Her knees crumpled, and she screamed as she fell forward into the middle of the Orion pattern.

"It will hold you," Sabrina found herself calling out. "The way it held me. You forfeit the power to me."

She didn't know if that was true. But maybe if Gwynn believed—

Sabrina darted past her attacker and out of the room.

Whatever was in the tea had fogged her brain, making it difficult to reason, difficult to make her limbs work.

Somehow Sabrina kept herself focused as she staggered down the hall. All the doors were locked.

Fighting a wave of dizziness, she struggled to think. She should go down. Out of the house. She couldn't drive, but she could run for help.

At the stairs, she hesitated. Every fiber of her being urged her to flee, but somehow she knew there was something upstairs she had to get first. Something that would free her once and for all.

Instead of going down, Sabrina began to climb. On the third floor, she began to try doors again. Finally she found one that was unlocked.

Certain the thing she needed was inside, she entered the room. It took a moment for her to remember that she'd have to secure the lock so that Gwynn couldn't follow. When she turned back to face the room, she tried to stifle a gasp of shock. Under ordinary circumstances, the place would have been frightening. It was an elongated chamber that could have been the set for a Dracula movie or something equally sinister. In Sabrina's present state, it was like a black hole ready to swallow her.

The walls were completely shrouded by midnight curtains, except for the strange symbols that broke the surface on either side of the door. The only illumination came from the candelabra fitted with tall white tapers placed at intervals around the room.

But more disturbing than the physical setting was the sense of ancient evil that permeated the place. There'd been echoes of it in the graveyard when she and Dan had come to look at the murder site. Downstairs in the workroom it had grown stronger. Here the malevolence hung heavy in the air as if it had soaked into the very fabric of the black curtains, which now gave it back in waves.

Sabrina wanted to back out of the door. She'd made a terrible mistake, but now there was no place else to go. She pressed her shoulders against the stout wood as she waited for her eyes to adjust to the eerie, flickering light.

She had run up here and trapped herself. This was what Gwynn had wanted all along.

The sudden knowledge that she wasn't alone was an icy breeze blowing across Sabrina's skin. Her eyes probed the flickering shadows, searching for danger—and searching for another way out. She moaned low in her chest and shrank back as the curtains at the far end of the room stirred and parted slightly. Paralyzed, unable to breathe, she watched as a figure shouldered itself partway out of the concealing drapery and stood in stark relief against the black background.

Her confused mind struggled to process what she was seeing.

Gwynn. Somehow the witch had gotten in here. Through another entrance.

Sabrina fumbled for the lock.

But the tall masculine figure wasn't Gwynn in her blaze of bright silk. Instead Sabrina found she was staring at a disheveled Dan Cassidy. His white shirt hung open where buttons had been pulled off. His blond hair dangled in his face. And as he tried to thrust farther forward, Sabrina saw that his hands were pulled in back of him and fastened to a stout wooden post.

He seemed to realize who had come into the room at the very moment she comprehended it was him. As his eyes sought hers out, his face went from agony to anger and back to agony. While she stared into their depths, he pulled himself up straighter, thrusting his face toward her, and she realized with a start that a flesh-colored gag prevented him from calling out to her.

Since she'd drunk the tea, she'd felt woozy. But in that blazing instant when her eyes locked with Dan's, her thoughts snapped into focus.

She hadn't seen Dan since Lowell had taken her off the boat and hustled her away to jail. In her hurt and pain, she vowed to forget Cassidy. Now a muffled, urgent sound welled up in his throat.

When she took a step toward him, he began to shake his head and twist his body furiously against the post. But there was no hesitation on Sabrina's part. He needed her, and she went to him. The anguished look on his face as he stared helplessly at her almost knocked the breath from her lungs. Then she saw the ugly red gash partially hidden by the hair that had fallen across his forehead.

"Dan. My God, Dan." With fingers that felt insensitive as metal prongs, she clawed at the beige scarf that served as a gag. It seemed to take forever. Finally she dragged it down so that it fell around his neck.

"Get out of here," he rasped as soon as he could speak.

"What?"

"Sabrina, it's a setup. The witch tricked me. Get out of the house while you can."

She blinked, trying to take the words in. "I'm not leaving you here." She dropped to her knees and began to inspect the coarse hemp that bound his wrists. It was wound securely around the wooden post. The way she'd been tied to the stake before they'd burned her. A long time ago.

As she worked at his bonds, Dan talked to her in a low, urgent voice. "Sabrina, she told me a lot of stuff after she tied me up. She's Lillias come back. She's got a whole group of people so frightened and captive to her persuasive techniques that they'll do anything she says. Sign over their insurance to her. Steal from their employers. If you try to cross her, you end up dead. Like the graveyard victims. She killed them as a warning.''

''And June Garrison?''

''She was working for her. She figured out some of what was going on and tried to get Gwynn to take her on as an equal partner. Gwynn drugged her and used her to spy on you and Davenport—and to set you up for his murder. She's absolutely ruthless. She's already killed four times that we know of and maybe a lot more. Now get out of here. Save yourself.''

Sabrina ignored the advice. If Gwynn had told Dan that much, she didn't expect that he was going to be able to pass the information on. But why had he fallen into her trap? ''How did she get you?'' she panted without pausing in her task.

''She said she had information that would save you.'' His voice was raw.

Sabrina's eyes shot to Dan's. They locked and held as her fingers gripped his.

The door rattled. Sabrina's heart leaped into her throat. Dan swore vehemently. The clatter continued as Sabrina's fingers began to work more frantically at his bonds. In her desperation, she tore off several nails below the quick. But she didn't stop unknotting the cords.

Somewhere in her mind it registered that the rattling had stopped, but it didn't affect her labor.

Dan strained against the bonds, making her task more difficult. ''Don't!'' she protested. ''Stay still.''

She felt the tension gathering in his body as he forced himself to stand perfectly quiet when every instinct urged him to pull away. Then he must have felt a loosening at the left wrist. He gave a mighty jerk, and the left hand came away with the rope dangling.

"Sabrina." He pulled her into his arms, clamping her tightly against him so that the medallion was squeezed between them. Then he lifted his hand to her chest, touching the sunburst through the fabric of her blouse. "You're wearing it. I thought you wouldn't." His voice was thick.

"I had to."

For a burning moment, neither one of them moved. Then Dan tore his eyes away from Sabrina's face. "We've got to get out of here," he grated. "Before it's too late." Turning to the wall opposite the door, he began to pull the curtains aside, searching for a window. White woodwork appeared behind one panel. But the opening was completely blocked by plywood nailed firmly in place.

Dan picked up one of the heavy candelabra, blew out the tapers, and bashed the metal base against the wood. It barely dented the surface. He swung again and again. Given time, he might batter his way through.

If they had the time. But they didn't. All at once, a sickeningly familiar smell drifting toward them.

Rotten cherries. Lord, no.

Holding her breath, Sabrina dashed toward the door and tried to twist the lock. To her horror she found that it no longer turned. She'd thought Gwynn was trying to get in. Instead she'd locked the door from the outside.

Dan redoubled his efforts. But the plywood held. Sabrina shrank away toward the far end of the room. When she felt as if her lungs would burst, she was forced to take a breath. As soon as she did, she felt her chest burn and her head fill with mist.

Dan raised the candlestick like a club.

"Drop it," Gwynn ordered, stepping into view. "Or I'll shoot your girlfriend." She must have come in through a door that was hidden by the draperies.

Sabrina caught the flicker of candlelight on the dull metal surface of the gun the witch held in her hand.

With an angry growl, Dan dropped his own weapon.

Sabrina stared from him to the tall woman. There was nothing she or Dan could do except watch in horror as the vapor filled the room.

Dan's face contorted. Finally he gasped in a draft of the drugging stuff.

There was no escape. It was only a matter of time until Lillias could do anything she wanted with them. Make them think anything she wanted.

Sabrina shook her head, trying to clear away the confusion. Not Lillias. Gwynn.

As she looked toward the end of the room where the hallucinogen was pouring in, she saw their captor standing still as a statue watching them.

"Erin didn't call anyone except me. I have control of her mind."

"H-how?" Sabrina choked out, clinging by her fingernails to sanity.

"Subliminal messages on the music tapes I gave her. A little trick I picked up from my late friend Dr. Davenport. Isn't it wonderful how many more tools there are nowadays?"

Sabrina flinched, knowing this was a woman sure of her power, sure of her control. Or had the drug garbled understanding? Erin? Had Erin really been helping the witch?

Gwynn laughed. "Your assistant was very helpful. She switched the cassettes in your pocketbook—for ones I'd drugged."

Speechless, Sabrina stared at her.

"And now I must insist you stay for the excitement of the ceremony. It just wouldn't be the same without the two of you." Gwynn turned to Dan. "You couldn't leave well enough alone. I didn't summon you, but you came back, anyway. You thought you could kill me. You were wrong. You should have died when I booby-trapped your car. Now I think you'll wish you hadn't joined the party." Gwynn's terrible laugh cut through Sabrina's flesh, scourging all the way to her bones. The room slipped in and out of focus. Tumbled thoughts careened around Sabrina's mind.

Gwynn's revenge.

Lillias had planned. For so long. Her and Dan together. No, not Dan. He was a wild card. But now she'd kill them both.

Kill them both.

Probably by poison. Or would she burn them? Sabrina cringed. No, not in the house. She couldn't do that in the house.

The room was filling up with the cherry vapor. It swirled around Sabrina, a rough blanket smothering her body. Thoughts slithered away like bugs skittering from the light.

They had to get away. She looked wildly around. Nowhere to turn. Nowhere to hide. Except perhaps one place. If they could get there.

"Sara," she called. "Sara, help me. Don't let it happen again."

"Stop! No!" the witch commanded. "Yield to my power over your mind."

Sabrina ignored the command. "Sara. Please, Sara. Come to me."

The air seemed to tremble. In the flickering light, the focus shifted. Back, back to another time. Before the scene could slip past, she reached out and clutched on to it, the way she'd clutched the pen when the writing had carried her back.

"No! Stop!" the witch cried out.

Sara ignored her. "Duncan, I need you, Duncan," she called. For an agonizing moment, she thought he wasn't going to come to her. Then he was beside her, grasping her shoulder. "Sara. It's not too late then, lass?"

"I won't let it be too late."

"Damn ye, Sara Campbell," the witch shrieked, her voice rising in a desperate wail. "Yield to me. Stop."

Duncan grasped her hand. With an urgent tug, he pulled her down behind the heavy table in the center of the room.

A crack of thunder sounded just as something hot and dangerous shot past Sara's head. Swearing, Duncan thrust her closer to the floor. "Give me the medal ye wear," he grated. "Be quick."

Thunder boomed again as Sara reached around her neck and pulled the medallion free. When she gave it to Duncan, he pressed her hand. Then he moved away from her so that he could swing the large medal pendant in a circle around his head the way he'd swung his sling and rocks when he'd taken her hunting. The disk whined as it flashed through the air. Standing, he gave a bloodcurdling shout and let the missile fly, just as the thunder cracked again.

The metal disk crashed into one of the candelabra, tipping the brass fixture on its side. The candles hit the curtains, and the dry black fabric instantly blazed up.

"No. Duncan. What have ye done? What have ye done?" Sara cried out.

The witch shrieked.

Terrified, Sara shrank away from the fire. Then there was only the cloying, sweet smell of the cherries, the shouts of the villagers calling for her blood, and horror of the crackling flames as they raced out to meet her.

Chapter Sixteen

With a terrible scream, the witch dashed to the spot where the curtains had caught fire. Cursing, she beat like a mad-woman at the flames, using the coils of heavy rope that had held Duncan to the post. But the frantic effort was wasted.

Heat billowed up as the red-and-yellow tongues lapped greedily at the hangings. While the witch rushed first in one direction and then in the other, the fire moved relent-lessly around the room, forming a flickering circle that lighted the secret chamber in all its lurid detail.

It was like a scene from hell. And Sara had been cast into the inferno once before. Speechless with horror, she tried to crawl under the table.

"No. We've got to get out of here." Duncan grabbed her, pulling her to her feet.

"Please. Not the stake," she choked out, coughing on the thick smoke that billowed around them. "Not the stake."

She tried to wrench out of his grasp, but he held her fast.

"Sara, stop. Don't fight me. You've got to trust me if I'm going to save you."

The urgency, the pain and the fear in his voice made her head jerk up. Her eyes locked with his, seeing both his anguish and the reflection of the flames flickering in their blue depths. There was no time for thought, no time to reason it out. Once and for all, she had to choose.

"Sara, please."

In the moment of decision, she gave him her trust. Her life. She reached for his hand. It might have been the only solid thing in the flickering red and yellow universe. Holding on to Duncan with all her strength, Sara stumbled after him, gasping on cherry vapor and smoke.

The fire surged at Lillias. With a curse, she jumped back, dropping the rope. Then, crying out her anger at the top of her lungs, she whirled and fixed Sara and Duncan with a terrible look.

"You haven't won. You'll die here. Together," she promised, as the thunder sounded one more time. "I'll send you to hell before I let you get away."

Hot pain sliced across Sara's arm. She cried out and stumbled.

With a shout of raw anger, Duncan lunged at the witch, knocking savagely at her hand. But she was almost his equal in size, and she was strong. In the flickering, diabolical light, the two figures struggled, coughing and wheezing. Then something heavy clunked to the floor. Somehow, Sara knew that Duncan had knocked a terrible weapon from the witch's grasp. In the next moment, he caught the large woman by the shoulders. With the victory cry of a Scottish warlord, he spun her around and sent her hurtling toward the burning draperies.

She shrieked as the flames caught her dress, then her hair. Crying out in pain and terror, she beat at her clothing.

Sara was transfixed in horror. Wasting no time, Duncan caught her up in his arms and began to stumble toward the door Gwynn had used. A line of fire raced from the wall and tried to snare them. He leaped out of its path and stumbled toward the door.

They were both choking and gasping in the smoky haze, and Sara pressed her face into his shoulders and squeezed her eyes shut.

He surged across the threshold into blessedly cool air, and they both dragged oxygen into their burning lungs.

Duncan started toward the stairs. Sara gripped his shoulder. "Wait."

He looked at her questioningly.

Twisting back toward the burning room, Sara raised her head and began to speak in low, measured tones. "I call on the powers of good in the universe to put a final end to the Servant of Darkness. Lillias will not return to this earth. Her second chance is spent. She is vanquished, now and for all eternity."

A terrible scream of defeat and pain came from within the burning chamber. Then the flames were leaping from the doorway, and a thundering crash shook the floor. That was the last Sara saw before the world went black.

SABRINA'S EYES blinked open. She lay on the grass under the shelter of a tree, a coat blanketing her. For a frightened moment, she tried to remember where she was and how she'd gotten there. Then her gaze took in the ugly stone castle several hundred yards away. Flames flickered behind the windows and shot through the roof, sending a column of black smoke into the air.

All at once she remembered being in the middle of the fire. And the witch. She cringed in horror, until she felt a gentle hand on her shoulder.

"Easy, honey. You're safe. You just fainted, that's all."

"Duncan?"

"It's Dan."

Sabrina stared up at him. Duncan had come to her when she called him. Dan was here now. When she saw his face and shirt were streaked with soot, and the arm of his shirt was singed, her chest squeezed painfully. She tried to reach toward him. Only it hurt to move her left arm, and she winced.

He came closer to her, hunkering down beside her on the grass, stroking the hair softly back from her forehead. "You need to lie still," he murmured. "She winged you. It's not bad, just a flesh wound, but it probably hurts like hell."

Sabrina looked down in confusion at the white gauze circling her arm.

"It's from the first-aid kit in my car," Dan explained.

Sabrina nodded and sank back against the makeshift pillow he'd made.

"It's all over." His voice was edged with relief—and regret.

Sabrina's heart leaped into her throat. "What's all over?" she croaked.

"The horror. The murder case against you. Gwynn didn't plan on my leaving that room alive. So she told me a hell of a lot before you got there. About how she'd set up the Graveyard Murders so I'd suspect you," he grated. "And how she trumped up the Davenport case against you. I could have sent her to the electric chair—if she wasn't dead already." Dan's face had gone tight with strain. "I want you to know you're safe. From the witch. And from the district attorney's office."

"Yes. Thank you."

"If you'd rather not have anything more to do with me, I'll understand."

Suddenly it was almost impossible to draw air into her lungs. "Do—do you want me to have anything more to do with you?"

He swallowed hard. "Yes."

She reached out toward him. It was all the invitation he needed. Leaning down, he gently pulled Sabrina into his embrace. Her good arm came up to circle his back. Her face pressed into his shoulder as she absorbed his scent, his strength, his essence. They clung to each other tightly.

"Oh, Dan, I was so scared. The fire. I'm so afraid of fire." She lifted her gaze from his face and stared at the burning building.

Dan found her hand and held it tightly. "I'm sorry. It was all I—Duncan—" He stopped and shook his head in confusion. "What happened in there is damn hard to describe."

"I know. I think we were all there. You and Duncan and me and Sara. At least that's the way it was for me. Sara was in control. But I was there, too."

Dan nodded. "Yeah, Duncan and me. I was pretty sure the witch wouldn't be able to handle fire, either."

Sabrina swallowed painfully. "You did the right thing. But I couldn't have gotten out of there on my own. You— you saved my life."

He drew back so he could look down into her face. "Well, I think you saved mine twice. Once on the boat when I was too crazy to know what I was doing. And then when you got me loose."

Sabrina fumbled for his hand and locked her fingers with his. "I'm not keeping score."

Far across the lawn, a terrible roar drowned out the conversation. Sabrina blinked and gasped as she saw the building caving in on itself. Massive stones showered down;

sparks and fire shot up into the air. Dan sheltered Sabrina's body with his own. But they were far enough away to be out of danger. Awestruck, they listened to the structure's groan of agony and watched it crumble until only one of the side walls was left standing.

"She built herself a castle," Sabrina whispered. "Now it's gone."

"She's gone. For good. You made sure of that."

"I did, didn't I?" There was a note of wonder in Sabrina's voice. "No, I think it was Sara who thought of it."

They stared at the wreckage of the house, the visible symbol of Lillias's final demise. When Dan finally spoke, his voice was gritty. "What happened to you this time is all my fault."

"No."

"At the graveyard, in the train station, the name Sara woke half-formed memories that terrified me. I should have trusted what was happening between us. But I couldn't cope with feeling solid ground shifting away from under my feet—feeling as if I were losing control."

"Dan, it was frightening. Even for someone like me. But you're so down-to-earth. You just couldn't handle it."

"Don't make excuses for me."

"All right, I won't. If you promise what happened in the past won't taint the future."

"*You're* saying that to *me?*"

"Yes. I need someone like you. Someone who's solid and down-to-earth and sensible. Someone who's all the things I'm not."

He gripped her hand tightly, but his face was still etched with pain. "Sabrina, I've got to tell you the rest or I'll never have any peace. I've been in hell. After Lowell took you away, I had to act as if I'd abandoned you again."

She took her lower lip between her teeth. "Laura told me they ordered you not to contact me."

"I didn't have any choice if I wanted to keep my job and stay where I could do you some good."

She held him tightly. "I know that now."

"I've been going over the evidence and every other damn aspect of the case practically twenty-four hours a day trying to find a way to clear you. Then Gwynn Frontenac called and told me she had what I needed, and I was stupid enough to go rushing over here."

"Not any stupider than I am. I fell into the same trap," Sabrina told him.

"When she had me tied up in that chamber, I thought I'd failed again." Dan's voice was raw. "I thought there was no way I could save you. That was the worst part. Failing after I'd been given a second chance." His mouth hardened. "The first time around Duncan should have married Sara and taken her away before it was too late."

"He couldn't do that."

"He'd decided to. He thought maybe they could make a life together in America or something."

Sabrina's eyes widened. "How—how do you know that?"

"I dreamed it. Very vividly. Just like when you were writing your story."

She looked at him questioningly.

"It happened when I finally fell asleep at my desk, the night after you were arrested." Dan's eyes were flushed with anger. "Duncan's father didn't want him mixed up with Sara. That's why he sent him away. When he heard about the trial, he came rushing back, but he was a few hours too late. They'd already burned her. But he went to the pyre at dawn and got the medallion."

Sabrina put her arms around him again. "You didn't hear Lillias's dying curse. She called herself and Sara and the doctor back. She didn't include Duncan. He included himself in. And this time he saved her. You were the factor she hadn't counted on." She stroked his cheek. "And I think that's where the violence came from. You're not really that way. But you were angry about what the witch had done to Sara. And angry that you couldn't punish her all those years ago."

"I thought of that," he admitted. "After the dream. I could have torn her to pieces with my bare hands—if I could have gotten them on her."

"Well, you have a primitive streak, but you mostly keep it under control." She gave a little laugh. "I knew that when you asked me to read your palm."

"Why didn't you tell me?"

"I did. In a kind of oblique way. When I was, uh, talking about conflict."

"Sabrina, don't ever be afraid to be honest with me."

"I won't. Not anymore."

"Do you remember on the boat when you asked me who we were?"

"Yes. You said a man and a woman who loved each other," she breathed. "Oh, Dan, I thought you couldn't really have meant it."

"I mean it, all right. I love you. I have for a long, long time." He traced his fingers over her lips and stared down at her as if he hardly believed his good fortune. He kissed her tenderly, lovingly, and then with more passion. And she returned the passion, murmuring her love for him against his lips.

When he finally drew back, they were both breathing

raggedly. "I think I'd better restrain myself until after I get you to a doctor."

She tipped her head, listening to the sound of a siren wailing in the distance. "I'd argue the point, but I think we're going to be interrupted by the fire department."

"Yeah."

Sabrina touched Dan's lips. "There's something else I want to do. Besides make love to you."

"Get married?"

"Are you proposing?" she asked, a smile dancing on her lips.

"It's about time, don't you think?"

She giggled, then turned serious again. "I want to go back to Scotland with you. To Killearn. That's where they lived."

"It won't bring back bad memories?"

"Some. But I can cope with them now. They're not going to interfere with the good stuff." She caressed his cheek with her palm. "I'd like to see if we can find the place where they met. And where Sara lived with her gran."

"If that's what you want."

"Only if you're with me."

He pulled her into his arms, arms that had finally led her to safety, to love. "Sabrina, I'll always be with you."

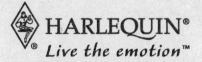

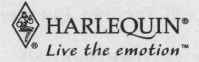

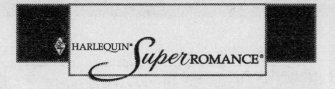

Harlequin Historicals®
Historical Romantic Adventure!

From rugged lawmen and valiant knights to defiant heiresses and spirited frontierswomen, Harlequin Historicals will capture your imagination with their dramatic scope, passion and adventure.

Harlequin Historicals... they're too good to miss!

HARLEQUIN®
INTRIGUE®

WE'LL LEAVE YOU BREATHLESS!

If you've been looking for thrilling tales of
contemporary passion and sensuous love stories
with taut, edge-of-the-seat suspense—then
you'll love Harlequin Intrigue!

Every month, you'll meet six new heroes
who are guaranteed to make your spine tingle
and your pulse pound. With them you'll enter
into the exciting world of Harlequin Intrigue—
where your life is on the line
and so is your heart!

THAT'S INTRIGUE—
ROMANTIC SUSPENSE
AT ITS BEST!

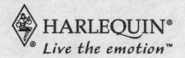

HARLEQUIN®
Live the emotion™